BLOOD LEGENDS

THE COMPLETE TRILOGY PART ONE

KIM PETERSEN

BLOOD LEGENDS

THE COMPLETE TRILOGY
PART ONE

KIM PETERSEN

WITH THANKS TO...

Beth Prentice, Paul Vander-Loos, Patti Roberts, Harley
Christensen, and Xavier Eastenbrick.
With special thanks to Joseph Nassise.

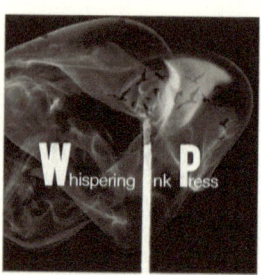

CONTENTS

BOOK ONE: UNDEAD

BOOK TWO: REBIRTH

BOOK THREE: ASCENSION

BLOOD LEGENDS
UNDEAD

KIM PETERSEN

FOOTPRINTS

"*D*id you ever want to step into someone else's feet?"

I tore my eyes from the gulls screeching above the waves that crashed against the jagged rocks, their wings beating against the briny air as they swooped the water's surface looking for a meal. A faint smile played over my lips.

"Don't you mean shoes?"

The breeze captured Scarla's platinum locks as amber eyes settled on me. Her smile was as meek as mine, dissolving just as fast when she dropped her gaze to grab a handful of sand. My throat restricted. The wind instantly carried a chord of torment as I watched her.

"No." She allowed the golden grains to fall from between her fingers. She raised her chin toward the sky and squeezed her eyes shut. "Thousands of footprints have marked this beach over just as many years; I'd give anything to step in any one of them."

My stomach hollowed.

"But then you wouldn't be here with me in this moment." I reached to catch a tear as it splashed over her cheek, folding my palm against her smooth skin while my gaze melted into her. She was all I saw in a disintegrating world. She was everything. "You would rather be elsewhere?"

She leaned her chin into my palm, her lashes dewy when she met my stare.

"Yes, with you, Jett."

"Where should we go?"

My gaze instantly fell to her lips when she smiled. Pale pink and plump. They reminded me of blossoms and lifted my heart in much the same way. She had a way of doing that. She had a way of bringing me undone.

"Florence." She pulled away from my touch, combing a hand through unruly hair as it wisped across her face. Her white blouse rippled and clung to her breasts.

"Ah, you want to immerse yourself in some Italian Renaissance, Bella donna? Where should we start? The Galleria degli Uffizi?"

She laughed.

"That will do just fine, signor. We'll spend our days exploring galleries, eating crostini di fegato and drinking chianti while we marvel at the architectural masterpieces. Afterwards, we will put on our best threads and go to the opera."

I feigned a frown.

"The opera? Hmm…"

"What?" She gave me a gentle nudge. "I'm sure you can conjure up your inner-aristocrat for a few hours if need be."

"Only for you, Bella donna."

I shifted, positioning myself behind her on the sand and pulling her between my legs so that her back molded against my chest. I wrapped my arms around her, burying my nose near her ear and breathing in her scent. She stiffened, her voice barely audible over the sound of the rumbling waters.

"Do you think the virus has spread that far?"

I shrugged.

"If it has, we'll get love-drunk on chianti at the opera with them. I hear the undead love high society."

"That's not funny."

"I'm not laughing." I pressed my lips against her temple. She tasted salty. *Sensually salty.* My voice was husky when I spoke next. "Can't we just pretend a little longer?"

She arched her neck so that her throat stretched beneath the afternoon sun. Her eyes closed as she leaned further into me, reaching to claw her fingers through the dark hair curling at my nape. I wanted her now, but I knew this wasn't the time nor the place for intimacy. We were alone on the beach, yet that could change at any moment. People were seldom friendly these days. Especially those that we call the hawkers.

My gaze drifted toward the horizon as I held her in my arms. If I could pretend on anything, it would be any place but here as long as she was by my side. It would be some place where the Vampiric virus ravaging the earth couldn't reach.

They say everything happens for a reason. Yet, I could think of no justifiable reason for the horror our world had become. Almost overnight, the lives of millions of people worldwide had turned into a living nightmare. A harsh reality where those infected by the virus feasted on humanity during the dark hours. Now, it was the kindred that were fast staking supremacy over the earth; humans had become the minority.

My thoughts shifted to my daughter, Avila, who we'd left behind in our hidden cottage; the meager refuge we'd sought after fleeing the city when it became obvious that I could no longer help contain the rapid spread of the virus. We were among the lucky ones who got out just in time.

"We should get back to the cottage," I said, knowing that she wasn't ready to leave. It wasn't often that we stole time away from the cottage. I'd come here for her. Sometimes, she needed to dream.

She squirmed in my arms, swinging around to face me. Her brows creased.

"Just a little longer? I want to trek through some footprints before we go back." She motioned toward the sand etched with shallow prints. "Will you join me?"

I held her gaze, smiling behind the pain of all I

knew she'd suffered and lost to the outbreak. She'd lost her little boy at the hands of a vampire. I shook my head.

"Go find your rainbow, Bella donna. I'll wait here."

"Okay." Her eyes deepened against the blue of mine as her lips slightly parted and she leaned toward me. I groaned inwardly as the sweet taste of promises to come found my mouth with her kiss. They say that the eyes are the gateway to the soul. I think lips are the same for the body. She pulled away and leapt to her feet, casting me a grin. "I'll be ten minutes. You can watch my rainbow from here."

I scanned the beach again, pushing away the apprehension that shadowed my every waking hour.

"Stay where I can see you."

My words were swallowed in the wind and the space between us as she walked toward the shore, but I knew she wouldn't wander far from me. She was more than aware of the lurking dangers in the form of hawkers. They were the ones who polluted the daylight hours by terrorizing the survivors. The profane remains of humanity who relished the aftermath with unspeakable acts of violence. Thankfully, we hadn't encountered any hawkers this far from the city. Still, you can never be too vigilant.

I watched Scarla for a few minutes as she stomped between prints, and looking back at me every now and then, smiling. She was safe enough that I took a breath and sprawled back into the sand. The warm grains cushioned my head as I closed my eyes beneath the sun, inviting the false sense of well-being its rays provided.

For the millionth time since the arrival of the V-Virus, I thought about the continuation of life. It isn't until you are faced with endless death and chaos that you realize the earth will stop for nothing and no one. There are no free rides out of here when evil comes calling. No help lines to pull you from the brink of insanity.

A few moments passed and I became aware of the breeze gathering speed, catching clumps of my hair as the sand sprayed like sharp needles against my skin. Suddenly, I felt cold all over, the breeze blowing in a sense of dread. I sat up abruptly, looking back to the place I'd last spotted Scarla scouring the shoreline but she wasn't there.

Scarla?

My heart thumped hard against my chest as I stood up and scanned the beach. I was confronted by a stretch of bronze sand in every direction as far as the eye could see, barren of life apart from the gulls that squawked and hovered above the waves licking the shore.

I could feel my head begin to spin as I called her name, but my words were instantly stolen by the wind as panic gripped me and my feet dug into the sand to seek out her footprints. Prints that I knew would haunt me for the rest of my days.

2

THE HAWKERS

a thick cloud of dust billowed above the road behind me as I slammed my foot against the accelerator of the pickup. Any other day, I would have taken extreme care to disguise the sound of the engine, much less leave an obvious path of smut leading toward the cottage. But today wasn't any other day. Today Scarla had vanished without a trace.

Hawkers. It had to be. But how they managed to slip past me to grab Scarla undetected in a matter of minutes was beyond my comprehension. And all without so much as a sound from her to alarm me.

Since when did those lowlife pilferers possess such stealthy tactics?

My thoughts harrowed over the severe truth. *Since vermin infected our streets and claimed most of the population.*

Anarchy and destruction have a way of bringing out

the best and the worst in humanity. Eventually, you cultivate the ability to ignore the suffering when desperation becomes second nature to every surviving human. But ignorance isn't an option when you're targeted by the wicked.

My knuckles whitened as I gripped the steering wheel and the tires slid over the rough terrain, just missing one of the dense and twisted tree trunks that fringed the road. I was covered in sweat and a thin layer of grime from searching the grassed hinterlands near the beach for signs of her. My face stung with the moisture that clung to the scratches I knew marked my face, but I barely felt it. It was all I could do to keep it together as I raced back to the cottage to get what I needed before starting back out to look for her.

Damn it! How could I be so foolish? How?

I let loose a barrage of four-letter words, fighting to keep control of what little resolve remained. I should have known better than to yield to Scarla's desire to escape the confines of the cottage. *Dying dreams on broken wings cannot fly.* There is no room left in this world for the dreamers. They were poached the moment the virus murdered most of humanity.

Avila was already out front and standing at the foot of the cottage porch stairs when the truck skidded around the final bend to emerge into the clearing. Her aqua eyes narrowed toward me while her usually chiseled features scrunched beneath the thick tawny hair framing her face. As I yanked the parking brake lever and moved to get out of the truck, her olive complexion paled as she rushed closer and pulled on the truck door to face me.

"Dad?" Her gaze drifted beyond me to the empty truck cabin. My breath felt like steel when she looked back at me. "Wha … where's Scarla?"

Her voice quavered but I could barely look at her. I shook my head fast before climbing out of the truck and pushing past her. I marched toward the cottage, bounding up the few stairs leading to the front door as she raced after me.

"Dad, stop!" She grabbed my arm, sinking her nails into my flesh as I reached the threshold. It was difficult to tame my racing mind when I turned to face her. Even more difficult to form the words I knew I had to say. Her brows dipped over a pinched expression. She clutched onto me. "What happened? Where is she?"

"I don't know, she vanished."

Her jaw gaped as I tore my arm from her and walked into the cottage. It was a modest dwelling with timber floors and burnt orange curtains that Scarla thought gave the place a cheerful vibe. I'd never agreed with that notion. I hated those curtains.

But curtains were the last thing on my mind as I stomped through the cluttered space that passed for the sitting area, heading for the room at the end of the short hall that stocked our supplies. The small room was filled with stockpiles of canned and dried foods, loads of water, kerosene, and piles of spare bedding among other things.

It was here that I'd kept the few weapons I had managed to salvage before deserting the city.

Admittedly, there wasn't a whole lot, and none of it would be of any use in the face of a vampire. Humans, on the other hand, could bleed when facing the blunt end of the few rusty hunting knives I'd collected. There was also a small-bladed axe, a cleaver and my prized possession, a machete that I used frequently to cut and gather firewood. I'd heard machetes were particularly useful for cutting limbs in addition to wood. Somehow, I got the feeling I might soon discover how to dismember a hawker or two. It was limbs and blood that I craved right now.

The blades were discreetly stacked on the shelf in the corner behind rows of water bricks, cans of fuel and oil, and dozens of bottles of bleach and candles. I began pulling them out as Avila burst into the room, stopping just short of me. I ignored her glare as her arms outstretched to take the knives as I pried them from the shelf.

"Hawkers?" Her boots squeaked on the timber floor as she swung around to place the weapons on an old coffee table pushed against the shelves.

"I didn't see them."

She took the cleaver from me, catching my gaze with solemn eyes.

"What are you going to do?"

"I'm going to find the bastards and cut off their limbs, that's what I'm going to do." I swung my gaze from her and reached for the machete, stiffening when I felt her hand on my arm.

"It's too late, dad. She's gone. We can't get her back."

My entire body felt as if an explosion was shredding every organ. But my heart fought ceaselessly against the onslaught. As much as I loved my 22-year-old daughter, those were the words I didn't want to hear.

I dropped my chin and sighed, the machete heavy in my hand as I allowed the blade to swing to my side. The inside of my head throbbed against my temple. It was pain that consumed me as Avila's hard stare begged for my acknowledgment. The moments stood as still as a tomb on a starless night. They were the same moments that forever sealed our fate like an impenetrable vault. When I looked back at her, it was the pain that thickened my voice.

"I won't let her go, Avila. I've already lost too much." I shook my head. "I looked away from her for only a moment and they snatched her away. I have to get her back."

Avila's jaw twisted. She gnawed on her bottom lip before gesturing toward the lone window in the airless room.

"Okay, but there's nothing we can do right now; it's almost nightfall." I was about to protest when she stopped me with a flash of a palm. "Listen dad, we can't do this alone. You can't do it alone. They'll kill you on sight. We need to contact Michal. We need help."

Michal was our sole connection to what little life

remained in the city. We'd been work colleagues at the Norbury Blood Research Center for more than two decades. He was one of the most gifted hematologists I'd ever met and had chosen to stay in the city to search for a cure for the V-Virus, working with a group of vigilante scientists in an underground laboratory.

Our communication with Michal was sparse and not always reliable, considering that the only means of contact rested solely on old CB radio transmitter. We'd agreed to reach out to one another only when it was necessary. Scarla was more than necessary, but what could he do? He was a few hours' drive away and I had no idea if he could handle a blade.

I swung my gaze toward the window, noting the diminishing light spreading through a gap in the curtains. Honestly, the way I felt, I could not care less about the threat of the kindred if it meant I could find Scarla and bring her home. But I was aware my thoughts weren't rational at that moment. There was Avila; I had to protect her too.

Reaching out to Michal couldn't hurt. Perhaps he could stay with Avila while I got this under control. My fingers clenched the machete handle as I glanced back at her, ready to concede when a loud knock thumped against the cottage door. The sound of my name spoken by an unfamiliar and gnarly voice reverberated through the flimsy walls.

What the hell?

Avila's eyes widened. I motioned for her to stay put

as I gripped the machete and raced to the front of the cottage, edging along the wall of the sitting room to steal a glance through the curtains at the yard. My blood drained to my feet as I caught sight of a group of hawkers spreading across the clearing and leaning against the timber porch frame.

There must have been about fifteen of them wearing ragged leather jackets above grimy jeans and carrying an array of long blades and rusted chains between frayed fingerless gloves. The voice called again; the sound of my name grating against my churning gut. I steeled myself, taking the few steps toward the door before flinging it open.

Stained teeth greeted me with a wry grin that split between wiry ginger whiskers. His tall, solid frame filled my vision as he toyed with a switch blade and cocked his chin to the side. Dark eyes bore into me above pockmarked skin.

"Ah, you're home! How fortunate that we caught you at the witching hour."

My eyes flashed dangerously.

"What do you want?"

He laughed, a few of his cronies joining in when he leered their way. He turned back at me.

"You're asking the wrong question, my friend." He leaned closer, his breath hot and rancid in my face. "I have what you want. The question you should be asking is how bad do you want it."

3

SUN

Forty-eight hours. That was the deal offered by the hawkers if I wanted to keep Scarla breathing. She now had a ransom on her head – a blood-ransom.

Myths and legends always seem to accompany major change. In a new world where blood ruled, it was blood that had become our most valuable commodity. Scarla's life had just become dependent upon a few drops of rare blood. Blood represented power to its possessor, and I was uncertain I could produce the payoff.

Avila lifted her head from the cradle of her arm and yawned beside me in the pickup cabin. I glanced at her before looking back to the road that stretched ahead in an endless brutal strip as we sped toward the city. It was brutal for the bloodshed it had silently witnessed and for that which dwelled at its end. We were headed back into vampire territory.

"Are you okay?" My voice was as rigid as the stupidity of the question, but I knew she was good at disguising her fear. My little tough nugget wasn't always as brawny as she made out. Still, her courage in the face of the epidemic was admirable.

She snorted and gazed out the passenger window. Fields of rotted vegetation and wild grasslands swayed beneath the morning sun, blurring the passing landscape.

"Of course." She looked back at me. "Is it really true, dad?"

"Is what true?"

"What the hawkers said about AB positive blood type. You've never mentioned it before. Can it transcend a vampire's supernatural powers?"

The sun's sharp heat already bit at my brow despite the early hour. When I lowered the truck window, the foul odor of spoiled crops instantly assaulted my senses. I flinched and tried not to gag.

"I wish I had the answers, Avila."

"Well, you of all people should know."

I flinched again, and this time, it wasn't because of the rotting crops. My eyes never left the road when I answered.

"It doesn't matter what I know or don't know. All that matters is that the hawkers believe it enough to keep Scarla hostage until I deliver it to them." I wiped my brow with the back of hand. My jaw clenched. "And that's exactly what I'm going to do."

Or die trying.

She was silent for a few beats, her fingers toying with one of the wooden stakes swaddled in a bag that lay on the bench seat between us. She sighed.

"Maybe Michal has the answers. Last night when you spoke to him, I heard him tell you he has one vial there at the lab. Surely, he's discovered something new by now? After all, you guys put in some grueling hours before … the end."

She was referring to the intense blood research program I had participated in when there was still hope the epidemic could be controlled. Of course, we'd failed. But when delirium had struck near the end, so too did the mysterious tales begin to circulate about a blood type that could provide the supernatural with even more extraordinary powers. Alas, by that time, most of the city had fallen and with it, the remaining blood banks ransacked and gutted.

No one really knew where the legend surrounding the rare blood type had originated. Some say the collapse of humanity was an ironic twist of fate handed down by unseen higher forces. That our most vital lifeforce would prove to be our undoing. Those same folks foretold a future time of reckoning in the form of a blood legend. Whether there was truth to those mystifying predictions did not concern me. I wanted no part in this new world. Once I got Scarla back, I planned on taking my girls and getting further off grid. Blood legends and myths be damned.

"Dad?"

I glanced at Avila, catching her eyes tapering as the wind blew fast into the truck cabin. She pushed strands of dark hair from her face.

"Yeah?"

"If Michal has a vial of this rare blood, why would he give it up so readily for us?"

It was a valid question and one that had already crossed my mind. I'd managed to contact Michal after the hawkers had left the evening before. He had been pleased to hear from me, posing little protest when I filled him in on our current predicament and what I needed to get Scarla back. We'd left the cottage at first light with the promise of the blood we needed awaiting us in an underground city laboratory.

I pushed away the unease rippling through me and shrugged. Even as I spoke my next words, I wasn't sure I believed them.

"Why wouldn't he, Avila? Heck, he's been a part of our lives for over twenty years. I trust him."

She gave a half laugh.

"The concept of trust disintegrated when the city fell and vampires overtook the world." She turned away, speaking toward the black tarmac that stretched before us. "*You* were the one that taught me that."

Indeed, I was. It was something I'd drummed into both Scarla and Avila. Keeping the guards up and the barriers firmly erected was as important to withstanding the new world as the basic needs for survival. As it was, we were fortunate to have enough supplies stockpiled at the cottage to last several months if rationed carefully. And as far as trusting Michal, Avila could be right, but I had no choice but to pursue the blood and this was my only option.

I was about to voice as much when Avila gasped and jerked next to me, lifting her arm to gesture toward a lone figure appearing on the hazy black horizon.

"Up ahead, dad. Look!"

My skin flushed as I squinted beneath dark sunglasses. My mind whirled with possible scenarios. You don't often spot lone figures walking along the deserted highways. You don't stop to ask questions either. Yet, as we neared the solitary person hiking in the middle of the road, my thoughts were lost when she spun around to face us, the sun catching the length of her wild golden tresses while her long black dress flowed with her movements.

A woman?

My foot automatically eased off the accelerator and my breath quickened with my knotting belly. The air in the pickup thickened with decaying pungent offerings as we slowed. When the woman raised a palm to wave us down, I noticed the rucksack slung over one shoulder and the wooden stake she gripped by her side. The sound of Avila's voice was the next thing I heard over the rumbling truck motor.

"What are you doing? Don't stop for her, dad. Keep moving." Her eyes were like frantic storm clouds when I tore my gaze from the woman to meet her stare. She shook her head wildly. "It's got to be a trick."

I took a shallow breath and scanned the area, the pickup now only inching forward as I clutched the steering wheel. The roadside was a tangle of high weeds and twisted bramble that suffocated farm fences and boarded rising fields of sloping grasses. Anyone could be hiding in those shrubs. Anyone. Still, I felt compelled to press my foot on the brake as we drew closer.

"Is your door locked?" My voice was taut as I double checked my own door and wound up my window until only a few inches remained open.

Avila checked her door and gasped loudly. "Have you lost your mind?"

Perhaps I had lost my mind. Either that or it was fast deteriorating beneath the precarious nature of the unfolding events, but something compelled me to stop for this woman and I had no idea why. I didn't look at Avila as I began to veer alongside the woman, maintaining a crawl in the pickup.

"Keep vigilant." I reached for the machete that was propped next to me.

"Ha! A lot of good that's gonna be if we're ambushed with weapons. What if they have guns? You have lost all your marbles."

She fell silent when the woman smiled from between chafed lips and fell into step on my side of the pickup. Her blonde hair fell stringy over slim shoulders clad in a faded denim jacket worn over a red singlet. Grimy fingers adjusted a pair of dark sunglasses poised on a petite nose.

"Thanks for stopping." Her voice was as light as the breeze drifting off the unkempt, sleepy pastures. The cawing sounds of crows circling over the fields clung overhead like an ominous warning as I stopped the truck. She looked beyond me to Avila. "My name is Sun. I'm heading back to the city. Can I ride with you?"

My jaw tightened and I dropped my eyes to the stake she clasped. A slight chill prickled my spine when I saw the dried blood that stained the end of the wooden stave.

"What's your business back in the city, Sun?"

She pushed her sunglasses to the top of her head and took a sharp breath. Eyes the color of gold peered at me from sunken sockets before she lowered her chin and swallowed hard.

"I'm going back for my daughter. I left her behind."

Avila scoffed next to me.

"Bullshit! If that's true, she's probably dead. Are you on a suicide mission or something?"

Sun's eyes instantly flew to Avila, and her lips quivered. She shook her head.

"Please. I have to know what happened to her."

Avila and I exchanged glances. Her lips pursed as she frowned at me. I gave a slight nod and ignored her look of disbelief as I turned back to Sun.

"Get in."

4

HOLLOW CITY

"So, what's your story, huh?" Avila glared at Sun sitting between us on the bench seat as we raced along the highway.

Sun shrugged; her fingers twisted in her lap. "What do you mean? My story isn't any different from anyone else's."

"Ha." Avila's lips curled as she indicated the stake leaning against the seat beside Sun. "I'm not buying the innocent act, *Sunny*. What's with the blood-soaked stake? Did you kill kindred?"

I glanced at Sun as her jaw squared while she stared straight ahead.

"No." She gave a rueful laugh. "Turns out, stakes can kill humans too."

Avila was silent for a moment. I could almost hear the gears in her mind turning over. Her eyes never left Sun.

"What happened? Who'd ya kill?"

Sun shifted slightly before she faced Avila. She frantically rubbed the back of her neck.

"Avila," I started, shaking my head. "Leave it alone."

Avila didn't even look at me. Her eyes were like fire in water as she scrutinized our hitchhiker. It was Sun's brittle voice I heard next.

"Hawkers. There were three of them. They stumbled upon me in an old church I was squatting in. They'd been drinking rum … and just as nasty as the devil's drink." She gave a half laugh and shook her head. "They'd been looking for some 'pink cookie', they said. For days, I couldn't stop them, couldn't leave, could barely breathe. On the fourth night, the ginger one got sloppy with his rope knot. I waited till the booze knocked them out cold and then I jimmied the rope from my wrists and drove this stake into each of their hearts."

Avila raised an eyebrow. She nodded briefly before turning her gaze toward the passenger window. Not much was said after that. We'd all been through our version of hell. Sun was right. Her story was no different to anyone else's.

The two women exchanged a few words every now then, but I tuned out for the most part. My thoughts were trained toward the rural landscape as it began to give way to desolate suburban streets that skirted the outer sections of the city. After hearing the disturbing scene Sun had just described at the hands of hawkers, I was having trouble pushing away visions of those barbarous humans pawing over my woman. Scarla must be beside herself with fear.

Swiney prickass lowlifes. If they so much as touched a hair of her head, I'll kill them all – one way or another.

I couldn't help but think of that last moment we shared on the beach together. The way the shade of her eyes deepened like copper inkwells when she looked at me. It haunted me. I'd failed her.

What if I couldn't get to her in time? What if it all went to shit?

I shuddered as feelings of helplessness and anger coursed through me. The hawkers had said they had a way of testing the blood type. If that were true, I couldn't produce anything other than the real thing. I had to keep my eye on the endgame. It was all I could do as I kept speeding through the streets, ignoring the stillness of the shopfronts, townhouses and buildings that only months before were part of a thriving city. Now, those dwellings were prey to vultures, crows and vermin that scavenged for human remains.

When the streets narrowed and the maze of suburban districts began to merge with clusters of tall city buildings, I slowed the pickup in search for a discreet place to park. The hidden laboratory was in Norbury's southern precinct, about a mile and a half away. I didn't want to risk drawing unwanted attention by driving the truck through the inner-city streets. We would walk the rest of the way.

Scarla's favorite Italian restaurant caught my eye.

We'd spent many an evening together drinking red wine and dining on boscaiola in that cozy joint. She loved it for its unexpected charm and authenticity. She loved it for its candlelit dining and checkered tablecloths. *Bella donna.* My gut knotted as peered closer at its gloomy facade.

Below the sloped faded green roof, the windows were covered in a slick of grime, the words "Bella E Buona" now barely visible. I recalled the off-street parking bay around the back of the small building. It was a perfect place to stow the pickup, and quite fitting given we were here for Scarla's sake.

I veered into the driveway and stopped the truck, the wrenching sound of the park brake shattering the silence in the cabin. I reached for my machete and the rucksack filled with rations and a water canister. I had also brought the hunting knives, a box of matches, a flashlight and a few candles. In the pickup tray, I stored a supply of fuel enough to get us back home. Avila and Sun gathered their belongings and climbed from cabin as I refueled the truck before setting off into the city.

Avila's boots scuffed the gravel parking bay as she crept around like a predator. She was clad from head to toe in black, her jeans appearing sprayed against her slim legs as she clutched the cleaver in one hand while carrying the swaddled stakes over a shoulder. She moved closer to me, gesturing toward Sun.

"What are we gonna do about her?"

I finished refilling the tank and twisted the cap into

place before straightening to peer at Sun. She rummaged through her rucksack before producing a canister and taking a sip. As harsh as it sounded, she couldn't tag along with us. I could not risk jeopardizing the location of the laboratory.

"She will go her own way."

Avila gazed at Sun and nodded. I knew what she was thinking, but we had helped the woman reach her destination safely. There was nothing more we could do for her. We had our own problems and time wasn't on our side.

We parted ways with Sun and set off toward the lab. The hairs on my neck tingled as we hurried through the wasted city streets. It was as if time had frozen, leaving behind a collection of vacant buildings and harrowing steel in the wake of devastation. My breath shallowed as I thought about those who had died at the claws of the undead that hid in city basements and underground tunnels during the daylight hours.

A chill ran through me as we silently pushed forward, keeping our ears to the ground and our eyes trained on every street corner and abandoned car. You never knew what could be lurking in the shadows by day. Those brave enough to linger in the city with the bloodsuckers were just as dangerous as far as I was concerned. They were the ones who sought to strike a deal with the wicked. The ones who vowed to protect them while they slumbered. We called them the Shadow Guardians.

By the time we reached the building where the lab lay beneath ground level, the sun was swallowed behind the towering smoky glass and concrete buildings. The air cooled against the sweat on my brow and was tinged with the sickening stink of decomposing flesh. It wasn't long before my fingers ached from gripping the machete so hard.

I stalled at the entrance of the building as I cocked my head to gaze toward its mirrored veneer. It was a building I was familiar with, having visited its plush interior levels on many occasions in the course of my career. The laboratory had been created for covert government research purposes. And while I had never worked for the agency, I did periodically have dealings with their ongoing intensive research programs. I was initially led to believe their sole purpose was to find a cure for cancer and other blood diseases. However, it wasn't long before I became aware of the experiments with biological weapons that went on here. Particularly when presented with an in-depth confidentiality agreement.

I took a deep breath and turned to Avila. "Ready?"

Her eyes darted around the street before she looked at the huge glass doors leading into the lobby. She gulped.

"What if they're inside?" Her voice wavered as she turned back to me. "What if we wake them?"

I reached out to stroke away a strand of hair from her face. I forced a smile, but it evaporated as soon as it had emerged. It was possible we could be walking into a vampire lair and there was nothing I could say to comfort her.

I steeled myself and took another sharp breath.

"Get the stakes out and keep close to me."

5

DEAD AIR

*T*he print of my palm smudged the slick of grime layering the heavy glass door as I eased it open. Dozens of contorted prints already smeared the surface. Avila's short breaths pricked the hairs on my neck as I peered into the lobby.

Dead air.

I scanned the dim spacious area. The foyer spread out in a flawless vision as my eyes darted, taking in the oversized couches and mahogany furniture among huge pots of faux greenery and sprawling rugs. On one side of the room, a vivid painting dominated the wall beyond a marbled countertop. On the other, rows of individual workstations lined the internal window-wall. My skin went cold as I spotted the solitary office chair lying overturned near the workstations.

My tongue suddenly felt like sandpaper as I inspected the black leather chair, which was the only evidence of the annihilated city beyond the heavy doors.

How had this building managed to escape the apocalypse?

It was an unsettling revelation. Other than that, I detected no movement in the lobby, but that didn't mean shit considering the vast space and dozens of upper floors I couldn't see from this viewpoint. My gaze trailed to the door leading to the building's stairwell which loomed unburnished and gray at the foot of the elevator corridor about fifteen meters away. I gripped the machete in one hand and a stake in the other, stealing myself to race to the door.

I glanced at Avila and gestured toward the stairwell. My voice was barely audible when I spoke. "Move fast and don't make a sound."

Her grim eyes nodded a reply. My heart lurched. I wanted to take her in my arms and hold her against my chest like I had when she was child. I wanted to make everything alright for her again. But it was a futile wish and wishes were yesterday's dreams. There were no words enough to take away the reality. She had become a child of devastation.

Our boots hardly touched the floor as we dashed through the lobby, keeping to the shadowed sections of the room before stopping short of the stairwell door. My chest constricted as I glanced down the darkened corridor where metal elevator doors glinted dully in the muted light offered by the grubby windows skirting the lobby.

The unscathed appearance of the place heightened the mood of eeriness.

Something doesn't feel right.

I tried to suppress the thought and the accompanying shudder as I grabbed the door handle before slipping into the gloomy stairwell. The narrow shaft immediately seemed to close in all around me as an inkiness infected my bones. I paused to allow my eyes to adjust to the diminished light while Avila slinked in beside me.

She gagged. "Argh!" She clutched at my elbow. Her was voice low and shaky. "Death is here."

She was right. The stench was unmistakable. It was distinctive and sickly-sweet and as familiar as the rising sun. I reached for the flashlight stowed in the side pocket of my rucksack, flicking it on to illuminate an endless flight of concrete stairs broken by short landings as far as the light stretched. A frigid draft filled the stark shaft. There were four flights of stairs between us and the lab. *Four flights.* I prayed that death lingered in the opposite direction as I reached for Avila's trembling hand.

Her skin was cold against mine. She clutched the stake in her other hand as if it were an extension of herself as she clung close to me through the dark. I gave her a squeeze.

"I'm okay, dad."

Her words tore into me as I wondered if bringing her along had been the right decision. *Was I leading her into a death trap? Would my choice forever change her destiny?*

There was no way for me to know and no time to second guess my decision. The alternative was to leave her alone at the cottage. Now that the hawkers knew where to find us, she would have been a sitting duck. I told myself that she was safer with me as I released her hand, ignoring the tension in every nerve of my body as I eased down the stairs toward the lab.

The building groaned and the shadows seemed to deepen with each step downwards. Like contorting, dark limbs, they writhed and expanded against the shaft of light from my flashlight before disappearing into the blackness we left behind. Avila's nails sunk into my waist as we crept along walls, her breath jagged in my ear while my senses went in overdrive. I pushed forward, progressing cautiously and with as much speed as I could, stopping when we reached the bottom of the stairwell to shine the light on the heavy metal door of the lab.

An odd sense of relief flashed through me as I skimmed the light around the bottom landing, seeing nothing but the gray slabs of concrete that enclosed the small area. The coast was clear but my fingers still tingled as they clutched the machete handle. I glanced at Avila and motioned toward the door.

"Come on."

I moved away from the wall as the sound of Avila's stake clanked against the floor as it slipped from her hand. My body froze as the sound reverberated along the steel balustrades, echoing up the lengthy shaft in a climatic staccato.

"Shit!" Avila cringed and scooped up the stake. She looked up.

I followed her gaze, catching sight of the balustrades glinting through the darkness as goosebumps covered my arms. My breath hitched at the faint sound of footsteps from above. Avila's gasp was followed by a sudden pinging noise at our feet. I looked down at a silver coin rattling against the concrete before coming to an abrupt stop.

Holy fuck.

Silence. I could barely breathe. Utter dread pulsed through me as I grabbed Avila's arm and dashed toward the door, gripping the handle at the same time that it opened an inch to reveal Michal's pasty face peering at me.

His dark eyes appeared spidery and wide beneath his glasses. His voice quivered.

"Jett?"

"Michal." I pushed on the door and ushered Avila into the lab, crossing the threshold as the cold draft carried the hideous sound of laughter. Two words clung in my mind.

Dead air.

6

RARE BLOOD

"Who or what the hell is out there?" Avila stalked between two long benchtops. She stopped to whirl around and glare at Michal. "You've set us up."

She had a point. It was clear we weren't alone.

Michal's bald skull gleamed dull beneath the emergency lights illuminating the laboratory. His finger's shook as he thumbed his glasses. "Wha – why would you suggest that, pigeon?"

Her eyes narrowed. "Don't you pigeon me, asshole." Her fingers tightened around the stake she waved with menace. She stepped closer to Michal who fidgeted beside me. "Who is up there, Michal? Have you become a Shadow Guardian? Are you their puppet now?"

He stiffened. His breath was hot and putrid as he slid closer to me, glancing between us. He began shaking his head and mumbling. I grimaced and stepped back. My thoughts were erratic as I scanned the workstations, dormant machines and the dingy spaces cordoned off by glass panels. *Empty space*. My gut flipped. A faint whiff of human waste lingered in the stale air. I looked back at Michal.

"Where are the others?"

He shrieked and his arms flailed. His filthy white lab coat swung wildly as he paced the lab.

"Questions! Questions!" He stopped abruptly. Beady eyes dropped and followed the pattern his fingers sketched along a bench surface. When he looked back up, a layer of spit foamed his lips. "Did they send you here to interrogate me?"

Avila and I exchanged glances. Michal had always leaned on the eccentric side. It became obvious his mental health was strained. Horror. It teased out our weaknesses. My back ached. I didn't have time for this bullshit.

"Where is the rest of the team, Michal?"

There should have been six other scientists here. They were the group that had stayed behind to keep researching for a cure. I knew all of them. They were the brave souls that had lost their loved ones to the virus. That had vowed to never give up.

Michal's eyes darted around. His fingers tangled together as looked up at the ceiling. I followed his gaze. It was a stick-built grid system. Some of the ceiling tiles were misplaced. I swallowed hard and increased my grip on the machete. He shivered visibly before he rushed toward me, his boots squeaking.

"They deserted me. All of them." His lips parted to reveal a set of stained teeth. He was about to say something else when was distracted by Avila who had begun stalking around the lab. She was headed toward the isolation spaces confined by glass panels. The experimental rooms were doused in darkness. Michal screeched as he set off after her.

"What are you doing?"

Avila ignored him. She stopped short of a glass wall to peer into one of the inky spaces. Her shoulders stiffened before she whirled around to catch my stare. I noticed her expression pale over trembling lips. Michal halted somewhere between us, facing Avila as he began pulling at his ears.

Dead silence. My blood iced as Avila's gaze settled on Michal. Her boots dug into the floor as she planted them wide with her hand firmly holding the stake. She stared at him when she spoke.

"Dad, I think the team are still here."

Fuck.

My nostrils flared. I lurched forward as Michal began stumbling backward. He spun around. He blinked rapidly at me before he tried to escape. But he was already within arm's reach. My blood ran hot as my finger's clamped into the back of his neck. He squealed as I yanked him toward me, and he struggled as I dragged him toward Avila.

She poised the stake at his chest. She looked at me and flicked her chin toward the glass panel. My knuckles tightened around Michal's neck as I leaned forward to peer past my transparent reflection into the glass.

Cold. It crept through me and jarred my senses. I shivered violently as I took in the grim scene confronting me. Blood was everywhere. It splattered across the floors and stuck to the chrome trolleys and benches. Severed limbs and body parts splayed across a wheeled stretcher and appeared distorted through the darkness. My head throbbed. I tore my eyes from the dismembered bodies and clawed Michal's flesh. He yelped as I growled.

"What have you done?"

His skin felt damp. His stench was putrid. He quivered and peered up at me, his words tripping over his tongue.

"Th – they were traitors." He shook his head, wincing as Avila pressed the stake into his chest. "The rare blood – I couldn't trust them – they all want it." He gestured toward the ceiling. His voice lowered. "What they say is true, Jett. The blood is power."

Avila twisted the stake into his coat. "Where is the damned blood, Michal? You told us it was here."

He became still then, his lips twisting into a grisly smile. "I hid it from them. I tricked the kindred." He laughed. "I had to kill them, Jett. If they had the blood and turned kindred, there would be no hope left to save what's left of humanity."

What the hell?

My thoughts reeled. I kept my grip firm. "The kindred are here?"

He nodded rapidly. "They've been here almost from the start. With some Guardians." He swallowed hard. "They call the overlord Marius. He let us live for the sake of our research. He's a cunning one … smart. He has a vision to build a functioning society for the clans. Humans will be hunted down, seized and kept alive as prisoners to bleed at their own discretion."

"They need scientists …"

"Yes! Specifically, hematologists."

Avila snorted. "That's why you're still breathing?" She dug the stake further into Michal's chest. Her eyes shadowed as he whimpered. "You've set us up. You've baited my dad here for them."

Michal shook his head furiously. "N – no, no. I might be many things, but I'm not a traitor!" He gave a rueful laugh. "I'm not suited for the world out there now." His gaze dropped to his arm as he slowly peeled back a grotty sleeve to reveal puncture marks trailing bruised skin.

Avila gasped. "It's already started."

Michal looked at me and reached into his coat pocket to produce a vial of blood. His fingers trembled. My stomach felt like metal as he spoke.

"You are the way to get the blood out of the city." He pushed the vial into my palm. "It's the gold our world knows now. It cannot fall into the wrongs hands, Jett."

I loosened my grip on him and took the vial. My head swirled and my body trembled as though with a fever. I glanced back at the dark room where the forsaken lay in torn pieces. Michal was utterly insane. Yet, an exceptional mind still lingered beneath the madness long enough to keep the rare blood from the enemy.

Avila lowered the stake. The sound of light footsteps drifted from the stairwell into the lab. Her eyes widened at me.

"They're coming."

Michal jerked. His eyes bulged as he gestured wildly toward the killing room. "Take the back-up stairs to the lobby. It's the door at the rear behind the benches and trolleys. Hurry!"

Back-up stairs? News to me.

There was no time to procrastinate. The sound of footsteps echoed down the stairwell shaft. I spun around with Avila as she flung open the heavy glass door and ran toward the back of the room where I spotted a discreet door beyond the stretcher and trolleys strewn with body parts.

I tried not to think about the blood or the blind eye sockets peering from mottled skin as I pushed Avila into the stairwell. As I stepped into the dark, narrow space and began to ease the door closed, the sound of the laboratory door cracked as it flung open.

I paused to peer through the slit in the door now inches apart to see a figure shadowing the threshold. His hair was glossy and dark above a milky complexion and crystal-blue eyes. He wore black leather and chunky boots. A swathe of crimson hugged his torso. My heart froze as he raised a jeweled hand to drum talons against the door frame and flash his white fangs. But it was the sound of his silvery voice that sent my blood cold as I quietly closed the door.

"Michal, Michal. What are you cooking up down here, hmm?" He chuckled. "My daytime slumber has been disturbed with the news you have received some visitors. You know how protective I am of my sleep …"

7

THE PROPOSITION

he vampire's image flashed through my mind. *Soulless eyes.* It wasn't even a thought. I was too pumped to think. My nerves felt stringy. My chest throbbed. I bounded up the stairs and every muscle strained. Sweat stung my eyes and almost blinded me as I shone the flashlight ahead. The stairwell was cramped, grotty and red. Dull scarlet lamps barely illuminated the landings. Human waste and stale iron snapped against my senses.

My breath was all I heard. *Or was it Avila's?* She took the stairs two at a time in front of me. My calves pounded. My ears buzzed. No time to think. Control was just beyond my grasp. We had to get out of here.

Three flights up, one to go. The door below creaked open, the faint sound grated into my heart. The jarred door blew in the sound of laughter. Lunacy. It was familiar. *Michal.* Avila stopped suddenly. She grasped the piped balustrade and swung around. Wide eyes peered at me through the dark as footsteps flew up the stairs behind us.

"Dad?"

I pushed a palm into her back. "Go!"

For Christ's sake – go!

The final landing loomed at the top of the stairs. Dark. Red. Hostile. My boots felt like a stampede. I pushed upwards. Avila was just about there. She yelped and tripped forward. I was so close behind her that she caught me in the offshoot. My chin slammed against her back and the machete slipped from my hand as I scrambled to get up.

I vaguely heard her behind me as she shifted to her feet and sprung onto the landing. The darkness was broken by a long hiss and golden eyes that glinted like firestones. Shallow breath. My fingers curled around the machete handle. I steadied my gaze to find him on the landing below me, golden hair like pink floss. Crimson lips appeared askew.

He leaned against the wall. His chin tilted and his lips twisted into a sinister grin. Shallow breath. My senses zoned in on him as I crouched on the stairs.

"Going somewhere without saying hello?" His voice was a singsong. He tapped long talons together. "Tsk. Tsk. Would-be warrior humans, when will you ever learn?"

My eyes never left his. The clock was ticking.

His eyes narrowed to slits. His voice throaty.

"You cannot outsmart or outrun a vampire. Give me the vial."

Shit. They know we've got the blood.

I took a sharp breath and grabbed the machete as he lunged up the stairs. He moved like speed. The machete blade slashed at his chest as his talons caught me.

He slipped to his knees, grinning. Blood spilled over the blade as I stood and swung again. He leapt to feet, catching the thrust of the blade with his hand and tearing it from my grasp. The metal clanked on the stairs and a roar tore from his throat as he lunged at me.

Time stalled as I dodged his yellow fangs and talons. Avila's low shriek clung in my ear as she slipped from behind and jabbed her stake through his heart. His nails dug into my arm as he froze. His jaw dropped and his expression paled before he collapsed.

His body crumbled onto the stairs.

Holy fuck.

I spun around to see Avila panting. More footsteps came from below. No time to think. My arms burned. So did my lungs. I grabbed the machete. We bolted toward the lobby door, bursting across the threshold and sprinting through the vast dim space that separated us from the streets. There was sunlight in the street. Relative safety.

The distance appeared unfathomable. I kept my focus on the big lobby door. Avila ran silently beside me. Adrenaline burned through my system, dulling the pain.

Fail and we were dead. Fail and the world would know even more evil.

My lungs silently screamed. Almost there. I reached for the chrome door handle and pulled. I heard a thump from behind. *What the hell?* Avila screamed beside me. My hand gripped the handle as I yanked on the door and turned to look for Avila. She was gone.

Sunlight flooded across the threshold and spilled into the lobby. I stood fast, jamming my boot against the heavy door as the warmth of the sun radiated over me. My chest heaved as my gaze darted around the lobby.

"Avila!"

"Dad!"

Her voice was followed by hideous laughter. That was when I saw her – trembling and ensnared between the claws of a vampire. My stomach dropped as I met her stare. They stood in the shadows along a wall painted gray that forked to give way to a series of long corridors. I hadn't seen him coming, and now, she was at his mercy.

The vampire's dark hair hung over his face and almost concealed eyes that glowed like neon lights as he held her firm. His fangs glistened only inches above her throat. She squirmed beneath his grasp and gritted her teeth.

"Let me go, asshole!"

He laughed, and his laughter was chorused by four other vampires as they emerged from the shadowy corridors to stand beside him. My heart felt like stone when I recognized Marius. It was defeat that gripped me.

I stood firm in the sunlight. I studied them as I struggled to gage the situation. The sun was neither friend nor foe in that moment. I wanted to burn to ashes as I beheld my daughter and took in her pallid expression and wild eyes. She swallowed visibly. Her eyes narrowed as she shook her head.

My little tough nugget.

I knew she meant for me not to yield to the bloodsuckers. Yet, I couldn't accept what that would mean for her. Hopelessness rimmed as Marius moved toward Avila. He clasped her hand and pulled her to him. His pale features were a striking contrast against his thick black hair as he regarded her before turning toward me, grinning.

"Jett, isn't it?" His brows raised as he looped an arm around Avila. He glanced down at her. "Such a beautiful daughter. Now, we both possess something that is precious to the other. What to do …"

I stiffened and lifted my chin.

"Let her go, Marius. I have what you want."

"Step away from the sunlight and give it to me." He went to stroke a strand of hair from Avila's face but she turned her head away and looked at me.

"No, dad. Don't give it to them."

Marius laughed. His barnacle cronies joined in behind him. I wanted to kill them all.

"Hmm … such fire!" Marius glanced at the others before giving Avila an approving nod. His gaze darkened when he looked back at me. "Quite an admirable trait, but one that will not keep her alive." He paused and took an exaggerated breath. "Tell you what; I have a proposition for you, Jett. I heard tell that you are an extraordinary hematologist – a skill I am in need of to help build the utopian world I have envisioned. Join us and no one needs to die today. In fact, no one need die ever. I'm offering you and your daughter the gift of eternal life. What do you say?"

I gaped at him as his words spiraled through my mind. It was despair that found victory over my emotions as I looked at Avila. She stood defiant and brave in the face of evil. Her eyes focused on me and my heart shattered as the weight of the situation shadowed me. If I handed the blood over to Marius, he would possess the power to transcend into a vampire with extraordinary abilities. He and his clan would become all powerful; monstrous creatures of the night that would ravage the earth and take every living being with them.

I could feel my veins bulging beneath my skin as Avila's eyes dampened and she mouthed the word 'no'. My heart lurched. I shuddered as I strained to provide an answer to a choice I'd never dreamed possible.

Dreams were yesterday's wishes on charred wings. The survival of humanity now rested on my shoulders and my daughter's life.

My beautiful little nugget.

8

CRY TO ME

*W*hen your baby leaves you all alone and nobody calls you on the phone.

Silence is a noise. Ragged breaths and the soulful sounds of Solomon Burke's *Cry to Me* screamed through my mind as I stared at my daughter. It was her favorite. The moments stalled. *My child.* Images of her long dark hair bouncing over her shoulders as she danced clung in my mind's vision. Flouncing yellow dresses. Small ruby lips breaking into laughter. The sweet sound of her voice when she called to me.

My heart ached. Her dewy lashes glistened despite the nod she gave me. The world spiraled with nothing beneath my feet. The lobby door cramped against my boot. My toes were numb. The beat of the sun slammed against my back. I wanted to die right then and there. Better that than to face the impossible choice confronting me.

Avila.

I was startled as Marius began humming the bluesy tune playing through my mind. My nerves spiked as I looked at him. His skin appeared luminous beneath the dull light as he spread his arms.

"Doncha feel like crying, Jett?" He looped his fingers beneath his chin, grinning. "Ah ... surprise, surprise! You weren't aware that some of us kindred have the ability to invade minds?" He laughed before snaring an arm around Avila. "It used to be my mother's favorite too. So, you see, we're going to be one big happy family!"

"Like hell we will!" Avila pushed against him, glaring. Her next words were delivered through gritted teeth. "You are a satanic brute."

She shrunk away as he hissed at her. Talons clawed at her hair. She didn't even whimper. Her jaw tightened as she glared at him. "Dick!"

He frowned at her with amusement before turning to me.

"I am growing very fond of your daughter. Her energy is ... intoxicating. Sometimes, we're not aware of what we're missing from our lives until we encounter it."

His grin dissolved as the noise of heavy footsteps came from the corridors behind him. "Play time is over. Bring me the vial or I'll have the Guardians take it from you."

A group of people suddenly spilled from the shadows into the lobby. There were about eight of them; men and women clad in dirty denim and knee-high boots with whips slung at their waists. Black bandanas hugged their skulls and their expressions were cold.

I could barely breathe as I surveyed them.

"When you're all alone in your lonely room and there's nothing but the smell of her perfume."

Time stopped as my gaze rested again on Avila. She was motionless, her image already fading as I took a step back. She mouthed the words *"I love you"* and my heart splintered into a thousand pieces.

Marius shouted as the sound of thudding boots charged toward me. The Guardians were on the move. It was time. I tore my eyes from Avila and spun around, sprinting from the lobby threshold into the street.

The air was a hot enemy and pain already an unwelcome friend. I was suffocating. *Dying.* My boots were concrete as I pushed forward. *Get to the corner.* The Guardians yelled out behind me. Lurking shadows filling doorways, watching the scene unfold. Manic laughter flooded the street. The corner came closer. *Closer.* My legs felt like pudding.

In the blur of the moment came another sound. *A machine? An engine?* My thoughts scattered. My tongue stuck to the roof of my mouth. *Breathe, Jett.* I fought for air. Go faster. My calves burned and I was blind. *Avila.* My ears pricked up through the deafening haze as a high-pitched screech crunched across the road.

Tires.

The muscles of my body tightened as I spotted the metallic blue Jeep come to a sudden halt at the corner.

What the fuck? My pace instantly slowed. I could feel the tremors in my body as the window lowered and the Guardians shouted from behind.

"Get the bastard!"

"Hurry!"

I glanced over my shoulder as swollen faces closed in fast. My fingers grasped the machete. There was no time to think. I swung my eyes back to the Jeep and the face that was distorted beneath golden hair.

"Jett! Get in!"

Sun?

I squinted, hesitating before bolting for the Jeep and flinging open the door to the shouts of the Guardians skidding up behind me.

"The bastard's getting away!"

"Motherfucker!"

I was still about to shut the door when Sun slammed her foot on the accelerator and sped off down the street. The Jeep engine roared and the hot wind gusted into my face as I yanked the door closed, my chest heaving as I stared back at her. Grimy slim fingers gripped the steering wheel. She chewed her bottom lip, glancing at me.

"Where's Avila?"

I squeezed my eyes shut as my body was racked with spasms. My throat hurt when I swallowed as I gazed ahead. All I could see was the image of Avila's bright lemon dress and her hair swinging as she danced.

I formed the words that tortured my soul. "She's gone."

Doncha feel like crying. Doncha feel like crying.

9

DEAD INSIDE

"Tea?" Sun's smile evaporated as fast as it had emerged. The dark circles beneath her eyes darkened. "You need to drink something … eat something."

I looked at the steaming mug she shoved toward me. My fingers felt numb.

"My grandmother used to say that tea makes everything better." Sun gave a half laugh. When I stared back at her, she bit her bottom lip and looked away as she sat down on the sofa next to me. "Take it. You're going to need your strength."

I took the mug and pondered the hot milky broth. My grandmother used to say the same thing about tea. It was a lie. No amount of tea could ease the constant stabbing sensation crippling my stomach, nor could it erase the evil that took my lover and claimed my daughter. Tea wouldn't make everything alright.

I tentatively took a sip and forced the liquid down my throat, grimacing. It hurt to swallow. It hurt to breathe. My skin was chilled from the inside out and it was guilt that weighed heavy on my heart. I was alive. Avila was not. I had forsaken her for a future hung on false dreams and unfounded myths. I'd failed my daughter.

Dreams have no place in this new reality. Dreams are nothing but feeble whims on the devil's tongue. They mean nothing.

I set the mug down on the coffee table and stood up, running my fingers through my dark hair and sighing. *Dead.* Everything inside me felt bloodless. I barely glanced at Sun as I paced the cottage sitting room.

"You should go. The hawkers will be here before long."

"I already told you, I'm not going anywhere. There's nothing left for me."

There's nothing left for anyone.

I stopped at the window and peeled back the curtain, scanning the cottage porch and yard. My gaze settled on the dense twisted trunks bordering the gravel clearing as I contemplated her sudden appearance in my life. She had said she knew where to find me in the city the day before; that she'd followed us before discovering her daughter's remains perishing on the floor of her living room. She said she had guns.

I spun around to see her bottom lip trembling, but her azure eyes blazed. I sighed.

"Stay with me and you'll probably die before the end of this day."

She gave a rueful laugh and rubbed her palms over her jeans. Her eyes moistened.

"You are the kindest person left in this world. You helped me when nobody else would." She shook her head, her stringy golden hair clinging to her cheekbones. Her voice lowered. "I'll die with you today, Jett."

Her words were delivered with simplicity, yet they struck hard against my heart. I shook my head. I barely knew this woman and didn't understand her reasoning, but there was no need to. In a world overrun by vampires, swindlers and criminals, nothing made sense anymore. She was a ray of light in an eternal darkness. She *was* like the sun.

"Your parents named you well."

She smiled as our eyes briefly locked before I looked away and walked to where her guns lay on the floor. I picked up a long-barrelled firearm. My hands were clammy against the cold metal, but I felt a sense of comfort as I drew back the hammer and cocked the rifle before propping it by the cottage door. I'd never been overly fond of guns, nor had I owned one. Things were different now.

Sun stood and came up beside me. She selected a Glock 9mm handgun from the small stash of weapons and started inspecting the dull black short-barrelled pistol. Quick fingers ejected and reinserted the magazine before expertly gripping the handle and stuffing it in the pocket of her jeans. My curiosity was aroused but I said nothing.

"Where do you want me?" She flicked her chin toward the front door. "You want me to hide out in the trees?"

"No, they use the forest grounds as their cover. Stay by the window and keep out of sight. Train your gun on whoever has Scarla. If it goes to shit, kill as many of them as you can."

"With pleasure."

Scarla.

Just saying her name caused the shadow in my heart to deepen. I turned away and headed back to the window as my thoughts swirled with a thousand questions. *Had I done the right thing by leaving Avila at the mercy of vampires for the sake of preventing further mayhem and horror? Had I made the right decision? Was she dead already?*

Whether she was dead or not didn't matter in that moment – or even if I'd made the right decision. The choice had already killed me on the inside, and I knew I would never forgive myself whatever the outcome.

The only thing that mattered now was Scarla and her safety. Rare blood and super-powerful vampires be damned. One of my girls had to survive this ordeal. Whatever became of the blood would be out of my hands once I traded it to the hawkers for Scarla's return. I had to believe their hatred for the kindred would be enough to keep it from falling into their clawed hands. At least until I could realign and plan to retrieve it.

I was thinking all these things when a movement in the yard caught my eye. I instantly stiffened as a dozen hawkers slinked from the shadowy trees into the clearing. I motioned to Sun who nodded and dashed toward the other window facing the porch. She meshed her slim body against the wall and stole a glance through the curtains, gripping her gun close to her chest as the sound of boots thumped on the porch stairs.

My heart thundered. Sweat pooled across my brow as I scanned the group of hawkers and spotted the tall nasty looking one that had delivered their ransom conditions forty-eight hours ago. He was clad in the same get-up – faded leather and dirty boots. His teeth were like rust between ginger whiskers as he grinned, and he fingered his switchblade as he bounded up the stairs.

He banged on the flimsy door and at the same time, I saw Scarla. My eyes widened as she emerged from the trees with her feet dragging between two male hawkers who gripped her arms. Her pale hair hung over her face that was blotched with angry welts. Her swollen lips fell apart above a bruised jaw while her shredded clothes barely concealed her body.

What the fuck?

Rage took hold. Death was my friend. It was hot steel that claimed my blood and drowned out any coherent thoughts as I grabbed my machete before stomping toward the door and flinging it open to face my enemies. A sinister smile greeted me.

"Right on time." The gingered hawker gave a wry laugh. His weathered eyes dropped to the machete I gripped at my side. He twirled the switchblade. "What ya think you're gonna do with that, eh?"

Cut you all to pieces.

"Touch my woman again and you'll find out, asshole."

He growled and his eyes flashed at me before he glanced over his shoulder toward his mob. I braced myself and followed his gaze, taking in the leathered men carrying an array of weapons. Some carried swords in worn scabbards that swaddled their waists while others held blades and chains. Two hawkers stood at the foot of the forest doused in the shadows and pointing rifles at me. But it was the gangly looking man holding a hunting knife at Scarla's throat that really caught my attention.

Dizziness threatened to overtake me when she lifted her chin long enough to blink at me through bloated eyes. Her head lulled forward, the afternoon sun catching the blood staining her scalp.

"Scarla." Her name clung on my lips and panic seized me. I stepped across the threshold but ginger-beard sidestepped closer, blocking my way to the stairs.

A thick layer of grime crammed the wrinkles around his eyes as laughter erupted among the group. He cocked his head. His voice was gruff.

"Let's start over, shall we? If you'd like to avoid

watching the tart bleed like a dirty pig today, I suggest you give me what I came here for."

My eyes stung as I glared at him and slowly reached into my pocket to retrieve the vial of blood that represented my daughter's death and Scarla's torture. The same drops of blood I knew would forever represent the death inside of me. Things were different now; everything felt bloodless.

10
THE VOID

"*M*arla!" Dark eyes flickered at me. Ginger-beard licked his lips as he clutched the vial of blood.

Void.

Some moments were barren of thought. His eyes bored into me. My mouth was a desert. A thin figure pushed through the hawkers crowding the stairs. A woman.

I glanced at her as she took the vial, pausing to look at me with a twisted grin. Her skin appeared cracked and discolored beneath the dull shine of the studs and hoops adorning her face. Her gray eyes were cold.

"How long?" Ginger-beard said.

"Six minutes." Marla pulled a small box from her jacket pocket – a blood test kit. She dropped to her knees and began fidgeting with it with tremulous fingers.

Ginger-beard scraped the end of his switchblade

across calloused knuckles and grunted a reply. Scarla sobbed as hawker fingers knotted in the hair at her nape. A rusty blade balanced at her throat. She trembled as she looked back at me. *Torment.* It killed. I could barely control the pain. The sound of his voice was like salt on a wound.

"People like you always thought you were superior to everyone else. White collar bullshit blinders. Used to get around like your shit didn't stink in your cars and shiny suits." He gave a half laugh. His breath was a stench. "I'm not a bloodsucker lover, but I can't help but take satisfaction in how things have turned out ... I always believed that one day people like you would get what's coming to ya; white collar crimes finally caught up when your biological poison went wrong."

He leaned closer. "Justice. That's what that is. You people were so caught up in your own asses that you never saw it coming, did ya? Where did all that education and privilege get ya at the end of the world, eh?"

I tightened my grip on the machete.

"I'm still here, fucktard."

He laughed. "I'm looking at a dead man walking. You don't have what it takes to see this out. This world isn't made for your kind anymore."

The hawkers lingering on the stairs chuckled but I ignored them as Marla stood up suddenly. She waved a piece of cardboard between filthy fingers. The silver rings on her brows lifted.

"Score!"

My breath quickened.

Void.

Some moments seemed endless. I swung my eyes back to ginger-beard. A pasty yellow tongue stuck out as he grinned.

"Well, well, the blue-eyed white neck delivered after all."

My throat felt like sharp glass.

"That's right. You've got your ransom." I flicked my chin. "Leave the woman and get the hell off my property."

His eyes pierced into me. "You might just have a half decent set for a club-fed." He gave a snigger and my blood ran cold. Marla laughed.

His voice filled my head. "Bleed the pig!"

Void.

Some moments swallowed you whole. My brain felt like an acute explosion as the hawker yanked Scarla's head back. The sound of her cry blasted in my ears as the rusty blade sunk into her throat and slid across her skin, releasing a flood of blood from the jagged wound.

"Scarla!"

I roared and swung the machete as I charged forward, collecting Marla in the back of her skull just as she spun around to move away. The blade cracked against bone. Manic gripped me. I drove the shank forward with the thrust of the motion as loud cracks rang out across the yard. The sound of the gunfire instantly purified my mind.

Clarity.

Some moments feel as if you see the following scene unfold before it happens. Time slowed. Marla dropped to the floor as the hawkers on the stairs lunged forward, propelling blades and swinging chains ahead of them.

Fuck.

More shots fired. My ears buzzed. I jabbed the machete in front of me, piercing leather as a stabbing pain detonated in the side of my gut. My flesh felt like sponge. The odor of blood mingled in the air along with the shouting hawkers. Pain was a welcome friend beneath the repeated strikes of ginger-beard's switchblade. I stumbled back, instinctively reaching to quell the wound as I managed to stabilize my footing.

My fingers were warm, sticky. My head began to spin. Ginger-beard cackled like an old hag. Sinister. Wicked. His ugly face contorted before me as I swung the machete. The effort was lost as the end of a chain caught around my wrist. Metal stung my flesh as the machete clanked to the timber floor and gunfire reverberated over the cottage. The sound of squawking birds mixed with laughter. I balled my fists and launched a right hook at a converging hawker. A blade plunged into my gut. Images distorted.

Scarla.

My heart felt like a blackened husk as I doubled over. My boots were awkward. I stumbled again. Sweat dripped into my eyes. Or was it blood? I couldn't breathe.

My hands clenched my stomach as my head filled with pain.

Thwack! A white flash zapped behind my eyes. Then I was spiraling. My legs gave way and I fell hard to the brutal blows of dirty boots and blunt chains.

Void.

Some moments are not spent within our fleshy exteriors. I drifted away. Darkness beckoned as ginger-beard bent over me to trace the switchblade across my cheek.

"I was wrong about you, white neck." He paused the blade, digging the pointy end into the flesh just below my eye. "You ain't got nothing between your legs that your high-end pussy didn't have. We did her real good. She was a running train and screamed just as loud as one." He gave a throaty chuckle and stretched to his feet. "I'll let you think about that while you bleed. We did ya solid."

The image of receding boots doubled as numbness took hold. A chill ran across the back of my neck and radiated through my body. My eyes felt heavy. *Heavy.* A whirling sensation overtook and then there was nothing.

Void.

"*Dance with me.*"

"*I'm an awful dancer.*"

"*You're wrong. Your soul dances with mine every day.*"

There are some places you can't remember but can't forget. She had a secret; a garden filled with precious blooms and wild roses. *Eden.* I had never known a love so deep; so pure. *She was a gift on earth.* Now, she was nothing. Her dreams were invisible dust on lost memories. Scarla was gone.

"Bella donna." I didn't recognize my voice as I hunched over the steering wheel of the pickup and struggled to focus on the road. Sun groaned. The sound of her voice startled me as her head lulled on my lap.

I glanced down at her, flinching as the moonlight struck golden hair stained crimson. Our blood mingled.

My hands were tacky as I reached to stroke her forehead. Her skin was ice. "Almost there. Stay with me."

Her body lay curled up on the pickup bench seat. She was limp and pitted from the bullets that had hit her. Her lips were tinged blue as her jaw slackened beneath fluttering eyelids.

"Wha – where are we going?"

I barely heard her above the rumbling engine as we careened through city streets. The broken white lines on the road flashed against the headlights like apparitions. *Death is unforgiving.* I was clawing at its door. *Stay or go?* Nothing left to breathe for; nothing except the score. It's strange how we find our greatest strength when looking down the barrel of oblivion.

"We're going to level the score."

My body felt raw. I was butchered and bleeding. It hurt to breathe and my mind was a hazy impression of honey-amber eyes and sensuous plump lips. *The place I can never remember; the place I'll never forget.* Grief lingered somewhere above me. Or perhaps it was grief that froze my heart and overrode my senses as the pickup skidded around the final corner, but it was hatred that motivated me when I slammed my foot on the brake outside the building.

An eerie quietness shrouded the cabin when I killed the engine. The moments stilled as I peered ahead at nothing. *Nothing.* I didn't see the darkness flooding the street nor the towering shadows cast by the buildings. All

I saw were fading memories of a life I would never know again.

Sometimes, the choices we make aren't ours to decide. Sometimes, the path forces us to unfathomable places. My choice to come here felt as if it was out of my hands. I'd come here for retribution. I'd come to do the unthinkable; to pledge the remainder of my days to darkness, violence and yield to the thirst of blood. I'd come here to be undead. But I couldn't make that choice for Sun. She had to choose for herself.

I gazed at her as she drifted in and out consciousness. She was pasty. Her breath was shallow and erratic. Like me, she wouldn't survive her wounds for much longer. My tongue felt thick as I swallowed and tried to rouse her, stroking back a lock of her hair and speaking her name. She groaned softly.

"You're a survivor, Sun. A ray of light in a world of fear and shadows." I paused as she opened her eyes to gaze up at me. I forced a smile. "You have to choose now – death or eternal life in death."

Her lashes clung together as she blinked and stiffened. Her bottom lip slackened before she lifted a hand and reached for my chin, wincing.

"J -Jett?"

I cupped my hand over hers and leaned my chin against her palm, squeezing my eyes shut as my heart shredded along with the blood oozing from my gut. Her skin was clammy and cold. Yet, the gesture was profoundly comforting and among the last I would ever know in my humanity. When I looked back at her, she merged with the tears blinding my eyes.

Her lips quivered as she inhaled sharply.

"I'll die with you tonight, Jett." She flinched and coughed. Her eyes dimmed as she looked at me again. "I'll go where you go."

I pressed my lips to her forehead. "Whatever happens, don't let them take your soul."

The sounds of unearthly screams caught in the still of the night and echoed along the street. My ears pricked and I felt my pulse quicken. I felt a sense of detachment as I climbed from the pickup and scooped Sun in my arms.

Cold.

I felt like a ghost despite the warm air that blew as I carried Sun toward the lobby doors of the building where I'd left my daughter the day before.

Weight. My knees almost buckled beneath the strain. I welcomed the pain. My veins throbbed but I relished the last of the fading warmth beneath my skin. I barely heard the distorted cries and harrowing shrieks carried on the slight breeze as they became closer. *Closer.*

The shadows came alive as dark figures emerged from the darkness. I balked as I clung to Sun and looked at them. Neon eyes glinted back at me from pallid expressions and milky skin. Scarlet lips curled up to reveal the dull gleam of fangs; hair glossed over shoulders clad in satiny attire as they regarded me. One of them started to move closer.

She regarded me from under a veil of vibrant red hair that cascaded to her waist. She reached out to stroke a talon across Sun's cheek before flicking her cat-like eyes at me. Full lips broke into a grin.

"Welcome to the Mysticus clan, your daughter awaits you."

12

BLACK HEART

*B*lack hole. *Black heart. Black everything.*

 I looked up at the night sky. Silvery clouds stretched across the half moon and the stars shone like cryptic messages. Bats soared on silent wings while the sounds of night creatures echoed in my ears. Nothing had changed. Yet, everything had changed. No single element appeared the same to my vampire senses. Everything was accentuated. Everything was striking.

 "Are you ready, dad?" Avila's eyes flashed electric blue through the dark. Her skin appeared luminous and as pale as the clouds overhead as we stood at the foot of the forest assessing the cabin in the clearing.

 The torment swirled in my gut and almost quelled the thirst biting at my veins when I looked at her. *My girl.* Ribbon laced braids and days at the fair. Lipstick on prom night. The way her eyes turned green before she was about to tell me a lie. Warm blood and a human heart. My girl had died and I wasn't there for her. She had been reborn into the cold-blooded beings now dominating our world. She was now a vampire. It was time to level the score.

I gave a slight nod and glanced at Sun who stood next to Avila. Her golden hair tumbled over shoulders clad in black leather. It was just as lustrous as the eyes gleaming back at me. Her long talons clung at her hips as her gaze deepened.

"Are you sure you want to do this?"

My jaw tightened.

"Yes."

Boisterous laughter erupted from behind the weathered timber walls of the cabin as the door flung open. A hawker male swayed as he gripped the balustrade to steady himself before making his way down the stairs. His voice slurred when he mumbled. Whiskey and tobacco mingled with the sickly odor of week-old sweat and carried on the breeze. His boots dragged across the clearing toward a tree. He belched repeatedly as he fiddled with his fly. The sound of his beating heart was intoxicating. I groaned inwardly and stepped forward, stopping when Sun grabbed my arm. Her fangs glinted with her hiss.

"Marius will kill you."

My veins bulged with the venom coursing through me. It took everything I had to tame the rage. I reached for her hand. Cold on cold. Darkness accompanied apathy. It was consuming. I held her gaze. My lips barely moved when I replied.

"He already has."

I released her hand and spun around before sprinting toward the hawker. The shadows were a part of me; the breeze was my ride. Blood was my lover. I stopped behind him and tilted my head to the side, watching as he stiffened before slowly cranking his neck around to look at me. Spidery eyes widened as I grinned.

"Hello, friend."

He gasped. The tips of his filthy beard fell as he stumbled back.

"Wha – what the hell?"

"Suitable word."

Black hole.

I could feel the pressure splintering in the pit of my stomach. My pulse throbbed desperately. I ensnared a hand around his throat. My talons cut into his skin as I rolled back my lips, hissing. My movements were effortless. The sound of his wail distorted in my ears when I flung my jaw forward to sink my fangs into his flesh, instantly relishing the taste of the blood he offered. His pulse was ecstasy.

Sweet. Salty. Warm.

In the cold-blooded creature I'd become, it was the warmth I craved above all else. But there was not enough blood to bring back my humanity. There was not enough vengeance to bring back Scarla nor return Avila to her mortality. But there was the blood of dreams and dreams were yesterday's wishes – and those wishes were my retribution.

I'd come here for more than just the blood of the hawkers that had killed Scarla. I had come with the promise of returning to Marius the rare blood he so desperately sought to possess. Promises made by the undead remained undead.

A growl tore through my throat as I released the hawker. He slumped at my feet. His blood coursed into my being. Elation gripped me. I felt my eyes blaze as Avila and Sun watched silently, the hunger in their stare unmistakable. I nodded and licked my lips.

"The ginger-beard is mine. No survivors."

Demons. That was the word circling in my mind as we took the steps onto the cabin porch before crossing the threshold into the sitting room. Demons for the merciless creatures we had become and for the treacherous acts we now bestowed upon surviving humans. We had become what I had despised the most – slaves to the darkness and forever damned.

Avila and Sun stood either side of me as we paused to take in the scene. About a dozen hawkers sprawled on the lounges and lingered around the edges of the room, cackling. One of them sat on the floor and strummed an old guitar. Smoke curled from makeshift ashtrays and glowing pipes. Through the haze a withered coffee table crammed with bottles of whiskey and dirty glasses was the center of their world.

Black heart.

Silence fell as they became aware of us. Promises of death foreshadowed. It had never sounded so pleasing. My nostrils flared as I inhaled fragrant gifts. Sour pickings. Riffraff lineage flowing in sanguine fluid beckoned as I curled my upper lip and my eyes settled on ginger-beard.

His dark eyes flashed as he stood up. The machete he fingered was familiar. Sweat formed across his brow and clung to the tips of his beard as he squared his shoulders, facing me. The machete balanced ahead of him.

Some of the hawkers gathered beside him; others cried out and made for the doors leading to other parts of the cabin. There was no place they could hide.

My gaze rested on the machete.

"What do you think you're gonna do with that, hmm?"

Ginger-beard swallowed. His heart thumped in my ear.

"I shoulda known you was a traitor to your kind." He shook his head. "Club-fed pussy. Taking deals with the devil and feeding on the blood of the innocent. This was the only the way you could make it in the new world."

"Perhaps you're right." I stepped forward. "But sometimes the people claiming to be our kind force us to make choices we never dreamed possible."

He took a sharp breath. His fingers tightened around the machete handle. Avila and Sun began to advance. The hawkers standing next to him started to back away. Ginger-beard's lips trembled.

"You came here for the blood – you can have it!" His fingers shook as he reached into his jacket pocket to produce the vial. "Take it – but hear this, blood-sucker – the time will come when the earth will know reckoning; an era when the Blood Legend will appear to right the wrongs of your kind and claim vengeance on all kindred. You will fall and you will fail." He tossed the vial at me. "And I'll be laughing from my grave."

I gave a half laugh. Failure already blackened my heart. I slipped the vial in my pocket before lifting my arms in a sweeping gesture. When I spoke, my voice was hollow.

"Bleed the pigs."

Black everything.

I lunged for ginger-beard as he swung the machete. The blade pierced my stomach but I felt nothing. His hair was like matted straw as I gripped his forehead. Bloodshot eyes swelled and brimmed from sunken sockets. Screams and wails reverberated across the room. Avila and Sun screeched as talons tore through flesh and fangs sunk into skin. I dug my fingers into his face. He didn't even struggle as I looked into his eyes and gave him a black smile.

"You stole a part of my soul and now I'll take yours with me to hell."

I roared before abruptly twisting his head between my hands. The sound of bone crunched beneath the impact, but I didn't stop. I couldn't stop. A red haze filled my vision as I tore his head from his neck in one fluid action. Blood sprayed over me. My eyes closed and I saw Scarla.

Warm honeyed eyes. Long dark lashes. Soft skin, platinum locks and sensual hips. Lips and love; my love. *Bella donna.* She smiled and reached for me as my heart cracked and my soul yearned for one last touch – one final kiss. And then she was gone, and everything was black and bloody, and curdling cries filled the air as I looked at the unfolding massacre.

Black everything.

I turned away and left the cottage. I bolted through the forest. My feet were like wings. My heart pumped darkness. I stopped at the edge of the sea to gaze down at the footprints that spread like golden illusions beneath the pale moonlight.

My fingers felt like steel as I reached for the vial of rare blood; blood that had the power to transform me into something more powerful than any other vampire on earth. The same blood that took my girls.

I removed the lid from the vial, dropped to my knees and gazed at the dark sea. The cold water rushed all around me with the incoming tide. I felt nothing. *Nothing.*

"Did you ever want to step into someone else's feet?"

Scarla's voice taunted the edge of my soul as I recalled the last of our conversations.

"Don't you mean shoes?"

"No."

I threw the vial into the receding waves and called her name. My voice was instantly stolen in the wind.

"Thousands of footprints have marked this beach over just as many years; I'd give anything to step in any one of them."

I stretched to my feet. Her name was a whisper on my lips as I began following the prints back up the beach toward the road.

"But then you wouldn't be here with me in this moment."

Prints that would haunt me forever.

BLOOD LEGENDS

REBIRTH

BL

USA Today Bestselling Author

KIM PETERSEN

1

DARK CHAMBERS

*I*ndifference felt like cold armor. Hunger gripped me. *Exhausting.* My mind contorted. I squeezed my eyes shut and hung my head. Strangled sobs tormented me. Each cry stoked the insatiable need to feed on their blood. My veins palpitated beneath my skin. I shivered and groaned as I shifted my back against the sandstone wall. My ass was paralyzed.

Avila's body curled on the ground. Her head was heavy in my lap and she trembled in a fitful slumber. Candlelight offended my senses. Sun's voice rasped over my pulse.

"Is this how it ends for us – starving in a filthy airless cell mocked by our food?" She gave a rueful laugh.

I lifted my chin to look at her beside me. Her skin was like chalky mesh sunk against cheekbones. Her hair fell in dull yellow clumps, almost concealing the stony eyes peering back at me. She licked chafed lips and flicked her chin toward the opposite cell. It was crammed with humans. There must have been about fifty of them.

"I can't tell which side was better."

I squinted toward the other cell. My joints ached; especially my knuckles as I clenched and unclenched them. The scent of fear and sweat carried along the shadowy shaft separating the cells. It hurt to look at them. Their offerings were too much to bear.

"Neither."

My gaze lingered on a woman who stood pressing her forehead against the rusty steel bars. Grimy fingers clutched the metal posts; burnt-red hair like straw. Brown eyes ebbed as she blinked at me. My ears pricked with the sound of her thumping heart. My mouth watered. I tore my eyes away from her and swallowed hard.

"We're all living the nightmare no matter which side we're on."

Sun grazed a hand across my arm. Her skin was like ice.

"I'm on your side, that's all that counts."

Emptiness gripped me when I looked at her. Time had lost meaning. *How long had we been here? Weeks? Months?* Endless time snatched in the shadows and feeding on sewer rats. We were prisoners now; thrown in the putrid cells beneath the city with the humans they hunted and collected. It was punishment for betraying Marius. I deserved it, but Avila and Sun didn't.

My eyes locked onto hers.

"I'm … sorry."

I'm so sorry.

She shook her head.

"Don't be." She leaned in closer as the sound of stomping boots drifted along the tunnels. "Remember what you told me; don't let them take your soul, Jett."

"What soul?"

She said nothing but her darkening stare conveyed her thoughts. The truth was my soul was sucked into a black abyss the day Scarla was murdered. It was the same day I'd made the choice to die. But even the apathy accompanying my human death couldn't erase the agony she left behind. Everything was meaningless without her.

Death could claim me again.

I looked away from Sun as Avila stirred. She sat up, stretching over sickly pale features and pitted eyes. Dark hair brushed at her waist as she cocked her head.

"The guards are coming." Her voice was hoarse.

"Yes."

Her eyes widened at me. Fangs glinted as she winced before she made the move to stand up. Her legs buckled slightly when she extended an arm toward me.

"Get up."

My girl.

She was the only reason I had to keep going. I reached for her hand and hauled myself up, steadying myself against the wall. I felt like cardboard. Weakness crept through me, but I ignored it as a low rumble began to rise among the human captives across the way.

High pitched shrills and disembodied wails erupted as

they began clawing at one another in an effort to distance themselves from the cell entrance. Terror was an intoxicating emotion. Excitement rimmed.

"The vampire guards are coming!"

"God, help us … Please, no!"

Limbs entangled. A few of them fell beneath the panicking mob. The blunt sound of crushing bones was a distinct melody in my ear. My gaze found the woman who still clutched the cell bars. Ragged lips mumbled breathless secrets. Her eyes were closed. She appeared in another world.

Sun stood beside me. We exchanged a look before I pushed off the wall and walked toward the cell bars. I stopped across from the woman and watched her, tuning out to the chaotic fever and the laughter that echoed along the tunnel walls as the guards drew closer.

She shifted her weight from side to side and squeezed her eyes shut even tighter. Her shoes were made of worn brown leather and fringed a pair of torn denim jeans. She flung her head back. Grime appeared like patchwork over the skin of her throat. Her words became frantic. Louder.

"Lygarou … Lygarou … the prophecy is born … the city will burn to ashes."

Avila and Sun sidled up either side of me. Screams escalated. Mayhem like wild alley cats. My heart pounded. My fangs ached for blood. Four guards rounded the bending shaft and came into view. Avila stiffened.

"Lygarou?"

I shrugged. My gut curdled as I looked back at her.

She froze suddenly. Shadows flickered across her face like an apparition as she steadied her gaze on me. Lips spoke cryptic messages.

"I've seen the birth of a Lystalker – the half-breed. She's arrived to ignite the Legends of Blood."

"Legends of Blood?"

I frowned and gripped the steel bars. The guards halted between the cells. They were clad in the usual black leather attire customary to the kindred. Chunky boots adorned their feet and twisted on the damp ground. They had their backs to me.

The woman's eyes darted toward the guards. They sniggered and cackled, nudging one another as they surveyed the humans. The prisoners quietened, albeit for a man who lay curled and groaning on the floor. Blood oozed from his skull and spilled over his fingers as he clutched the wound.

Thirst stabbed my stomach like a serrated knife.

I looked back at the woman as one of the guards hissed and held up a set of keys, shaking them. He laughed even louder when some of the people sobbed, shrinking further into the shadows. Just as the cell gate creaked open, the woman took a quick breath before she mouthed two words at me: "Blood Legends."

Blood Legends.

A chill went through me. Mysterious predictions and farfetched superstitions haunted me. They were the same words that had passed from the ginger-beard hawker before I tore his head from his neck. Words that foretold a time of reckoning that would bring the kindreds undone. Our greatest existential threat.

I had to know more.

Two of the guards converged on the human prisoners. The crowd instantly became restless. A few women screeched as the guards hunched over them, hissing before ensnaring sharp talons around their arms and dragging them closer.

I looked away. My attention was captured by the guards that had turned our way and were now opening our cell door. All thoughts of Blood Legends and folklore evaporated as eyes the color of bright lemons pierced into me.

Conceit. I could smell it. He leaned against the cell bars and regarded us with a dark grin. His mouth was a shock of scarlet, parting to reveal stained fangs. His crony had a neck like a bull. He grunted and pushed into the cell behind lemon-eyes, stopping with a sneer. An inky stare settled on Sun.

"It appears as if fortune has bestowed upon you this day." Lemon-eyes ran bony fingers through his hair, giving his head a toss for good measure.

"How so?" Avila gripped her hips and glared.

His grin widened. Screams shattered my ears. I looked back at the other cell to see the guards hauling three prisoners from the chamber. Two women; one man. The redheaded woman was among them. Lemon-eyes' voice grated into my bones.

"The Masters have decided it is time for your citation. You are to have an audience with Master Zaros."

Zaros? The name was unfamiliar. My thoughts scattered as the three humans were shoved into our cell. They stumbled and immediately cowered together as the guards returned to the other cell. Hunger overwhelmed me as I eyed the fresh blood now within arm's reach.

"Yes ... you are permitted to feed before your attendance." Lemon-eyes motioned toward the man and two women who began to sob uncontrollably. Not the redhead though. She stood trembling but her eyes daggered into mine when I looked at her.

Lygarou. They're coming; the prophecy holds true. I can show you.

The words weren't spoken yet I heard them clearly. I turned to see the guards dragging the wounded humans from the other chamber. Some of them were dead. Agonizing wails reverberated all around.

Lemon-eyes spoke again.

"Well; what are you waiting for?" he laughed. "You must be famished. Your feast awaits you."

Sun and Avila didn't hesitate. Desperation was like a vapor as they moved forward. The guards yanked the injured who were still alive over the cell threshold, dumping them near my feet. My eyes darted back to the woman. Her gaze widened. My pulse screamed as I stepped forward.

"Wait!"

All eyes turned on me. I squared my chin and gestured toward the woman.

"That one is of use to the Masters. Let her live."

"Why?" Lemon-eyes glared. Talons twirled the ends of his hair.

"Because she's a witch with valuable knowledge."

The guards laughed but Lemon-eyes didn't. He slinked closer to me. Eyes like deadly firestones burned into mine.

"What knowledge does the witch possess?"

"She knows about the Blood Legend prophecy."

His features twisted and paled beneath the dim light.

"Very well. We shall inform the Masters." He flicked a wrist toward his cronies. "Return her and fetch another!"

An odd sense of relief flooded through me. My gaze fell to the groaning man at my feet. I bent to my knees and gripped his head roughly. My pulse quickened. Anticipation had never been so sweet. My fangs sunk into human flesh and reprieve was mine. I fed like a demon.

Hunger did have a soul. It was created from human flesh and blood, and death was its heart.

And it owned me.

2

TREASON HAS A SCENT

"*W*ell, well, look at what the fangbangers dragged in!"

The guards halted abruptly either side of us. Lemon-eyes tittered. They'd led us down a series of dank tunnels that eventually gave way to an open burrow deep beneath the city. It was part of the subway grid.

My boots scuffed against gravel. Sun and Avila stopped either side of me as I searched for the speaker who I assumed to be Zaros. I saw no one. *Moths.* Their wings sounded like an acoustic tune as they sought out flames.

Fact: *They don't hand out instruction manuals when you turn kindred. Humanity eludes me. I'm not sure how I feel about that yet.*

The area was spacious. My senses flared with stale air and candlewax; burning candles balanced on wrought iron candelabras. Shadows stretched and writhed over black glyphs and symbols across the walls. Red satin adorned lengthy lounges and appeared viable. The kindred loved red. Perhaps it was because the color now represented our lifeforce.

My gaze lingered on scarlet satin. I felt heady. *Drunk.* Fresh human blood fused in my veins. It was euphoric. I shook my head. I had to keep it together. *Who knew what they had in store for us?* Provocative sensations and red visions shattered when the throaty voice spoke again.

"I detect the scent of treason in the air."

I frowned and whirled toward the sound of the speaker, spotting a dark figure doused in the shadows in a far corner.

"What say you, Blade?" The figure stepped forth and lingered at the edge of the gloom. Onyx eyes glimmered. Thick pearly fangs were the next thing I saw as he grinned. "How would you describe the stench of treason?"

Fact: *Lemon-eyes has a name.*

Blade's lanky figure shifted. A satanic smile erupted as he tossed his long mane and looked at us. His nostrils were like a bonfire.

"Worse than the decaying rats they've been feeding on."

The bullnecked vampire chuckled as he gripped Sun's arm and pulled her closer.

"This one smells like a canary." A chunky tongue swept across meaty lips. "I always had a thing for little birdies."

She scowled and yanked her arm free.

"Take your *thing* elsewhere, dipshit. I'm no birdie."

He responded with a hiss. I grimaced. His breath was distinguishable even from my position on the other side of Sun. It was disgusting.

Laughter chilled me to the core.

"Now, now, children, there will be plenty of time to play later."

I got my first real glimpse at him as he emerged entirely from the shadows. A short clump of jet hair spread over his scalp and shone almost violet above ebony skin. An engraved silver buckle was all that broke the black leather covering all his body. Bejeweled fingers stroked his jaw as he regarded us.

He was striking … captivating. But I didn't dwell on his appearance too long. My thoughts were stolen by more urgent affairs. Like how was I going to get us out of this mess for one?

The dark vampire tilted his head.

"But first we must tend to the matter at hand." He grinned. "We must decide the fate of our betrayers."

Question: *How could I be deemed a betrayer when I felt nothing for the kindred?*

Answer: *It didn't matter. I was a pawn beneath vampire law now, whatever that meant.*

Suddenly he was in front of me and breathing in my face. Black eyes flashed red. "I am Zaros." His stare crept over Avila and Sun before settling back on me. I tried not to swallow visibly. "No doubt you have heard of me?"

I shook my head.

"Can't say that I have."

"Regardless, I am to decide your misfortune for your actions against the clan."

"Have we not experienced enough misfortune rotting and starving in that deplorable cell for weeks on end?"

He leaned closer. "And you think that is adequate penance for intentionally discarding the one vial of AB positive blood known to exist?"

I held his gaze. My thoughts collected but I said nothing.

"You broke your word to Lord Marius."

"Yes."

"Why?"

Words cut over my tongue. "Because that blood destroyed everything I loved and held dear."

Lips barely moved in a half-laugh.

"There is nothing precious left in this world now. Nothing save for the blood you destroyed." His face contorted as he growled and lunged for me. Talons plunged into my throat. "You eradicated a chance at evolution for our kind and you speak of love?"

"Love was the only thing worth living for."

He laughed as his talons sunk deeper into my flesh. Blood rushed to the surface.

"So, what do you live for now, hmm?"

He grinned and I stiffened as his gaze trailed to Avila. The scent of my blood spilling over his fingers quickened my pulse. A bright flash pulsed behind my eyes and he was gone just as fast, ensnaring his claws around Avila and hissing.

Bullneck grabbed Sun. She shrieked and pushed against him. He laughed. The sound was hideous. Blade combed a hand through his hair and sniggered. My eyes pierced into Zaros as he gave a drawn-out snarl.

"Perhaps I was wrong." He went to stroke Avila's hair. Her face flushed with resistance, but months of existing from the blood of rodents rendered her useless against his strength. "I never fathered a child, but I do believe the love of a parent is unsurpassed in its power."

Question: *Did I want to find out what happens when a vampire kills one of their own?*

Answer: *Think more on that one. Later.*

I gestured toward Avila and Sun.

"They had no part in discarding the blood. I acted alone."

His eyes blazed. Avila winced as he clutched her tighter.

"And yet, I hear no trace of repentance in your voice." His features dimmed. "Killing one of our own is against clan code. You should know this information if you wish to survive the kindred life. If you survive the kindred life."

Bullneck chuckled.

"Lord Marius wants him alive. The daughter too." Thick fingers stroked Sun's hair. "I want this one."

Sun responded with a sharp elbow and a heated glare. Zaros glared at him.

"Thank you, Athan. Lord Marius wants many things … but I see him nowhere in this moment, do you?"

"Err … no."

"Ding, ding!" He laughed and released Avila.

The sense of relief was fleeting as I pulled her closer. His boots barely touched the ground as he began pacing before us.

"Unfortunate accidents have been known to occur in these tunnels. I for one, am not as forgiving as our Lord Marius." He stopped short of Athan. His face was brutal. "They deserve to die for denying me the opportunity to transcend my powers. Knowing there exists enemy clans out there, do you dare disagree?"

Athan shook his head fast.

"No, sire."

Shit. We're done for.

Zaros turned toward Blade who smirked silently.

"And you?"

"Never, sire. I am with you one hundred percent."

The inky room condensed around me as Zaros grinned before turning back toward me. Ebony skin glistened like slated crystals.

"It is true that Marius senses value in you, but I sense otherwise."

He turned away and sauntered across the room to retrieve a wooden stake propped against the shadowed walls. His features were like stone when he began walking back. He stopped before me and my heart went wild. Avila and Sun gasped as he raised the stake above his head. "I see no use for traitors. There are others that can aid our blood-work endeavors."

He was referring to my hematologist skills, but that was the last thing on my mind right now. I flashed my palms and stepped back.

"Wait!" My words were desperate. "I can help the clan's survival. I have information about the Blood Legend, the prophecy holds true with the birth of the first lineage. Vampires are under threat."

He paused the stake mid-air and regarded me. His voice was a sliver.

"I don't believe you. The Blood Legend prophecy is a myth conjured by the frailty of frantic humans fighting to believe in something when their god failed them."

"You're wrong. Legends and myths are always born from the ashes of truths. The witch in the cells saw it come to pass; she trusts me. I can help destroy the threat."

I didn't know if that woman trusted me, but it was all I had.

My breath stalled as his lips curled into something sinister, but I didn't miss the fear flicker across his eyes. Blade and Athan tittered, and at the same time, the room suddenly erupted with the sounds of other kindred as they came in from the tunnels behind us.

Zaros snorted. He lowered the stake as male and female vampires glided toward the lounge settings. Some of them glanced our way with disinterest. Others grinned and treated us to a mocking wave before settling in to watch the scene unfold. Then his eyes lasered into mine as he leaned closer.

"If I discover you are lying, I will force you to watch while I do unthinkable things to your daughter before I kill you." He pulled back and gave a dismissive wave, flicking his chin toward the guards. "Return them to the cell. We'll continue with this affair later."

I released a breath as he whirled around. He puffed up his chest as he strode toward his clan. Silky hair flipped and lashes fluttered as they greeted him. The burrow filled with sickening croons and sensual murmurs. My stomach lurched. Sun and I exchanged glances. It was repulsion that flooded into me as the guards yanked my arm and pulled me from the lair.

3

IN THE STILL OF THE NIGHT

"Zaros has got it in for you. Clearly, he's defiant in the face of Marius' reign." Sun stopped pacing the cell and spun around. The gravel beneath her boots split in my ear. "He is power hungry. Greedy. I know the look. He's dangerous."

Weariness sunk into my bones. Human waste and rotting rat carcasses drenched my senses. It was rank. I peered up at her from my position on the cell floor.

"He's no more dangerous than Marius."

She shook her head.

"You're wrong. Marius at least is somewhat diplomatic in his thinking. His plans to construct a dome city will grant us freedom to live decently beneath a UV protective canopy. We won't have to be slaves to the night forever. We will know daylight again."

"Not to mention an endless supply of blood," Avila added.

She leaned against the wall. Her eyes shone like sapphires from the shadows. "Marius realizes the importance of humanity. Succumbing to our vampiric urges will eventually result in our demise as the human species dwindles."

Sun grunted.

"Yes, something needs to be done before they become extinct. It's evident who among the kindred leaders has the ability to think ahead." She paused. "There is already dissonance brewing amongst them."

She was right. It was only a matter of time before the new species would fracture into a hierarchy of sorts. We existed in an emerging society. Rules had to be set. Systems needed to be formed. Resistance would inevitably unfold as they vied for power. It would be the most cunning and intelligent vampire who would prevail.

"Zaros is beginning t0 form his own faction. One of the masters will fall."

I wasn't a big fan of Marius, but after having met Zaros, I knew which side of the fence I'll be landing when the shit hits the fan.

Ah, vampire politics. Let the games begin.

"It's obvious that Zaros allows his primal instincts to influence his decisions," I said.

Avila smirked.

"You give him too much credit. He's just pure asshole, Dad. It is our most undesirable human traits that become accentuated in this condition if we don't learn to tame them."

She shook her head and gestured toward the cell across the way. The hour was late. Human captives slumbered fitfully among the filth and putrid. "Marius speaks of development and normality. He wants to create a blood-letting program. The leftover humans will be sanctioned to live in one half of the city where they can lead a dignified life under Mysticus protection."

Unease rippled through me.

"He told you this?"

"I spent some time with him during the days before we ambushed the hawkers."

The unease deepened to disturbance. She might be a grown woman, but she was still my daughter. I hadn't missed the way Marius had looked at her. I didn't like it. She must have caught my expression because the next thing I heard was her snorting.

"I'm no longer a little girl, Dad." She moved closer and took my hand. Her skin felt like cool rubber. "The world is different now. We're different now. We play by new rules and abide by new kings. Marius is the way toward a peaceful future. He will look after the Leaving humans; give them everything they need. In exchange for their blood, of course."

Of course.

Disbelief. It was a familiar feeling of late. I could hardly fathom my daughter now. The way she spoke of blood and humans as if she had never experienced a mortal life was unnerving. I didn't know if I'd ever get used to it; despite that human blood was now my own weakness. It was an overpowering weakness that repulsed me.

I could barely control it. I didn't know that I even wanted to. My gaze lingered on the human cell. *Irresistible pickings*. Never had human frailty been so acute to me. I groaned inwardly.

"I don't know that Marius' intentions toward the humans are that noble, Avila."

She gave me a squeeze and stood up.

"It's better than living on rodents in a disorganized world with Zaros at the realm." Her voice became grave. "His way would mean a life of squalor and violence."

I grunted a reply as Sun made noises that conveyed her agreement. *Meh*. I could think no longer about smoke-filled bureaucracy and blood-hungry villains. I felt jaded and out of touch. My empty gut cramped. *Blood lust is an insatiable affliction*. The energy borrowed from the humans I'd fed on earlier was fast waning. I needed more.

I'm to live out the rest of my days preying on humans.

I should have let Zaros kill me and be done with it. With death came the promise of tranquillity – peace from the torment haunting my soul.

Scarla.

Her pale features danced behind my eyes like a sweet vision. Velvety skin I longed to caress taunted me. I'd give anything to hear her laughter just one more time. *Anything*. But even in death, I knew she'd never forgive me for the brutality of her murder. I was forever damned to the pain of the undead.

I deserved it.

"Dad?"

I looked up at my daughter. I stared back at a replica of someone I loved; someone who would forever appear youthful despite the stretching years ahead. Feelings eluded me. Coldness prevailed. *Can I still love?*

"Yeah?"

"How do you know the witch woman speaks the truth about the prophecy?"

I shrugged.

"Gut feeling."

She was about to respond when the tunnels suddenly erupted to the sounds of strangled screams and unearthly screeches from the city above. My ears pricked and I stood up. *Instinct overdrive.* My pulse dashed as the disembodied wails clung along the putrid tunnel walls. Sun and I exchanged a look. She frowned.

"What the hell is that?"

I didn't know. It wasn't unusual to hear the occasional scream catch on the night hours. After all, humans were hunted down when the sun sunk on the horizon. But this sounded different. This sounded like the terrified wails of the kindred.

Spectral. Wraithlike. Supernatural.

I didn't utter a word. Clarity evaded me. Avila and I followed Sun as she moved toward the cell bars. We peered out along the dark narrow shaft. The shadows loomed and frolicked in the faint light of candles. Distant water dripped between the walls, broken by the noise of heavy footsteps and harsh shouts; the kindred were on the move.

Urgency.

My hair felt static. Inhuman whines were like sirens and froze my blood. Some of the people in the opposite cell began to stir. But it was when the distinct sound of a lecherous howl filled the dank chamber air that my heart almost exploded.

Avila gasped.

"That was no vampire."

A sudden mass of long-winded screams erupted to reach an ear-piercing peak. They sounded primal. Havoc reigned overhead. Guards yelled at one another. Boots stomped along the sludgy tunnel ground. My stomach flipped as the witch woman caught my eye.

I grasped the steel bars and peered at her as she walked toward the edge of her cell and looked at me. Hair like rusty water almost concealed eyes that glimmered through the space between us. Her lips quivered before forming into an odd grin.

"The lunar is full. The Lygarou have awakened. It has begun."

Sun scowled beside me.

"Stop talking in riddles, woman. What the hell is a Lygarou?"

That was when another hideous howl rang out across

the city and seeped through the tunnel walls. It was followed by more shrieks and desperate yells.

My breath stalled and my eyes felt like steel when I looked at the woman. When I spoke, my voice was unrecognizable.

"Answer the question, witch. What is a Lygarou?"

She laughed spontaneously. Grotty fingers clutched the cells bars as she pressed her forehead against the flaking steel poles. She licked her lips and stared heavenward.

"They are wolves born from the sorcery of another era. They are the reason you are what you are; and they will be the death of every vampire and human on earth, including you."

Wolves?

Absurdity.

Sun and Avila gasped in unison. A snarl reverberated. Shrieks like distorted chimes reverberated in my veins. The woman laughed again. *Hysteria.* Suddenly, my body felt numb. Her next words were delivered on the wake of a scream.

"The wolf mother has ignited the Legends of Blood with the birth of her baby. But the power is too raw. The legend genes must mature through the bloodlines. The earth will turn to death once more if the legend isn't silenced."

A gnarly growl followed by a shrilling shout erupted. Then there was silence. My heart missed a beat.

4

LYGAROU BEWARE

A nervous vibe hung over the human captives. Wide eyes blinked from caved sockets and dirty skin. They cowered and trembled. Some of them wept uncontrollably while others murmured to themselves while rocking back and forth. I couldn't blame them. The revelation of the existence of yet another supernatural species was perplexing to say the least.

Werewolves.

It was a chilling thought. I sensed that somehow there was a vital link between their emergence and the rise of the clans. The witch had vaguely mentioned as much. I had no doubt that she spoke the truth. My gut feelings never failed me. I urgently needed to discover more before earth and all its occupants perished at the hands of the Lygarou.

I had to get us out of this cell.

The city above had remained eerily quiet. No longer

were the tunnels reverberating to the sounds of stomping footsteps and strangled cries. A feeling of isolation was bestowed upon the chambers. We had no way of knowing the outcome of the attack or how many Lygarou had descended on the city. We could be sitting ducks down here. We could be dog food.

All these thoughts circled through my mind when Sun grabbed my elbow. It was horror that I saw brimming in her eyes.

"Wolves that attack and kill vampires? Can things get any more bizarre in this world?"

Ironic words coming from the mouth of a vampire. The notion fizzled as I clenched my teeth and prepared to answer when the witch woman piped up. She stood apart from the others crowding the cell behind her. She appeared calm.

"Not just any wolves; they are of the Lygarou bloodline. The purest of werewolves created by a powerful Demilune French witch named Evanora a long time ago." She paused to brush a lock of hair from her eye. "I believe the modern term for the reawakened is Lystalkers."

"That doesn't sound so comforting." Avila pushed off the wall to face the woman. "How do you know all of this? Who are you?"

"My name is Clio. My ancestry belongs with the Demilune Circle; the buried and secret coven of witches and sorcerers who originated in the mountains. I know all of this because the stories and folklore have passed through the generations." She gave a rueful laugh. "I'd always thought the Legends of Blood and the Lygarou to be fanciful fables conjured by the ancestors to entertain. I was wrong."

Sun snorted.

"Clearly." She shook her head. "Why now?"

"It was etched to unfold the moment one of Evanora's Lygarou defied their peaceful mountain existence to seek a life among the humans. Shane. He was the first created and the reason behind the curse that rendered the species dormant." She swallowed hard and her voice became urgent as the sound of boots trudged along the passage shafts. "The baby has broken the curse and awakened the pack, but the Lystalkers are unaccustomed to their werewolf genes; they're primitive. This new breed has to be stopped."

Guttural bellows spiraled ahead of the guards heading our way. My eyes darted to their shadows stretching along the walls as they rounded the bend. I frowned and leaned forward.

"How do we stop them?"

Clio began stepping back, dousing herself in the gloom among her captives. Her lips barely moved but I heard every word regardless.

"The wolf mother and her child must be destroyed. It's the only way."

Murder a newborn?

I knew that some part of me should have rejected that notion, yet there was no trace of resistance within me. My mind whirled. The guards hollered and sneered at us as they came to a stop in front of the cells, and one of them began rattling the keys to unlock the cell gates.

"Back up, convicts."

It was Blade and Athan, and they were joined with others I didn't recognize. I swallowed a pang of annoyance and moved away from the cell gate. Another rendezvous with Zaros was the last thing I needed to deal with right now. Not with the appearance of the Lystalkers.

Blade grinned as he stepped over the threshold. Despite his smirk, he smelled like fear.

"Lord Marius has requested your presence at once." He barked an order at his cronies, but his eyes never left mine. "Fetch the witch. We're all going on a trip to reckoning."

"Sounds cheerful," I said. "Should we pack light or heavy?"

Yellow eyes glowered.

"Well, look who has a case of the smart-ass. See how that works for you in the immediate future."

We shall indeed.

He tossed his shiny mane in a fast pivot and I looked at my daughter. She stood defiant, glaring and grasping her hips as she watched the guards when they began ushering us from the cell. *My tough little nugget.* Her eyes skimmed to me and I forced a smile. A tinge of affection shimmied through my heart and there it was – love. It still existed in my core. I was grateful.

"Come on, hurry along!" Athan yelled. "We don't have all night; it's almost daybreak."

I braced myself and silently followed them from the cell as they began leading us and Clio from the underground chambers. I focused ahead and tried to still my thoughts. It would be the first time that I'd be in the company of the vampire that had sired me since our capture months before.

He had branded me a traitor, but I knew he wished to keep me and Avila alive. Otherwise, we'd be long dead by now. My experience as a hematologist was the one card up my sleeve – the knowledge I'd acquired during my humanity. Still, there was little trust among the kindred, and I was certain he had a plan of retribution for me.

The night air was warm and stale, but I welcomed every breath as we finally stepped out from the underground passages and into the city streets. I inhaled deeply, savoring the stars hanging between giant glass towers. I took a beat before marching after the guards. *Tangy iron.* It was salty and sweet, and hung all around. My stomach churned with the scent of fresh blood and strewn body parts littering the pavement and roads along the way.

Shivers.

Cold snapped through me. I sought out Avila's hand with my own and gave her a reassuring squeeze. She pressed her palm into mine. Her fear trickled into me.

"It will be okay."

She nodded.

"I won't let anything happen to you."

The words were out before I could catch them. Promises meant nothing anymore. Not in this new world. I'd promised the same thing to Scarla. She was dead. I couldn't fail Avila again. Whatever was coming, one thing that I knew for certain was my belief in my daughter. I would grip that faith with everything I had.

Zaros was right. The love of a parent is all-powerful. Her survival was all that mattered now. Even if that meant the death of a newborn baby and her mother. Even if that meant my own death.

5

THE RECKONING

*I*t's strange how easily we adapt to new concepts and realities when left with no alternative. The fact that I had died to my humanity to embody a creature I'd only ever known as a fictitious character in books and movies should have been a shocking notion, and yet the opposite was true.

I carefully stepped over a severed head laying in a pool of blood on the stairs leading toward the building entrance. Matted hair the color of strawberry clumped across a gaping bloodied jaw and shockingly frightful features. The fading moon cast silvery shadows, distorting bruised lips and hollow eye sockets. I didn't even balk at the sight of it. Death had become customary.

Derangement.

The streets mirrored a garish Halloween scene. Torn flesh and spilled innards were everywhere. My nostrils blazed. It stunk like an abattoir. Not that I'd ever visited one, but I didn't need to in order to make that comparison. This blood-soaked world was enough.

Lystalkers.

It was clear their bygone genetics were underdeveloped upon their rebirth. *Then again, could the jaws of a werewolf ever be anything but savage?* The hairs on my arms rose. Another supernatural species that sought to replace a new reality. I was dealing with it well, all things considered. Not much could surprise me anymore.

Avila shuddered.

"Barbarous creatures. Do they have no finesse?"

We stopped behind the guards as one of them opened the lobby door. I glanced at her.

"Is *there* a sophisticated manner to murder, my dear?"

"Well, yeah. *We* might be killers, but at least we carry out our indiscretions with competence."

My jaw fell.

"Is that what you call it?"

She shrugged but said nothing as Blade ushered us inside the building.

"Hurry up slayers."

I grimaced, barely noticing Athan leer at Sun as I stepped across the threshold. Avila's image flashed in my mind the day I'd first brought her here. She had tried hard to control her terror as she clutched a stake at the lobby doors. It was the same day I had delivered her into the hands of Marius. She was different now. The world was green.

Guilt lingered like moss growing at the bottom of a pond. It was relentless. But this was no time to dwell on a past I couldn't change. It was time to receive Blade's promised reckoning. This was apparent when I spotted Marius striding across the lobby toward us.

Clio gasped but I didn't look at her. My eyes were glued on Marius. He appeared like a cinematic vision and moved with formidable force. It was clear that he was pissed. I began to suspect that his reckoning might be about to take on a whole new meaning. I tried to keep calm as he stopped short of me.

"So, here you are. The one I entrusted to return to me what I most seek."

His black hair was slicked across his scalp to accentuate dark penetrating eyes and his sallow complexion highlighted thick ruby lips.

The guards shrunk back. Sun and Avila were either side of me with Clio behind as we stood near the lobby door.

"Marius."

The lobby felt dreary and desolate. Murky corridors ran off into darkness and a chill hung in the air despite the heat outside. A sofa marked the center of the room, and scantily dressed women moaned softly as they draped themselves across lounges. Their heads lolled.

Humans.

I felt a rush through my veins, but the sound of Marius' brash tone quickly quelled the taunting hunger. I steadied my gaze back on him.

"I trust you've enjoyed your time with the cockroaches and sewer rats these past months?"

The guards sniggered and Avila scowled. She shrunk closer to me when Marius gave a black grin. His eyes settled on her.

"I expected more from you, Livvy." He reached to stroke her chin.

Livvy?

My thoughts whirled and I almost missed the flicker in her eyes as she gazed at him. *Since when did this happen?* My blood felt like mercury. Marius cackled.

"Still, I don't suppose that you would be disloyal to your father. Love can be a powerful force that drives us to carry out the unthinkable – like discard rare blood – that had you kept your promise, would have been extremely useful considering the threat of what we are now facing." He glared at me. "Do you have anything to say?"

"There is nothing I can say that will change what I've done, but *Livvy* and Sun were not involved in the decision to destroy the blood. It was all me." I shook my head. "Whatever plans you have by way of retribution, leave them out of it. They've suffered enough."

"And because of your decisions, we're all suffering now!" He growled and stepped closer. I could almost taste the fresh blood on his breath. "I lost at least two dozen vampires tonight to a pack of flea-bitten mongrels and you speak of suffering?"

I kept silent and tried not to focus on the inflamed blood vessels at his temples.

"I expect nothing but loyalty from those I have sired. Have you forgotten the gift I readily bestowed on you when you turned up practically begging for eternal life? Do you have no gratitude for all that I've done for you and your family?"

The guards grunted in agreement. I ignored them.

Gratitude?

I almost choked.

Clearly, this vampire had a selective memory. It was he who had destroyed my family.

I bit back words and reined in my thoughts before he could collect either of them. My voice was much more even than I'd anticipated.

"I accept that I am now kindred and a member of the Mysticus clan, and I will honor my position as such."

Fact: *I had no choice at this point.*

He gave a half laugh and moved back, peering beyond me to Clio.

"You shall indeed. If you want those that remain precious to you to keep breathing, that is. It is time that your loyalty is renewed through acts of demonstration and service to the clan." His fangs glistened like pearls. "The witch woman knows secrets about the dogs?"

"Yes."

"I'm listening."

I glanced at Clio. Her dark eyes looked wild.

"The birth of a baby has broken a curse and awakened the Lygarou blood genes. Those reawakened are feral in their transformation and are unable to control their natural instincts." I shook my head. "Apparently, the only way to destroy them all is to kill the child and her mother. I don't know the details surrounding the curse or the sorcerer who originally created the Lygarou, but I do know that the species is somehow linked to the origins of the Vampiric virus and I'd like to consult with Michal on this subject."

"Why?"

"Because knowledge is power."

Black eyes gleamed like metallic paint.

"Agreeable. Your scientific skills are an asset to the clan that I will need when the creation of the dome city is completed – Bloodfaye will provide us protection from enemy clans and ..." His lips curled. "The wolves. Ascension for us, if you will. We shall live a dignified future where we will co-exist with the humans. After all, we cannot afford to behave bestial if we are to thrive as the dominant species. I need those who can think beyond their bloodthirst. Given your educational background, I sense that you are more than capable to adopt a grow mindset. Am I correct?"

I was about to answer when a voice bellowed from someplace deep within a corridor cavity. It was familiar. *Zaros.* An instant ache sprung in my head.

"Ha! A grow mindset would not have so easily destroyed the blood capable of defeating the Lystalkers!"

His boots squished on the tiled floor as he emerged from the shadows. Long, black trench coat tails flowed behind him. I didn't miss Marius' grimace as Zaros came to a stop beside him and glared. "I'm not convinced this vampire has the clan's best interests at heart. Even in his undead affliction, he remains romantic."

Marius didn't even look at him.

"Whether you realize it or not, Zaros, it is the undead heart that remembers his humanity that will further the clan into evolution. Perhaps this is something worth pondering on your part."

Zaros snorted.

"We are different creatures now. Romantic hearts are a sign of weakness that belongs in the days past, as is our humanity." He paused to glance at Athan and Blade. They stifled sniggers and Zaros grinned. "What of soft-cock's punishment?"

Marius and Zaros glared at each other for several tense moments. Sun and I exchanged glances. Marius licked his lips and looked at me.

"Some of us are still learning the vital qualities required in order to solidify the clan's future survival," Marius said. He ignored Zaros' loud snort. "I will grant you access to Michal and the lab on the condition that you take the witch, a few of my men and hunt down that wolf-mother and her baby."

My thoughts began to reel.

"You will not return to the city until you have killed them both."

Sun stood defiantly with hands on hips.

"Are you crazy? The wolf-mother and her baby are hidden some place in the mountains and probably heavily guarded. It's too dangerous for any Mysticus vampire to venture that far from the city, let alone face a pack of wolves on unfamiliar territory. The journey will take days. How are we supposed to shelter from the sunlight? What if we are ambushed?"

Marius laughed.

"Tsk, Tsk. You have it all muddled up in your sweet little head. You little vampire ladies will be staying here with me as leverage. If he fails or attempts to flee the clan, I will slaughter the both of you."

Zaros began laughing. I cringed.

"Perfect! Let's see how the sob story handles the big bad new world." He leered at Avila. "I daresay daddy will be the death of you yet."

I wanted to murder him.

6
WITH THE WIND

"*H*aaa!" Michal screeched. He rounded the laboratory bench and scurried closer. He stopped abruptly when he got a good look at me. His face paled beneath layers of filth. Grotty fingers knotted franticly. "Ya ... you're a vampire?"

I barely nodded. His freckled eyes skirted the floor.

"You were supposed to get the blood out of the city; you were the one I chose to protect it."

"I got it out of the city."

His gaze darted owl-like through clouded spectacles. His voice was tremulous.

"Then where is it? Is it safe?"

"It's gone."

His mouth formed a huge "O".

"Gone?"

"With the wind."

I pushed past him, striding further into the lab and

scanning the area. Not much had changed since my last visit. The lighting was dim, and it was cold, and it still reeked of human waste and rotting flesh. However, a glance into the killing room cubicle revealed no mangled bodies this time around.

Repulsion.

It was overpowering. His feet sounded like a mini stampede as he trotted after me. When I stopped and turned around to face him, he almost collided into my chest. I moved away, stretching the distance between us while vaguely wondering how any vampire could desire his blood.

I wouldn't feed on him if he were the last human on earth.

In the next instant, he was hiking up sleeves that knew better days and thrusting his wrists toward me. Beady eyes popped.

"For you, Master."

"Huh?" I grimaced. "No."

Lord no.

"Why? I wish to serve you."

I forced a part smile.

"Marius keeps me well fed, thank you."

It was true. Days had passed since forming our agreement. Well, if you call it that. We had been promptly moved from the cells and into more pleasant living conditions where hot showers and human blood were freely available.

It is amazing how fear can drive us. Marius was

beside himself with the threat of the Lystalkers attacking again on the next moon. He was certain they were gathering in numbers during their dormancy stage. That they sought to form a strong outbreak against the clan.

I agreed.

The next series of attacks will prove more dire if we didn't do something to protect ourselves. It was an ironic twist that we were no longer at the top of the food chain. What Marius had not realized was that he needn't have used my daughter as leverage in order to gain my assistance. I would do anything to make sure she stayed safe. *Anything.*

The stakes were higher now because I had no choice but to kill that baby and her mother or it meant Avila's death. I couldn't allow that to happen. I'd already lost her once to the kindred.

However, other matters dominated my thoughts right now – matters of government secrets, blood and viruses. I watched Michal as he hunched and shifted awkwardly, his eyes steadying on his boots as he spoke.

"No more AB positive blood type means no way to study its astonishing effects on those infected by the virus. It could've been the path to finding a cure."

"I think it would've empowered ego-driven vampires and caused much more destruction before a cure could have been cultivated. There is no way you could have worked the blood here with their knowledge. You know that; that's why you gave it to me."

He rubbed a palm over his balding scalp. Sweat glistened.

"Tell me about Shane."

He jerked suddenly. He lifted his eyes toward the roof and froze before swallowing hard.

"Sha … Shane?"

"Did I stutter?"

"N … no, no, Master." He shook his head furiously. "How do you know about Shane? That was confidential information that very few had access to."

"Call it a hunch."

It was the truth. I mean, it didn't take much to make the link, what with Clio mentioning the connection between vampires and Lygarou. Then Shane seeking a life among humans.

"Huh. Nice hunch."

"Yeah, now talk. What is the connection between the V-Virus and the Lygarou?"

He chewed on his bottom lip and shook his head.

"Makes no difference now. Shane was special. I don't know how the agency discovered the gifts in his blood; he was already here when I was recruited. He told me they hunted him down for years before his capture. He told me that he was the first werewolf; the alpha."

"He became their guinea pig."

He nodded. "More than that, he became the crux of a series of biological experiments. His blood was unbelievable! I'd never seen anything like it." His voice pitched and he blinked rapidly. "The rate at which his blood cells regenerated was phenomenal; his white cells were abnormal, and his iron levels should've rendered him dead."

"What happened?"

He laughed.

"The V-Virus was born, that's what happened. It all went to shit."

"Yeah, no shit." My fangs began to ache. "Where is he now?"

Michal shrugged. His next words hit hard.

"He escaped not long after the virus took hold, but not before vowing to destroy every one of us."

"So, he pro-created to unlock the curse and awaken the Lystalkers."

"Exactly."

Terrific.

Turns out we have an alfa wolf with a vendetta on our hands. *Could things get any worse?* I shuddered to think but think I must. My thoughts unraveled as I spun on my heels and began pacing. Talons combed through my dark hair, and I was aware of Michal's fixed stare.

"The witch woman who knows about the Lygarou says the baby carries the Blood Legend gene, whatever that means. What if I can get a sample of her blood?"

His brows rose. "Her blood could be the pathway toward finding a cure for the virus. It could be the missing link that eluded us all along!"

I strode up to him and gripped his collar. He shrieked and whimpered as I twisted the fabric between my talons.

"I'll bring back the blood of the baby, but you had better keep those flappy gums of yours closed or I'll remove your heart from your chest with my palm. Do you understand?"

He nodded fast. "Yes, Master!"

I could feel my veins bulging at my throat. "Good." I released him and stepped away, throwing my next words over my shoulder as I walked from the lab. "And don't call me 'Master'."

7

BLOOD BATH ON THE HORIZON

Motionless air clung to my skin with the balmy night and half-moon. It was comforting. I couldn't get warm enough. No amount of natural heat could thaw my cold blood.

What am I? I was neither alive nor dead. *Limbo.* I lingered some place in the in-between. Perhaps it was hell on earth. Happiness was a memory, and an emotion I never expected to feel again. Still, the warm night air was the closest I could get to feeling normal.

The tree leaves bristled slightly. *Bats.* They were abundant and appeared to follow our movements through the dense forest grounds. Night creatures hunted. The sound of a long howl broke in the distance.

"Wha … what was that?" Clio said.

She smelled like wild daisy.

"Obviously it was a wolf."

The snappy reply was delivered by Lena. She was one of the two Shadow Guardians who accompanied us on the quest to hunt the wolf-baby. She was a tough middle-aged Latino woman with braided yellow hair and black roots. Her skin appeared like overused leather and her legs went on forever.

Clio scowled.

"Yes, but was it …" Her voice trailed and I glanced at her. Glossy red curls accentuated the dark eyes peering back at me. They'd cleaned her up. Even given her fresh clothes. There were perks to being a witch with valued knowledge. You got the treatment.

She gave a nervous laugh. "Na … it's not a full moon. It's their cousins. I bet they sense their alpha's rebirth."

Lena snorted. I felt irritated. She wasn't the most pleasant human. Her attitude sucked harder than a newborn vampire.

"How do you know all this shit about the Lystalkers?"

She grabbed Clio's elbow suddenly and yanked hard, causing Clio to stumble back. The earth crunched as she shrieked and fell against Lena's chest. I stopped walking and whirled around as Lena spat her next words in Clio's face.

"Are you some kind of freaky sorcerer leading us into a trap?"

Clio wriggled her arm against Lena's grip. Her eyes blazed.

"Let go of me, wench!"

Lena grinned. She flicked opened a blade with her other hand and pointed it toward Clio's throat. Her elongated neck gleamed as she bent forward and sneered.

"What if I let you go in pieces, witch-bitch?"

I groaned inwardly.

Humans. Have they not experienced enough violence?

Clio balled her fist along with her face. I saw the oncoming actions long before the sequence could play out. It was time to intervene. My feet barely touched the ground as I slid between them, snatching the blade from Lena's grasp and growling in her face.

"Leave the woman be."

She shrunk away as the rest of our group closed in around us. It was Blade and Athan, and the other Shadow Guardian whose name was Hugo. He resembled a cross between Bob Marley and a fart. His personality was like moldy cheese. So was his breath as it vapored in my face.

"Let it go, Jett."

I turned on him with a hiss. Blade and Athan laughed. Adrenaline surged. *Hunger.* It was hard not to think about it and Lena just spiked my radar. I was edgy. We'd been hiking for two nights without a decent feed, albeit for the small amounts of blood offered by the Guardians.

Clio and her blood were off limits. I'd made that clear at the onset. Not that she was offering. For some reason, I felt compelled to protect her. At least until we made it to the wolf-mother's den.

Hugo stood in all his graceless glory. Putrid dreadlocks spilled over his shoulders and glued against a spotted brow. His lips looked like deflated tires and one eye twitched franticly.

I took an even breath. My talons itched.

"Keep her leashed, brute."

He nodded. Lena scoffed but I ignored her as I tossed the blade at her feet. Hugo understood. It was enough. I was fast learning their language.

Clio shuffled closer to me. She said nothing but her eyes spoke volumes. Her mind too when I tuned in hard enough. But I couldn't focus that hard right now. I needed blood. She said we'd arrive at our destination the following night. I knew I'd need to replenish before facing whatever awaited us in those mountains.

All of them looked at me. Expectation was apparent. Somehow, this little circus quest had become mine.

"There is only about three hours left until dawn. I know of a small settlement at the foot of the mountains near the river. We can shelter there."

I was about to stalk away when the faint sound of voices drifted through the twisted tree trunks.

I instantly froze to the spot. My eyes trailed back to Blade and Athan. *Excitement.* It had a destiny of its own – a path difficult to ignore. I closed my eyes and tilted my head, sniffing out the sweet claret afforded by bottom-feeder rabble camping in the woods.

Foolish humans.

"Hawkers." My lips hardly moved. "I can smell them a mile away."

"Only hawkers would be stupid enough to be out in

the woods after sundown." Blade grinned with elation. "In the mood for a dirty feast?"

Hell yeah.

"Beggars can't be choosers." I looked at Hugo and motioned toward Clio. "Don't take your eyes off her."

I didn't wait for his reply. Saliva formed in my mouth as I anticipated the rush of a feed. It drove me forward. I was a ghoul. *Heinous.* Not even inhuman.

Athan and Blade were velocity. The three of us moved like force. The night ignited. I saw everything and nothing at the same time as we flew through the forest. Discreet gruntles, subdued laughter and stale whiskey led the way.

We slowed when the clearing came into view and we lingered in the shadows. Athan and Blade stood either side of me as we peered past the trees to survey the scene.

It was a tidy mob of hawkers. Three small tents were pitched at even intervals. Muted light glowed from within worn canvas. Their shadows stretched like a taunting dream. I groaned. A few men sat between the tents drinking ale and smoking pipes.

"There be a rumor running rife about striking a deal with the vamps. I heard tell that they will offer us protection if we agree to give them blood. It might be in our favor to concede what with the state of the new threats."

A big hawker with a wiry beard spluttered. He took a swig of ale.

"Screw that shit. The vamps are as trustworthy as them snotty smush kittens who think they're too good for what we've got packing. Me and Brad made a deal with one of them hoes last night; didn't go as planned."

Laughter erupted.

"What happened?"

"I wanted to eat her out. Show her some tenderness. She turned me into a vampire. She got the bloody dick instead. The bitch got it hard!"

More laughter followed but I didn't really hear it. My boots felt heavy as I was catapulted back in time. *Scarla.* Her name was a sigh on my tongue. It was hawkers like these that had raped, tortured and murdered her. My heart shattered. Her image filled my mind and I was lost.

Secret amber smiles.

"Dance with me."

Sweet laughter.

"I'm an awful dancer."

Lingering glances and soft skin.

"You're wrong. Your soul dances with mine every day."

Twisted memories and yearning tore at my soul. She had been my Yin; my everything. They took her from me. The pain never stopped. I could never get used to her absence from my life. Black hate twisted through me. The next thing I heard was Blade.

"Bon appetit!"

I looked at him and smiled. The moment was nothing

and everything as it bore new revelations. *Truth.* I slipped from the trees and bolted toward them.

I was a vampire.

8
BLOOD LOVER

I breathed deep and stretched my neck back, catching sight of an owl perched among the branches above. The darkness was no barrier as large eyes peered at me from a flat face. I was gorged and reborn with the sanguine liquid flowing through me. I grinned and wiped the blood from my chin with the back of a hand.

"Hello my feathered friend."

My image flashed in his yellow eyes. A stranger peered back at me. The blues of my eyes appeared animated and unnatural against my dark hair. *Incubus.* The thought stole my grin and everything around me dissolved along with the occasional whimper and shriek offered by the surviving hawkers.

The owl knew acts of bestiality and cold murder. I looked away. It almost felt like God was peering at me through those eyes. Another helping of guilt was the last thing I needed right now. Not that I was feeling ashamed. My father used to say that life was too short to live with guilt and regret. Now, life spread before me like an endless black tarmac. I had plenty of time to wallow in guilt and regret if I so wished. Tonight, I would do away with such notions and be who I was reborn to be – a killer.

Feathered friends be damned.

I gave a half laugh. Euphoria was seduction. Blood my victory. I felt more alive than I had in months, and I couldn't help but respect the unbridled beast within me. *Supernatural energy.* It was disturbingly empowering, and I was fast becoming hooked.

Speaking of beasts, it was Athan's colossal figure that caught my vision as he released a dead male hawker and stood up. His face gleamed the color of red wine and his eyes were inky torpedoes. *Blood-drunk.* He was as delirious as I. He grinned.

"Jett the owl whisperer."

"Ha! Screw the owl. He's too uptight up there on his squeaky clean, high-horse branch."

He laughed and picked up a stone.

"Fucking owl, like *he* doesn't kill to survive."

I had hardly registered that he had pitched the stone when I heard a dull thump as the owl landed at my feet. I looked down at it and grimaced. It was as dead as the hawker Athan had just drained and dumped.

Goodbye feathered friend.

Athan laughed as Blade's throaty cackle broke out

ahead of him as he strode toward us. He stopped short of me and slapped me on the shoulder.

"Looks like the soft-cock just got himself a hard-on!"

Athan laughed.

"Yeah, he's evolving alright. I'm not sure which Master will be more pleased."

Blade licked blood from his lips. Lemon eyes were ablaze.

"Hmm ... let me see ... the one with the vision, or the one with the vision?"

They broke into laughter, but I ignored them as I looked around. Mortality and oblivion hung heavy in the balmy night air. The scene appeared as if straight out of a Dracula movie. Corpses and torn flesh were strewn all around while evidence of blood was splattered across the earth and the tents.

Hmm ...

Apparently, some vampires relished the kill more than others and took pleasure in shredding their victims before draining them. Avila would be affronted. Oddly enough, I looked forward to filling her in when I returned to the city.

My gaze settled on the small cluster of hawkers huddled against a flimsy tent canvas. I counted two men, one woman and a child. They dared not move as they sniveled beneath wild stares. My attention settled on the boy who looked to be about ten years old. I could smell his tender blood from here. Thoughts vanished as I fixed my stare on him.

Desire. My heart thumped as my senses spiked. Dark velvety eyes brimmed and peered back at me as he curled into his mother's chest. A lock of brown hair fell over one brow while rosebud lips pouted, and his pulse became my rhythm.

Remarkably, I felt famished again. My nostrils fired up and I began to move forward, led by the promise of young blood. It was thrilling. *Impelling even*. Resistance was unattainable until Blade grabbed my arm and shattered my trance. His voice boomed.

"Taking children is forbidden, greenhorn. It's against clan code."

My eyes flashed as I fought to contain vigorous impulses. Including the dumbest response ever.

"Why?"

"Because we have to conserve our future blood supply, that's why." He laughed. "Hell, even Zaros adheres to this code despite that the blood of the young is the most difficult to resist."

Athan smirked.

"Yeah, children's blood is what caviar and white truffle used to be to the rich folk. It's a delicacy denied to us, so learn to control yourself, slayer, or you'll find yourself burning to a crisp come dawn."

It was the longest statement I'd heard him utter thus far. I remained silent. *What was I thinking?* Self-disgust erupted as I looked back at the child, and it was a question I knew I would ask myself repeatedly over the coming days. It was also one I couldn't answer.

I barely knew myself anymore. I felt like a modern-day Dr Jekyll, however my alter ego was more terrifying than a psychotic serial killer who liked to slice up hookers for pleasure.

The supernatural powers and urges that accompanied vampirism were overwhelming, particularly when confronted by blood and insatiable hunger. I knew that I would have to learn to be a vampire without allowing the beast within control me, at least not all the time.

That was much easier said than done. I was discovering rather quickly how easy it was to succumb to ruthlessness and apathy because it was now my second nature. Marius was right; it was those rare vampires who held onto empathy that were needed if we were to have any kind of future, and not only to preserve our blood supply. I sensed something much more profound at play here.

Philosophical thoughts took a backseat when I caught sight of a figure dashing from one of the tents. A whirring vision of scarlet fabric and long dark tresses disappeared into the woods. *A woman.* My pulse quickened. Blade and Athan laughed, and their banter followed me as I instantly took off after her.

"Ha, would ya look at that!"

"She's got more balls than a juggling circus act."

"Go on, slayer – go get your wild cat!"

I tuned out their chortles as I entered the dense vegetation. I became still, closing my eyes to focus on her. *Ba-bump. Ba-bump.* Her heart was a melody that merged with the forest sounds and set me in motion. My breath was shallow. The earth didn't even feel me as I weaved through the twisted trunks like a firebolt.

She stopped running and I immediately paused. My eyes darted over wild bramble and vivid ferns as I searched her out. A twig snapped followed by a gasp. I licked my lips and whirled toward the sound as she began running again. A flash of red blinded my vision. She veered around a tree. I grinned and leapt forward. She couldn't outrun me.

The wooded air condensed around me. Her feet crushed timberland turf, dragging over fronds and leaves just ahead of me. I slowed and rounded a trunk to see her grasping a branch and heaving. Black dewy eyes shone like a starless night sky beneath pitch hair. Her lips quivered like crushed cherries on creamy skin. She looked to be about Avila's age, maybe a little older, and she was flawless.

I drummed my talons against a trunk.

"Are you done running?"

She squared her chin; eyes reduced to slits. My gaze fell to the rise of her full breasts straining against flimsy fabric. Her skirt swirled at her feet. She carried the faint scent of musk. I was captivated.

"I … I guess I am." She struck out her hips and clasped them. Her eyes glimmered. "What are you going to do?"

"I'm going to kill you."

She inhaled sharply, and her eyes never left mine.

"Do what you must, vampire."

Arousal overload.

"Thank you, madam."

She didn't flinch when I walked closer and roughly grabbed the back of her skull. Her hair felt silky for a hawker woman. But I didn't dwell on that for any longer than necessary. Her blood screamed my name. I tilted her head so that the skin of her throat revealed itself to me. *Glory.* Blue veins stretched like wonderous candy. I couldn't stop even if I wanted to. I didn't want to.

Her heart raced as I gripped her hair and curled back my lips to sink my fangs into flesh that revealed sweet offerings.

Blood Lover.

It was all I could think as the moment claimed me. A whimper reverberated into my ear. Her pulse throbbed like a lilting symphony as I siphoned her blood and relished the warmth as it filled my mouth and made me whole again. Ecstasy found me.

Was this my heaven on earth now?

Then suddenly:

"Jett – no, stop!"

Hands clawed at my back and small fists pounded my arm.

What the hell?

The woman slumped against me as I turned with a fierce growl to catch Clio's wild eyes glaring at me. Blood dripped over my chin and my hiss deepened, but it didn't seem to faze her. Instead, she shook her head and scowled, before she went to the woman.

"She's only a young woman and you've just about killed her!" Her lips pulled tight. "You can't kill this one, Jett. Do you understand?"

Understand? Now there's an interesting word for a world where very little made sense these days. I looked at the woman who I still held in my arms. She appeared lifeless. My voice was unrecognizable.

"It may be too late."

9

PURE HEART

"This wasn't part of the plan."

Lena wrenched the curtains closed. Brass on brass chinked into my ears as she turned to glare at whoever was listening. Unfortunately, her abrasive voice was difficult to ignore.

I leaned back into the armchair and regarded her. It was overstuffed and stunk like old mac-and-cheese, but that was the least of my concerns.

"Welcome to the discovery plan."

The others laughed. Lena didn't. Her dark eyes turned to slivers.

"This is the witch's doing. It's all going to shit, what with babysitting these hawkers. I don't like it and I don't trust her."

A tiny weathered wood cabin plus one witch, two Guardians, three vampires, an almost dead woman and hawker prisoners made for one brutal headache. Not to mention the state of the shack. It was crammed with timeworn furniture over filthy rugs that barely covered the gaping cracks in the floorboards. At least there was light. *Bonus.* Whoever dwelled here in the past had possessed a fetish for oil lanterns.

I pushed my hair back. Weariness radiated in my bones.

"Trust is overrated in the new world. You will do as instructed and leave for the city with the mother and child at first light."

Grotty fingers dug at her hips. She held my stare for a few tense moments before looking away.

"Very well," she said. "The windows will need thicker coverings if you are to slumber here for the day. I'll see about fetching blankets."

I gave a curt nod as she stalked from the room. She made no attempt to disguise her frustration. This was made more evident when the sounds of cupboard doors being slammed and banged was heard from other parts of the shack.

It was Hugo I heard next.

"Heh. She's going at it like killing snakes!"

He lingered awkwardly by the threshold of the room where we had stowed the surviving hawkers. His broad shoulders hunched below a chronic eye twitch as he laughed. He looked like pig on ice.

I ignored him. My mind was a whirlwind. We hadn't quite made it to the town at the foot of the mountains. Instead, we were holed up in a half-rotted cabin that Clio had found. Our friendly local witch was full of surprises. Perhaps she wasn't as far removed from her genetic origins as she had made out. Blade brought me back to the present with his clucky mouth.

"She does have a point. What of this discovery plan – couldn't we just let the woman die and leave the mother and child to their own devices and carry on?"

I wanted to roll my eyes. *Did nobody pay attention?*

"We could but we're not. The child's blood and his mother will be safer in the city. I think the masters would agree considering we're talking *delicacy* blood. We can afford to continue one man short."

"How can you be so sure?"

I shrugged.

"Wolves remain in their human form between moons. I'm certain we can overcome them easily enough provided we arrive before the next lunar."

Lemon eyes squinted. "You're certain of this?"

"I've seen *The Wolfman*, I know how it goes."

His brows raised but he said nothing more as Lena returned with an armful of blankets. Her nose scrunched with the flick of her braid.

"They reek of mothballs and rat shit."

I grinned.

"That's the least of your problems."

She snorted as she set about draping the bedding over the windows; an act that instantly strangled the already constricted space. Her mouth offered a running dialog.

"I watched *The Wolfman* once at my aunt's place. She

lived on the Northern Fringes. I was just a little girl. Thought she was the coolest adult until I couldn't sleep for a week."

Athan cackled. His massive figure almost concealed the sofa.

"You mean you weren't always a tough bitch? Hard to wrap my head around that one."

She whirled around to face him, delivering her words through gritted teeth.

"Wrap your big head around this, vampire. I saw those wolves with my own eyes when they attacked the city. They make *The Wolfman* seem like Scooby-Doo." She looked at me. "You best pray that you're right; those wolves were more savage than any vampire I've seen."

"I don't pray."

They continued exchanging remarks, but I tuned out for the most part. Talk of savage wolves turned my thoughts to Avila and Sun. They were safe for now and I needed to keep it that way.

The truth was, I didn't know crap about the wolves and how their shifter phase worked, but it was obvious the moon cycle was involved. Otherwise, we'd all be dog meat by now. As it was, there was about five nights before the next full moon.

Time is of the essence.

I tried to relax in the knowledge that we had plenty of time to get to the wolf mother's den, slaughter some canine and get out before they had a chance to transform into heinous gobblers. After that, it was happy days. No more wolf problem and no more threat on my daughter's life.

I did have to find a discreet moment to steal a bit of the puppy's blood via the syringe I carried before I killed her. No way could the others get wind of that little side angle. It was too important.

Who knew what treasures the blood of this baby held?

I was curious as to what secrets her blood may unlock, if at all. I could only hope that it may provide a pathway into discovering a cure for the V-virus, or at least give us something to hope for. *Imagine a world without werewolves and vampires?* That would be a world in which I would pray.

All these musings were lost at the sudden ear-piercing shrill that echoed along the shack's short hallway. It was Clio. She had opted to stay with the wounded woman who lay on a thin cot in one of the rooms.

I didn't react immediately but my stomach did clench when she called out my name. Trepidation rose as I stood up and made for the room. Honestly, *wounded* may not have been the most appropriate choice of words to describe the woman's condition. I mean, she was literally drained of blood.

Does that count as wounded? Stupid question, Jett.

But stupid is, is stupid does and the world is now full of stupid questions; like the fact that Clio had stopped me from completing the kill and then had us haul the woman to this dump for a start. I didn't like it, yet something compelled me to take heed of the witch's words.

Discomfort would have to take a backseat. Time for the big-boy pants. Although, as soon as I got wind of Clio's next words, those pants weren't feeling so great.

She knelt beside the cot where the woman lay as still as a coffin. Clio's knuckles whitened over the woman's flaccid hand while a shock of her red hair almost buried the woman's face as she whispered in her ear.

"Hold on, Bella donna. Hold on."

I froze. My talons sunk into the timber threshold. *Bella donna.* They were the same words I had often used for Scarla. My heart squeezed and Clio looked up at me. Her eyes were wide.

"Jett! Hurry!"

I frowned as my gaze fell to the woman. Her black hair was a striking contrast against a pale pillow and the blue tinging her lips. Thick lashes appeared like bottlebrush. Comprehension eluded me. I shook my head.

"What?"

She stood up and marched toward me. She gripped my hand and pulled. "You need to make her kindred now. We need the blood of a newborn vampire."

"Huh? No!"

"You must, Jett!" She tightened her fingers around mine. "It's the only way to protect any hope of reviving humanity in the future."

I couldn't think.

"What? Why?" I snatched my hand away. "Why me?"

Her voice lowered. "Because it was you who discarded the transcendental blood and kept me alive.

You are the one; the pure heart that remains in vampire form. You are a vital part of conserving the prophecy." She gestured toward the woman. "As is she."

Tingles spread along my spine and my pure heart almost stopped.

10

I SOLD MY SOUL AGAIN

*M*adness. I had been drawn into a world I didn't want. My insides churned with all kinds of protests as I sat leaning against the wall in the corner of the room. I longed for the rotting floorboards to swallow me whole. Oblivion was an enticing affliction, and yet it eluded me just as the sun remained evasive.

What did I just do?

There was no way back now. I had done the unthinkable. Clio said that my heart was pure and that my presence and participation was important to the prophecy. *Strain.* Everything racked on the inside. I gripped my skull. The taste of my own blood was fresh on my lips. I could hardly fathom the reality. If indeed my heart was as pure as what she had said, then it was no longer. I had just crossed a threshold with no option to return – I had sired another, and in the process, I sold my soul again.

"You've done the right thing." Clio sat down next to me. She pushed a lock of hair from her eyes and smiled. "Thank you."

Shouldn't the right thing feel right?

"For what, exactly?" I motioned toward the woman who had fed off my blood. She was motionless. Dead. "She didn't ask for this life. I'm a fiend."

"You're wrong, she asked when she told you to do what you must. In that final moment, she didn't resist your vampire bite."

"I didn't interpret that as a request to become kindred, Clio."

I rubbed my wrist where the puncture marks were fast healing. I could still feel the sensation of her sucking the blood from my veins. It had felt critical.

She frowned. "We can't always see through the blur in front of us. This world has become an altered reality of the past. The same rules don't apply; everything has changed. We must cultivate and use our higher senses to help guide the way back."

I swung my gaze to my boots and studied the dried earth that clung around the edges. My father used to say that we couldn't control how the world and people changed, we could only manage our response to it. He said those were the qualities that defined us. I felt defined alright and I couldn't say I was digging it.

Still, perhaps this why I felt compelled to trust her. She was like a rainbow in a blackened world. Still, I needed more than just an abstract anecdote. My breath felt like glass when I looked at her.

"Back to what? You mentioned the woman was vital in reviving humanity, but how?"

She gave a rueful laugh. "My grandmother was one of the last practicing Demilune Sisters. As a child she would take me up into the mountains where she spent time honoring the ancestors and brewing magical potions. I'd help her collect wild berries and rare herbs like blueleaf and darknut. Those days seem like a dream now." She paused and her eyes glazed. "She used to tell me that I was special, and that someday my gifts would reveal themselves at a time when the earth turned to darkness. I never believed her … until the V-virus took hold and activated something within me."

"Your gifts?"

"Yes." Her eyes narrowed. "I … I don't even know myself anymore. These feelings and visions wash over me like messages from an invisible realm … a higher place or something. I have to trust it. I'd like you to trust it too."

"Your grandmother was right, Clio. You are special. Whoever you're becoming in this new world, don't allow the evil to steal your light."

She reached out and stroked the back of my hand. Her skin felt warm. Longing swelled.

"I don't have the answers. I'm not exactly sure of her role yet, but I do have faith. Do you, Jett?"

Ha. Faith was a blind resolve based on nothing but an

unfaltering belief you find true, good and beautiful. *Scarla.* My faith in the love I had for her had propelled me into greater states of appreciation during our time together. She made me want to be a better man. Of course, that was before the apocalypse, and faith didn't prevent her death.

The woman stole my thoughts and attention as she began to stir. She groaned softly. I stood up and looked at Clio as she stretched to her feet beside me.

"Why did you call her 'Bella donna' earlier?"

Her shoulders slumped in a half shrug.

"I'm not sure. Why?"

"No reason."

She was about to say something when the woman groaned louder and sat up suddenly. She blinked repeatedly beneath a dark wide stare that settled on us. Her features were a milky compilation of sharp cheekbones, a petite nose and full lips that slackened. She was obviously perplexed, but she was striking nonetheless.

Clio rushed to her bedside.

"Hello, Bella donna. How do you feel?" Her gesture to stroke a strand of hair from the woman's face was met by a fast hiss as she shrunk back. Clio faltered. "I'm not going to hurt you."

The woman's eyes shaded and her chest heaved as she regarded Clio. I knew the look. Hunger. It was ravenous upon reawakening as the undead, and her sights were firmly set on Clio.

Crap.

My nerves shot through me and we moved at the same time. The woman lunged for Clio and I lunged for her. A shriek erupted. The frail cot scraped over the floor as I ensnared my talons around her delicate neck. A percussive sound rang in my ear. She clawed at my face like a wildling. I grimaced and grunted. The cot gave way beneath the kerfuffle. Then, we were an awkward tangle of limbs and bedsheets that reeked of BO and pubic hair.

Next thing I knew, fists were pounding into my jaw.

"Get off me!"

"Calm down, woman!" My words contorted with the incoming slam. *Sting.* She had a punch. I was on top of her and managed to grab her flailing wrists. I glared down at a twisted vision of lips and fangs. "I'm going to get up now and you are going to stop doing what you're doing, okay?"

Spidery veins splintered her brow. She clamped her mouth shut and nodded. That was when the door sprang open. Blade's voice was a cannon.

"What the hell is happening in here? We're attempting to sleep!"

Terrific. I had hoped to keep this little fiasco under wraps until dusk.

I climbed off the woman. She ignored the hand I offered to help her to her feet and fast adopted an indignant pose with hands on hips. I looked at Blade.

"We have a newborn clan member who needs to feed. Go and fetch one of the hawker males."

He gave a drawn-out whistle and looked beyond me to the woman.

"What's your name, sweetness?"

She gave a flick of her hair and lifted her chin.

"Leandra, and I'm not your sweetness."

11

THE FRENCH DEMILUNE WITCH

*T*he air thinned as we ascended the ranges far west of Norbury city. Night sounds were few. My senses came alive despite the rough and uneven terrain. Branches slapped in my face as I led our group through twisted shrubs and thorny nettles. Clio was adamant that we veer off deeper into the wilderness. I hoped she knew where we were going because I had no clue now.

Irritation was a tic in the back of my throat. I tried not to think about the wasted nights spent in that damned shack. Four to be exact. Turning Leandra kindred had slowed down our progress due to the time required for her to replenish her new energy. Now, we were tight on time, considering it was full-moon-glory the following night.

Fricken wolves and prophecies. They were the reason

the world went to shit and so many lives destroyed. The reason I'd lost Scarla.

I groaned inwardly as Leandra's querulous voice rebounded from some place behind me. The regeneration process had no bearing on her temperament. If she was sassy before the transformation, she was now a pistol with a mouth.

"Argh! How much further?"

I didn't stop. She had fast acquired an entourage willing enough to cater to her every whim and she milked it for all its worth.

Hugo's deep drone replied. "Here Leandra, let me help you."

"Get your filthy hands off me, brute or I'll drain you of every last drop next time I feed."

He laughed. "Sounds promising."

A sharp inhale was followed by a slap. "You are a deplorable human. I'm sure Lord Marius will be interested to know how you disrespect female kindred members."

"I … I'm sorry, Leandra. Forgive me."

Blade and Athan cracked up. I grinned.

"Yeah, cut him some slack, Leandra. He's just love-drunk on ya, is all!"

"He's like a Bryan Adams' number; he knows not what he does."

They broke out into an off-key version of *Please Forgive Me*. It sounded dreadful. Leandra huffed. Clio laughed. Hugo cackled. I smirked and imagined her snotty features twisting with her next words.

"Eh! How boring … I hated Bryan Adams."

Athan guffawed.

"I heard tell he turned Death Metal since the apocalypse, jamming it up with Slayer these days."

More laughter ensued but I tuned out and picked up my pace, pushing through the dense undergrowth while Clio struggled to keep up beside me. Slivers of moonlight streamed through the thick forest canopy. I glanced at her.

"You chose an interesting candidate for your prophecy protection scheme."

She gave a subdued laugh. "I didn't choose her, you did."

"God help me."

"Ha. You mean God help all of us. She's a force to be reckoned with, but it's not her personality I'm interested in."

"Give it time."

I rubbed my temples. My thoughts strained. According to Clio there was a little under an hour left between us and the wolf den. Why she needed Leandra's newborn vampire blood was a mystery. I had to keep focused on the endgame – kill the baby and her mother. Return to Avila.

Simple. Well, it sounded simple enough in theory. I could only hope it played out the same way. *Lygarou. Who could've predicted the existence of such creatures?*

The fact that top federal agencies had not only known

of the Lygarou but proceeded to abolish most of humanity through their defective ambitions to possess biological warfare, pissed me off no end. I had spent hours in their underground city laboratory studying blood, blood-forming organs and blood diseases under an entirely false pretense. I felt like a fool.

Governments have a way of doing that. Can't say I looked forward to the backroom jungle awaiting our new bureaucracy. I repressed a shudder.

"Tell me about Evanora and Shane. Why did she create the Lygarou?"

Clio shook her head. "As far as I know, Evanora was a French Demilune witch who lived an isolated life in the mountains some time ago."

"How long some time ago?"

She shrugged. "About a hundred years or so. Folklore says that the mountain wolves were drawn to her." She gave a half laugh. "A bit like the movie *Dances with Wolves*, only she was powerful enough to conjure a spell to bring the wolves into human form – with a sidekick that they would shift back into their former skins every full moon so that she was able to enjoy them as both animal and human. She called them Lygarou."

"*Dances with Wolves* in the literal sense."

She tittered lightly. Freckles like flecked gold. "Yes. Evanora and the Lygarou lived peacefully in the mountains for decades with no interference from the outside world."

"So, what happened?"

She pushed an overhanging branch aside to climb over a mound of earth. Her breath shortened, and she moved ahead of me on the path before answering.

"Shane is what happened. He was the first to be spawned – the alpha wolf. He grew bored of their isolated life and defied Evanora's sacred commandments." She stopped suddenly and looked at me, her voice grave. "The Lygarou were never supposed to be revealed to the world. They are a sacramental Demilune species with extraordinary gifts."

"Yeah, gifts that mutilate and kill."

"It was never supposed to be that way. The reawakened are not of the sacred breed. They are Lystalkers."

Lystalkers. Lygarou. I didn't much care for labels when my daughter could be shredded. I didn't say as much though.

"Why are they different from the original breed?"

"Intent. When Shane deserted Evanora, she was beside herself with grief and fear. But she knew his decision to leave would inevitably expose her beloved Lygarou. Their utopian existence was gone. Everything was at risk – their lives and livelihood; their great honor, beliefs and tranquil code by which they lived. Even more so, Evanora was well aware of man's insatiable thirst for power. She couldn't have her wolves become subject to the scientific arena ..." Her voice trailed. "We all know how that goes."

"What did she do?"

"She did what any witch in her position would do; she conjured a dormant spell to suppress the species. Apparently, they sleep in peace within hidden caves some place deep in Sweetwater Valley."

I frowned. "Never heard of the place."

"Why would you? You're no witch."

"Good point." My thoughts were haywire. I didn't know which question I wanted answered next. I chose the obvious. "Why didn't her dormant spell work on Shane?"

Her fingers clutched at her jacket hem. She pulled the thin fabric tight around her. Her voice sounded somber.

"I think it was because he was the first to transform and mature into his werewolf abilities. His defiance was more than just an act of desertion; it caused a shift. Something to do with the time-belt; major alter fate-of-the-world stuff that eventuated into the V-virus." She shook her head. "He couldn't resurrect the original Lygarou without witchcraft, but he knew he could awaken an adapted breed by spawning a child."

Hmm ... the revelations were pouring forth and the cords in my neck vibrated. I looked ahead. My vision was exceptional now, particularly since my diet had been re-established into something sustainable. I caught sight of movement among the thick brush bordering the trail. I halted and grabbed for Clio's hand just as the sound of Leandra's shrill voice blasted along the track.

For a split second, I froze, and everything happened at once. I spun around as a deep growl reverberated. Hugo screamed. Blade yelled blue murder. I went to move but

Leandra's pale, stricken features stole my vision as she sprinted toward me. She gripped my arm. Blade and Athan hissed, and Clio shrieked. Then, Leandra's hysterical voice stung my ears.

"W ... wolves!"

Fire ignited my veins. Thoughts evaporated. I flung my words over my shoulder as I pushed her aside and ran toward Hugo, Blade and Athan.

"Stay with Clio!"

12

PURE WILD

The winding trail blazed beneath my feet as I launched forward. I felt nothing but the mountain air whizzing across my skin. A hiss and a holler rose in the night. Rumbles and snarls erupted. The distinct sound of tearing flesh pricked my ears as I halted near Blade and Athan.

Incandescence. They were startling amber and pale blue, and they peered fiercely above exposed gums, thick canines and silver-tipped fur. I scanned the scene in a beat. Three wolves tore into Hugo. His massive figure writhed on the ground, and his wails were muffled.

Shit. My nerves were like razor wire. Three wolves stood between us and Hugo. Their legs were stiff; black hair bristled. Jaws dripped and teeth milled. One of them began to stalk back and forth. My nostrils scorched. *Wet dog.* It was blood and innards, and the musty odor of old rain that hung heavy in the air.

There was no time to dwell. I arched my shoulders and let out an insistent hiss. Supernatural adrenaline coursed through my veins. My vision flared. I surged forward, my talons shredding the air ahead of me. A roar ruptured in my throat. Athan and Blade moved like dynamite. The wolves hunched low, ears flattened. The stalking beast and I leapt at the same time. My bones crunched against solid matted hair and a wet snout as we collided in midair.

We plunged to the ground with a thud. His legs kicked in fury and his jaws enveloped my arm, his teeth sinking deep into flesh and veins. I barely felt it. I was hyped up. Thunderous growls detonated the air as I thrust my fist into his face and he shook his head, tearing at my arm.

Fuck. He wasn't letting go. Bats screeched with riotous shrills. My flesh stung. The others were going at it like monster alley on steroids. Dirt billowed. I let out a hiss and went for his eyes, plunging my talons into his sockets. I drove my talons deeper into his skull. The wolf yelped and instantly recoiled. Quilled paws slid across gravel. His eyes avoided mine as he gave a bark and a whimper and backed away. He raised his head and let out a long howl.

My stomach was a storm. Icy blue eyes flickered when he looked back at me. I hissed again and advanced toward him. I was ready for round two when the pack stopped suddenly and began to withdraw. Hugo groaned behind them as they retreated in seconds.

Blade's breath was heavy beside me. "Holy mother of all things wild, what the fuck was that?"

I glanced at him and Athan. Their features were spidery lines of blue on white. Blood stained Athan's skull and hands. Blade's golden stare was a crimson moon.

I shrugged. "Wolves."

"Yeah, no shit." Athan said. "Wolves on what? Animals don't usually behave like that."

I gave him a frown. "And since when do humans behave like vampires, hmm?"

He said nothing as Leandra and Clio emerged from the trees unharmed. Relief was fleeting. If this was the welcoming party, I shuddered to think what was waiting for us at the wolf-mother's den.

Clio faced me. "You okay?"

Stupid question. I was a vampire. I healed fast. I nodded and she promptly went to Hugo. The dirt trail beneath him was clotted with blood. His dreadlocks were soaked through and his clothes were shredded to reveal torn flesh and many gaping holes. I didn't hold out much hope for him considering his state.

Clio crouched over Hugo and glanced at me. "He's still alive!"

"Yes." I moved closer to peer at him. His face was a mash-up of meaty flesh and blood soup. I shook my head. "I don't think he will be for much longer."

He gurgled and squirmed. It was arduous.

"We best be getting on with it," Blade said. "The sun will be up before long."

He was right. It was only a matter of hours until dawn and we still had to face the wolves if we were to secure lodgings for the day. Of course, we had no choice but to set our sights on the wolf den as coverage.

Clio stood up and scowled. "We can't just leave him like this! It's seriously undignified!"

She might be right. I may have been indifferent toward him, but he did provide mouthfuls of blood here and there to keep us sustained. I studied him. Big mammoth human who had chosen to be a Shadow Guardian in our new world. *Schmuck.*

I was about to respond to Clio when Leandra pushed past me and halted in front of him. Her hands gripped her waist and her breasts pushed forward as she peered at him. She gave an exaggerated flick of her long hair before narrowing her eyes at me. "May I?"

Surprise rippled through me, but I remained silent and nodded. She mirrored my move before dropping to her knees before him. Her scarlet skirt fanned out like a blossom dream as she tenderly took his chin between her palms and murmured in his ear.

"I'm sending a dove to heaven." She pressed her lips to his forehead and spoke against his skin. "I forgive you, dummy."

He groaned and blinked as he reached to stroke her cheek. She smiled down at him and everything began to feel hollow. *Heart.* It banged in my chest. My breath stalled as she stretched his neck to the side and sunk her fangs into his throat. He didn't make a sound. His chest deflated and his body slumped further into the dirt. I was completely floored.

13

RUMBLE IN THE WOODS

*I*llusion. *Horror. Savagery.*

Treetops swayed with the slight breeze and silver clouds doused the moon. The forest hummed. We stood amid the dewy trunks that fringed the clearing and we peered at the wolf den. I inhaled. Wildflowers and rotting wood lingered along with the scent of hostility.

"Well now, I can't say that my visions of the wolf den resembled anything remotely like that." Blade rubbed his chin and glanced at Clio. "You sure this is the right place? Maybe you need to check your witch GPS again."

He had a point. The wolf den turned out to be an enormous log cabin with lofty peaked rooftops, sprawling verandas and floor-to-ceiling windows that glowed from within. It was a far cry from a den, whatever that looked like.

Athan laughed.

Clio scowled. "Dick."

Blade stepped up to her. "You negate me with your name calling?" He reached to stroke a lock of her hair. "Let's see how that works out for you in the immediate future."

She gave him a sharp elbow. "Is that a threat, Barnacle?"

He backed away, his face contorted with the shadows.

"Just pointing out the obvious. We're all equipped to handle the Lystalkers. I don't see no fangs on your honeypot gums."

She was about to retort when I cut in. "Shut up!" I flicked my chin toward the den. "We've got the right place."

Illusion.

Sometimes reality felt surreal. This was one of those moments. The log cabin door flung open to reveal a brawny hooded figure. He paused at the threshold. His eyes were shadowed above a protruding chin spread with dark stubble. His broad shoulders were like a giant as he stepped from the cabin to stand at the top of the stairs.

He looked straight at me as a pack of wolves emerged from around the back of the cabin along with ten other men who spilled onto the veranda. They clutched an array of weapons – stakes and swords, and a couple of chains. They stunk offensively and stood with pinched expressions and glassy stares as one wolf raised his head to give a long howl.

A chill went through me. *Was this a waking dream?*

My hammering heart suggested otherwise. That and Leandra's sudden needled grip on my arm.

"There is only five of us, Jett!"

"I'm aware." I pried her fingers from my arm. "You're about to get a fast lesson in supernatural combat. Watch for stakes and avoid wolf jaws. Be who you were reborn to be and stay close to me." I glanced at Blade and Athan whose eyes were like hot steel. "Keep an eye on the witch."

They grunted a reply while Clio flicked out a switchblade. She held it steady and nodded. I braced myself before we moved from the trees and into the clearing. Adrenaline rushed. My veins felt twitchy, and the wolfmen were on the move.

They descended the stairs and strode toward us. The Lystalker front line sneered, exposing grotty teeth. They were clad in dirty denim and checkered shirts. I could only be grateful they were still in human form but their menacing grins were accompanied by a disturbing chorus of snarls emanating from their four-legged friends slinking alongside them.

Horror.

I was a creature of death who longed to kill. My fingers prickled. Aggression pulsed. The earth felt spongy and the air hung dense as we stopped mid-way and faced them. Bestial blood called my name as the big fellow shrugged his hood from his head and looked at me. Cold eyes dilated.

"I figured there would be more of you."

"We don't need more."

His bulbous nostrils flared with his grin. "Now that's a bold statement if I ever heard one."

I laughed. "Want to hear another one?"

Gray eyes flickered. His grin dissolved as I moved with the swiftness of the wind. Roars and growls crackled in my ears. My hands found his throat in a searing flash. He resisted. His strength was a revelation, but I was a demon. A fiend searching for blood. My talons etched deep as my fangs pierced the flesh as I bit down hard.

He bellowed. It was hellish. Twisted shrieks became the night as fists like cannons punched me in the side of the head. The impact jarred me. Thwacks and grunts, and butchered flesh. I grimaced and gripped him harder. Bones crunched against my fangs. One brutal shove and I was reeling backward. A chunk of raw wolfman meat filled my mouth.

Salt and metal.

I regained my footing and crouched. I spat out his flesh, scanning the riot. *Massacre.* It smelled like home. I caught the scene all at once: Wolves prowled and ravaged. Vampires were like light. Blade danced with iron jaws snapping at his ankles as he thrashed his claws along a wolfman's face and hissed. Chains whizzed. Athan growled like an inferno and tore off a head. Swords clanked to the ground. Leandra was spectral – grace and evil. Clio was nowhere in sight.

"Jett!"

Leandra gestured quickly. The big guy howled and

ran for me. He had a stake. I sprung to my feet and charged for him, dodging the sharp end of the stave and plunging my fist through his chest. Bone on bone. His ribcage shattered. *Warmth.* He froze. His stubble jaw slackened as my palm encircled his heart.

Savagery.

I felt nothing as I leaned to speak into his ear. "Bold statement is bold heart."

He gasped as I clenched the throbbing organ and yanked it from him. I spun around, barely hearing his body thud to the ground as a wolf lunged at me. *Boom.* It was solid. I hit the ground to gaping jaws, hot breath and a soggy nose.

I shoved him hard. My flesh ripped. I hooked an arm around his thick neck and slammed my fist into his head. An ensemble of high pitched screeches peeled across the night sky. I glanced up. *Bats.* They were everywhere. A vision of black wings as they swarmed and swooped.

Disorientation. It was momentary. Pitch wings, red eyes and sharp beaks were our allies. They barraged the wolves in an incessant onslaught. The mammoth beast on top of me grizzled as bats tore at his ears and eyes. He yelped and I rolled from beneath him.

A fast breath and thumping hooves. *What the hell?* I turned toward the forest to catch sight of a herd of deer. They appeared from the brush like a doe-eyed vision and were heading straight for us. That was when the bats receded to a low hover and wolf ears pricked. Alert eyes were reduced to slivers; jaws salivated, and canine hair bristled before gigantic paws were set into motion.

My mind whirled as bleats and squeals rose like a city circus. Dust clouded. Jaws clipped furiously. The herd bolted from the clearing and made for the forest as the wolves gave chase beneath a flock of wild bats.

I frowned, and it was as heavy as the cloak of silence that followed. My back panged as I looked around. Leandra, Blade and Athan stood like blood-soaked mullets staring into the woods. Bodies and carnage littered the clearing. It was a mess. The wolfmen were goners. *Dead.* A moment felt like forever.

"Where's Clio?"

"I'm here!"

She stood at the top of the log cabin stairs and waved at me. Respite was my next breath until I spotted the woman behind her crossing the cabin threshold. Skintight black leather appeared sprayed to her body and contrasted against the tumble of golden hair that fell over one shoulder as she sidled up beside Clio. Her thick lashes blinked over large amber eyes as they settled on me. My heart lurched.

Scarla?

Everything was numb after that.

14

WHEN THE PAST COMES CALLING

"*J*ett?" Leandra's touch startled me. My boots seeped into the earth. "Are you okay?"

Did my eyes betray me? I couldn't stop looking at her. My bottom lip slackened but I managed to nod. "Let's get inside."

I walked like a ghost. My mind was a fog. Perhaps the blows to my head had more impact than I thought. The wolfman *did* pack a meaty punch.

I saw her throat split. I saw her die.

My breath splintered when she turned away and vanished inside the cabin, and I barely heard Athan and Blade's discussion as we took the steps up to the veranda. Clio's dark stare held mine. Her features were unreadable.

"What was with the Zootopia scene?" Athan said.

"Mystery. Maybe the witch is in the know." Blade came to an abrupt halt in front of Clio. He gazed at her through the bloodied flaxen locks shadowing his brow. "It was you, wasn't it?"

"Some simple spells stuck from the time spent with my grandmother."

He gave a low whistle before grinning.

"Respect!" He gestured toward the cabin. "I need to get cleaned up before my slumber. Do they have running water in there or what?"

Her nose scrunched. "How should I know?"

He grunted a reply before moving past her, and Athan and Leandra followed him into the house. A strange feeling took hold as I watched them. Half of me wanted to get to the woman inside as fast as possible. The half couldn't move. It was Clio's voice that set me in motion.

"Come on. The sun is almost up, you need to get inside."

She was right. I'd hardly noticed the perpetual murky hues on the horizon. My chest felt tight as I followed her inside, and I halted as soon as I crossed the threshold, barely hearing the door slam shut behind me as Clio set about shutting off the house to the impending sunlight. The sounds of yanking curtains, banging doors and clanking shutters were lost on me as I looked around.

Evergreen and Peach.

It was those soft woody scents of cedar that encapsulated my senses. It was rather nice, and so was the lofty timber ceiling that was suspended over oil-stained floorboards and sandstone walls. If you were inclined to notice it like that. I couldn't go there. But as my gaze swept over the thick pile rugs that sprawled beneath oversized sofas and polished furniture, I did notice the set of stone stairs that created a focal point that spiraled toward the upper levels.

My nostrils twitched. The place had a somewhat calm vibe, but that was the last thing I felt when my vision settled on the woman who sat in the far corner nursing her child. My nerves were as sharp as the look in her whiskey colored eyes as she held her swaddled baby and scowled. A slice of heaven moved through me. *I knew those eyes.* My gaze latched onto hers and I was transported to another place. *Scarla.* She was just like her – the clean shape of her cheekbones beneath porcelain skin; the delicate etches of her lips and the way her hair wisped around her jawline. Even the slight crease on her brow mirrored the woman I had loved.

Bella donna.

The resemblance was uncanny. Nothing was making sense, but I knew I had to get my shit together. We were on the home stretch. We'd faced the wolfman pack and their hounds protecting her, secured the wolf den and now she was within arm's reach. All I needed to do was to kill her and the kid and this entire Lystalker fiasco would be behind us. Peace would be restored to the clan and my daughter would be safe.

Pièce de résistance. She was mine.

I ignored the others buzzing around the place as they called out to each other from unseen parts of the house. They were scouting every nook and cranny before our slumber. We all knew the threat was far from over and we were at our most vulnerable through the day. Luckily, we had a witch on our side who could keep watch.

Grace eluded me as I moved ahead. The woman reacted instantly by shrinking back into her chair. She clutched the baby tighter and her paling lips quavered.

"Who … who are you? What do you want from us?"

I gasped and paused. *Silver bells.* The timbre of voice sounded just like Scarla's. I shook my head and said her name without thinking.

"Scarla?"

"Huh?" Her mouth fell apart and she sprung to her feet. The baby gurgled as she rushed closer to me. I could smell the powdery scent of the newborn baby and the sweet sweat glistening on her brow. *Blossoms.*

She sneered in my face. "You're a vampire; how do you know my mother?"

Every so often, life presents us with information that blows our minds. I was nullified. Words felt distant. Her jaw squared and eyes like transpicuous lanterns flashed as she scrutinized me. Tingles shimmied up my spine and that was when I knew it to be true. The wolf-mother was Scarla's daughter. A daughter I never knew existed.

"You're Scarla's daughter?" I could barely keep my voice steady. "Scarla Mage?"

"Yes. Who are you?"

"Jett."

"Jett?" Her eyes widened. "You're Jett?"

This was getting too much. Ludicrous even. She had

obviously heard about me. I was about to answer when the baby cooed and squirmed in her arms. My gaze went to the little bundle to catch sight of tiny fists jarring through the air. All at once, I felt pitted as I watched tiny knuckles turn white. Her mother began rocking back and forth as she watched me. My throat rumbled.

"You're the wolf-mother." It wasn't a question. Hardly even a coherent thought. She responded regardless.

"My name is Sienna and this is Shana, Scarla's granddaughter."

"She carries the Blood Legend code in her genes – half wolf, half human."

Her eyes darkened to inkwells.

"Half human with the rare blood. That's why her birth is so critical for the future. You have to help me protect her."

Whaat? Rare blood? Scarla's bloodline carried the AB positive blood that had eventuated in her death?

I struggled for clarity as a heaviness weighed in my limbs. I couldn't even summon a response. Her next question nailed my tongue to the roof of my mouth.

"Is my mother with you? Is she safe?"

My stomach dropped. She didn't know Scarla was dead. I ground my teeth and met her stare. I didn't need to say the words out loud. My expression revealed all she needed to know. Her face twisted and went gaunt as realization dawned, and the look in her eyes tore at my soul.

"I'm sorry …" My voice was unfamiliar. This scene was unfamiliar. Her raw pain reminded me of my lost humanity. A glimmer in the eye. *Light.* I wanted to touch her; to offer comfort of some sort. It was at that moment Clio decided to make an entrance, walking into the room with her energy all keyed-up.

"Okay, I've battened up the house as much as I can. There are showers and soap upstairs. You should consider using both before your slumber." She halted abruptly but I didn't look at her. I was too busy watching Sienna's heart shatter before my eyes. Guilt was a creeping shadow, as was Clio as she drew closer.

"What's going on?"

My eyes darted. "She …" I gestured toward Sienna. "I know her."

"Huh?" Clio balked before her hair became a scorching vision as she shook her head. I briefly wondered if her eyes would pop from their sockets. "Umm … well, isn't this a surprise?" Hands clasped hips; a cool stare sized up the situation. "You realize this doesn't change anything, Jett. The kid needs to die to stop the Lystalkers."

Sienna shrieked. She began to edge backward. "What? You came here to kill us? My baby? No way!"

I held up my palms and moved toward her, stopping when her wild eyes pinned my boots to the floor. The baby began to cry as she spun around and made a dash for a door at the far end of the room. I called out to her, but my voice was lost against her high-pitched scream as Blade suddenly burst through the door.

His face was contorted with a vicious hiss. She gripped the baby and stepped back as his face split into a sly grin.

"Going somewhere, my sweetness?"

Her throat swelled slightly before she whirled around, almost tripping over a rug as she bolted toward the center of the room. Athan and Leandra appeared from another doorway. Her boots twisted on the floor and the baby wailed in her arms as her eyes skimmed between us. She shook her head.

"Please … don't hurt my baby."

Scarla.

She blinded me. Everything felt knotted and my mouth ran dry as Blade's voice grated over the bawling baby. Lemon eyes gleamed my way.

"It's time for you to complete your retribution, Jett." He gestured toward Sienna. "And make it quick; we could all use an early slumber."

Sienna's eyes were dewy when they met mine. Agony gripped me from the inside out. I had no choice but to kill the daughter and granddaughter of the woman I had loved more than anything. The woman I couldn't keep safe from this ugly world. The lives of the surviving humans and the clan depended on their deaths. So did the life of my own daughter. I couldn't even feel the tips of my fingers. I was obliterated.

15

THE SILENCE

S *ilence.*

It felt like violence. The moments preceding death were anointed with annihilation. It chilled me to the bone. Clio's breath was audible. She stood somewhere behind me. Shana's cries muffled beneath my thumping heart as I lowered my chin to gage the situation with my senses.

Blade, Athan and Leandra advanced toward Sienna who began to sob and shake her head. *Heat.* I could feel her throbbing pulse as they closed in around her. Blade cackled. His footsteps were like synaptic impulses in my brain.

"There, there, my sweetness. It will be over in a jiffy."

Sienna's shrill deafened. I closed my eyes. Vampire fever burned my nostrils. Headiness rimmed like vitality. Athan's voice was an explosive staccato.

"Wake up, slayer! Plenty of time to slumber after you complete the kill."

His chunky tongue ran across his bottom lip as I looked at him. He grinned and motioned toward Sienna.

"You gotta do it now, before the Lystalkers get a chance to re-skin tonight."

I knew that he was right. If the half-breed wasn't destroyed, the Lystalkers would attack the city tonight with the full moon. Vampires and humans alike would perish, and Marius would know of my failure long before our return to the city. He would kill Avila and Sun.

I gave a heavy sigh and looked at Sienna. She stood stiff as she clutched Shana near a coffee table. Her lips were like jelly and her eyes stole my breath as she silently pleaded with me. *Torment.* It was Scarla all over again and the scene felt the same. The day the hawkers came to slice her throat and dump her body in the dust near my feet. The day I had lost a part of my soul.

Leandra's sudden outcry broke my reverie.

"Hurry up, Jett! We haven't got all day; I want to go clean up."

It was time. I inhaled sharply and strode toward them. All eyes were glued on me as I stopped short of Sienna. She gazed up at me through the tears that now splashed against her cheeks. I shook my head.

"I'm sorry."

Her eyes widened and terror claimed her features. Blade laughed. Athan grunted. *Exhale.* My senses were acute. I clenched my fists. Adrenaline pumped as I whirled around and smashed my knuckles through Blade's chest. Shock struck his face as Leandra shrilled and Athan roared behind me.

Athan barged into me. Meaty arms ensnared my chest. I braced myself and snarled. I grabbed the back of Blade's skull. Broken ribs splintered as I followed the thrust of the motion and palmed his heart.

Life.

His was literally in the palm of my hands. Athan growled and yanked me hard. This time, I didn't resist. My boots stumbled backward with the weight of him behind me. Blade's eyes bulged like neon lights as his heart slipped from his body as I fell against Athan.

He slumped to the floor, but I didn't hear the thud. Athan's inky eyes raged as I turned to catch him lunging for me.

"Motherfucker!"

His talons ripped through the air and slashed across my cheeks. I sprung back and pegged Blade's heart at him, following with a hiss and a round of blows to his head. He didn't even budge with the impact. His growl was like the grim reaper as he caught one of my flailing fists.

Silence.

Pain erupted in my hand beneath his vise-like grip and my bones shattered as he squeezed with brutal force. I grunted. It sounded contorted as we staggered around before I flung my other hand at his face, going for his eyes. My razor talons scratched at cold flesh and blood rushed beneath my nails. He dodged a jab to the eye. His putrid breath blew over my face and his other fist was solid muscle as he pounded it into my temple.

Dizziness threatened. Black spots stained my vision. Infant wails and screams cut through my head as my legs gave way. I fell hard. Athan's weight was debilitating as he clambered on top of my back. He had me pinned to the floor. He clobbered his fists into my spine and let out a barrage of profanities.

"You double-crossing, wolf-loving piece of shit!"

A hiss sounded nefarious. My ears began ringing. My jaw felt like a boxing match against the hard floor as my whirling vision found the leg of a coffee table. Timber. My thoughts tunneled as he paused in his barrage and leaned over me.

"You killed my friend and broke kindred law. I'm going to take your heart before I murder the mongrels. And then I'm going to tear your daughter apart with my big vampire cock before I slaughter her."

I tensed. Blood oozed like sticky paint.

"Like hell you will."

Violent silence.

It was a fleeting second. He went to move and as his weight shifted, I reached for the coffee table leg and wrenched it as hard as I could. The timber paling cracked as I tore it from the tabletop and a series of clunks followed. I gripped the wooden stave and roared, twisting my body around at the same time that he went to plunge his fist through the flesh of my back.

Strike. The stave found its target. His lips sagged and his catapulting fist went off course as I shoved the paling through his chest and into his heart. Time stalled. Burly fingers fumbled at the stake as I drove it in harder. He wheezed and gasped for air. His chest sucked against his ribs like a deflating balloon as scarlet saliva pooled over his bottom lip and his face went ashen. Then, he dropped like a sack of potatoes and I rolled away from him.

Silence.

No longer did it feel like violence.

16

LITTLE SECRETS

"What the hell did you do?" Leandra struck her heels into the floor and peered down at me. Blue veins lumped across her brow. "You killed them, Jett!"

My eyes fixed on the timber fan blades that suspended from the pitched ceiling. I felt depleted and my back hurt. "I do know that, Leandra."

She huffed and puffed like a dragon and flailed her arms wide as she hissed down at me. "What were you thinking? Now, we're all dead. If Marius doesn't get us first then the Lystalkers will, thanks to you!"

I knew she was not too far off the mark; my thought process wasn't even clear to me. *What was I thinking?* Only hours before I was hankering to kill the wolf family and get on with my new kindred life. Now, I had just done the one thing that I had vowed to avoid – I'd jeopardized the life of my daughter. *Have I lost my mind?* All I knew was that I couldn't allow Sienna and Shana to die today. Scarla had been too precious and too important to me. Even in death, I wasn't going to fail her again.

Unfortunately, that choice came with dire consequences that I now had to face, and I had no plan for the immediate future. I grimaced and stood. My legs felt like pudding as I regarded Blade and Athan. They slumped on the floor like shriveled gray carcasses smeared with blood. It was too bad. A part of me was just beginning to warm up to them. Somewhat.

"What are we going to do, Jett?" Leandra gripped her hips. Dried blood and grime shadowed the creases on her scrunched nose. "You sired me into this dumb-ass mess. How are you going to get me out of it?" She gestured toward Sienna who now sat nursing the child and silently staring at us. "We can still kill the half-breed and save ourselves."

Sienna was all volcano. "Like fuck you will, barnacle-bitch."

Leandra's eyes narrowed. "That's tough talk for a rabies-bitten slag without her dogs."

Sienna stood up. "Oh, they will come. Do you really think Shane would leave his child for too long?" Copper eyes boiled. "He's recruiting more of us for tonight's full lunar when *you* get to become vampire stew."

"All the more reason to dice the kid." Leandra hissed at me. "Did you hear her? We have to do something!"

God help me.

"Shut up, Leandra. Go take your shower so I can think."

I rubbed my temple. My hand felt like a bag of grainy sand; the one that Athan had so lovingly crushed. I wasn't regenerating as fast as usual. Blood and sleep deprivation will do that to a vampire. Throw in a few violent brawls and I was naked. My veins felt like withered spaghetti. I hadn't had a decent feed since we shared the last hawker male a few days ago. If you could call that decent.

Leandra's mouth formed a huge "O" before clamping shut. I could almost see the gears turning in her head. *Ding ding.* Something appealed. She gave an indignant nod. "Very well, but I hope your *thinking* wields more desirable results than our current predicament."

I ignored her glare. "Go."

She gave a dramatic flick of her head and about-faced before stalking from the room. I exhaled and immediately collapsed onto a sofa, momentarily relishing the soft folds against my back and searching out Clio with my eyes. I found her standing in a shadowy corner by the cabin entrance. Her fingers knotted and she chewed on her bottom lip.

"You're awfully quiet," I said. "Nothing to say about the sudden turn of events?"

She moved from the corner and her eyes appeared somber as she walked closer. I kept quiet and watched as she pushed back unruly hair and stopped in front of me. I swallowed a knowing sigh. She had been adamant that the baby's death was the only way to protect what was left of humanity against the Lystalkers. I'd be lying if I didn't say that I wasn't expecting another tongue-lashing. I was ready for it.

She caught me off guard when she slid to her knees and reached for my hands. A moment of respite found me as skin like a sunny day wrapped around the chill of mine.

"You're weak," she said.

"I've had better days."

She pulled her hands from mine and my insides instantly protested. I barely noticed that she had rolled up her jacket sleeve until she thrust her wrist into my face. "Drink."

I gaped at her and briefly considered a refusal, but then the sweet rhythm of her pulse caught my ear in a lullaby and my willpower was none to zero. Hunger brimmed in my eyes as they met hers. She gave a nod and I cupped her wrist between my palms and paused. *Ba boom. Ba boom.* The sound of her heart became a rapid beat. I dropped my eyes to the smooth flesh of wrist before my own heart surged and I lowered my lips to find the tangy bliss of her blood.

Delectation.

It raptured in my veins like rich merlot, but I was careful not to take too much from her – only what I needed to nourish my body before slumber. Her quickening breath and frantic pulse were my cue to withdraw from her flesh. *Sour cherry and spice.* It clung to my lips as she immediately wrapped her arm in a cloth as I leaned back into the sofa and allowed the fresh blood to fuse within me. After a few moments, I began to feel normal enough to gather my thoughts.

Time to think my way out of this situation. I looked at Sienna. Her expression was passive, but her eyes flickered at me as Shana slept bundled in a bassinet by her feet. She gave a waning smile.

"Thank you."

I nodded in reply as Clio clasped my hands again.

"Feel a little better?"

"Yes." My voice sounded awkward. "Thank you, I never would've asked."

"I know." She grinned. "Look at you go, pure heart."

"Pure heart just committed murder against his own kind and disobeyed his kindred master." I flicked my chin toward the infant. "Nothing is alright, the kid still breathes."

"She does. The Blood Legend legacy will pass through the generations because of you – you've protected the prophecy."

Huh? Hold on a second.

"This pleases you? You wanted her dead; you said it was the only way to ensure the survival of humans."

A smile split her face. "I did say that, didn't I?" She leapt to her feet and her mouth offered a fast script as she began pacing. "It had to be this way, Jett. The choice had to be yours despite the pressure from others and the outside world – you did this – it was the only way a cloaking spell of this magnitude could work."

"Cloaking spell? What are you talking about?"

She stopped abruptly and looked at me.

"Shana can't die, Jett. If she dies, the Blood Legend gene dies with her, leaving us facing a bleak future with no hope." Her eyes gleamed. "Her blood is just the beginning. She must procreate to allow the genes time to evolve through the generations. It will be her granddaughter who will arrive during the transition era to ignite the second apocalypse."

My mind was a ticking timebomb. "But what about the Lystalkers? They're still going to be around to wipe everyone out long before that. They're too primitive, not of the original bloodline. You said so yourself."

"The Lystalkers won't be a threat when the cloaking spell is created. It will render them dormant."

A sprig of hope shimmied through me.

"Then, Marius won't know the difference between the kid being alive or dead." I was almost afraid to believe it. "Avila will be safe."

"And so will the humans – at least, the ones you lot don't kill. The ones who are becoming the first generation of Leavings." She gestured toward Sienna. "But I have to get them to Sweetwater Valley before the full moon tonight; and somehow, I will have to find Alvin."

"Alvin?"

"Yeah, he's the only one that can do something like this. All I need is Leandra to bite the kid so that her newborn kindred blood merges with Shana's – this acts as a blood shield and bonds the two bloodlines." She frowned and began pacing again. "I'll also need some kind of matching lockets to act as dual components to hold each supernatural element and guard the cloaking spell; Alvin can do the rest. He lives in the valley, I think."

"You think? Clio …"

She cut in. "Remember what I said about faith?"

My eyes narrowed but I said nothing. She wasn't waiting for my reply anyway.

"Well, I'm asking you to have faith now. It's either that or things are going to get a whole lot worse come tonight." She paused to look at Sienna. "Only Alvin can make a spell of this magnitude happen. Will you come with me?"

A few moments felt like forever.

Sienna squared her jaw. "Marius has your daughter, Avila?"

"Yes. He will kill her when he discovers my betrayal."

Her eyes glazed. "My mother used to talk about Avila. She was very fond of her and said that we would've made great friends."

My heart hollowed at the mention of Scarla. But it was confusion that prevailed over my emotions.

"I don't doubt that for one minute." I shook my head. "Your mother told you about us? Why did she never tell me about you?"

She gave a rueful laugh. "She had no choice. Nobody

could know about me. The risk was too great, what with Shane being kept prisoner for all those years in a government lab."

"Why could no one know of you?" Clio asked.

Sienna lifted her eyes to mine and for some reason, my breath almost stopped.

"Because not only do I carry the rare blood now sought by the kindred, but my father was a direct descendant of the Lygarou originals."

Clio's gasp hardly penetrated my astonishment.

17

STARGAZER

"*Stargazer, you call the shots and I take em.*"

She used to whisper to the stars and speak with angels. Of that, I was sure. My stargazing woman was too good for a world like this. She had to leave. Her soul was too pure. The vermin now infecting the world would have spoiled her from the inside out. Yet, I would selfishly give anything to have her back.

She out of mind and simply out of soul.

Stargazer: Mother Love Bone.

It played in my mind and dragged at my heart as I watched Scarla's daughter lay down her child to receive the bite of a newborn vampire. That song could have been written for Scarla – the best thing I'd ever seen. My eyes fell to the infant who lay on top of a small white blanket. Rosebud lips and dimpled cheeks. Golden hair and innocence. She would never know the woman I loved.

The moments felt as if shrouded with divinity and I

knew they were among the last that I would spend with Scarla's family. Another piece of her would be ripped from my life as fast as it had appeared, but they would survive, and that, along with Avila, has become my priority. Scarla and the magnificent secrets flowing through her bloodlines were the key to the future. Even beyond her death, my woman was still a gift to the world. I felt privileged for the little time I had shared with her. Somehow, my love for Scarla had brought me to her daughter and reminded me of all that was lost to the kindred existence – our ability to feel emotions and love.

Sienna hesitated before stepping away from the baby. *Myrrh and Frankincense.* It was distinctive and floral, and it burned with the curling scent of incense as strong as the uncertainty filling her eyes.

"If you see Shane, tell him that I'm sorry. Tell him where I've gone."

"I will. You're doing the right thing."

She bit her lip and gave a fast nod. This wasn't easy for her. She was choosing to take her daughter and abandon her lover for the sake of preserving the survival of humans. These were the days when every choice made was accompanied with critical consequences. Her choice would see the end to Shane's quest in taking vengeance against those who had mistreated him – a vendetta that would cause more suffering for humanity.

Clio rested a hand on Sienna's shoulder. "It will be okay. Alvin will take good care of you and Shana."

Her dark gaze skimmed to me briefly before she went

to the baby. She held a small bag of salt and two heart shaped pendants suspended on thin gold chains that Sienna had produced. She paused over Shana and smiled.

"Hey sweet little one, you're going to save a lot of people; you're going to do great things but you have to brave now, okay?"

Shana pushed a balled fist into her mouth. Her eyelids began to close. That was when Clio began to whisper in a dialect I couldn't decipher as she placed one pendant above Shana's head and the other at her feet. After that, she created a wide circle of salt around the infant before positioning five white candles on the circle at even intervals and lighting them. She stood up and reached into her pocket to produce a switchblade, flicking it open as she motioned for Leandra.

"Show me your wrists."

Oddly enough, Leandra was silent as she exposed the smooth flesh of her wrists to the sharp end of the blade. Clio sliced into her skin and blood rushed to the surface.

"You must enter the altar to bestow on her the Threefold Kiss. You will bite her lips that shall utter sacred names; her heart that shall form her strength, and her third eye that shall see all." Clio's voice deepened. "Your bite must break her skin only so that she may take your blood with her own. Do not feed on her, do you understand?"

Leandra nodded. Her expression was passive, but the slight tremble of her lips betrayed her nerves as she stepped into the sacred circle. Her feet anchored apart as she looked down at the sleeping baby. Her voice was barely audible.

"I'm sorry ... this is going to hurt just a little bit."

She bent to her knees and Clio began to chant words that sounded charming and foreign. Witch lingo. The pitch of her voice rose and fell in a lilting melody and created an unusual sensation through me. It felt profound, as if the unfolding ritual was a momentous event that would forever alter history. It was everything surreal.

Dancer, dancer. I'm all wrong.

Shana's cries rose above Leandra as she performed the Threefold Kiss; gently pressing her fangs into the soft folds of baby skin before allowing her blood to drip into the broken flesh. Sienna tensed beside me. I cringed and looked away to the fragrant haze that hovered over them. I gasped when I saw Scarla's figure dancing in the curling incense smoke.

Scarla?

Hands clasped sensual hips that swayed beneath a swirling white dress. Long lashes shadowed her cheeks while lustrous flaxen hair flowed down her back as she moved with grace. *Angel.* Lips like swollen cherries smiled as she whirled around before fixing her eyes on me. The sound of her voice was heaven in my soul.

"Dance with me."

"I'm an awful dancer."

"You're wrong."

My heart cracked wide open as her essence shrouded me. *My love.* Clio's chants became an intense backdrop as

I arched my neck and lifted my arms and surrendered to her. I would have fallen to my knees and given her everything I had left. I would die all over again for her. Anything for her. I closed my eyes and my lips moved without a sound.

"I'll dance with your soul every day. Wait for me."

"Always."

The faint sound of her reply echoed through my mind as the Threefold Kiss ritual was completed. Scarla was gone and I felt heady. I blinked to see Leandra wipe her lips with the back of a hand as she stepped from the circle. Sienna immediately went to console her child and the energy in the room shifted into the stark reality we faced. It was Leandra's voice that hit me next.

"May I go upstairs to slumber now?"

"Yes, go. I'll see them off and join you shortly," I said.

She gripped her hips.

"Good. Let's hope all this hocus-pocus stuff keeps us alive long enough to replenish ourselves."

I forced a smile. "You better go get your head start then."

She didn't say anything else as she strutted from the room. I was relieved that she didn't stick around to bid the others farewell. While she had obviously taken a crucial role in what had just transpired, I sensed that she was about as trustworthy as a shady King Street pimp on ICE. To say I was concerned was an understatement.

Clio stuffed the heart pendants into her jacket pocket.

She ran a hand through her unruly auburn hair as she came up beside me.

"We have to get going while we still have enough daylight."

"I know."

They were making the journey to Sweetwater Valley alone. I couldn't join them; my place was back in the city with my daughter. Besides, no one could know for sure if they would make it to the valley and find the elusive Alvin before tonight's full moon. I planned on leaving here as soon as I could to get to Avila. This was far from over yet.

Clio reached for my hand.

"Get some rest; you're going to need it."

I was indeed. My body ached. Sleep was a relentless tendril pushing behind my eyes. At least we didn't have humans to slow us down during the journey back to Norbury. Leandra and I could run like the wind.

"What about Leandra? She might speak of this. She's a risk."

"Not for long. Her blood is now infused with Shana's. As soon as Alvin completes the ritual that I just began, her memory of this will be cloaked along with the spell."

Relief didn't come. "If you find him, that is."

"You got to believe in something, Jett. It may as well be this."

"I don't have much choice."

She cupped a palm over my heart. "We always have a choice, pure heart."

I couldn't help but smile. "You're a rainbow, alright. Make sure you ride the colors to the end." I gestured toward Sienna who now stood near the cabin door with a rucksack and holding a bundled Shana. "Look after them."

"I will. Goodbye, Jett."

I stroked the side of her cheek with the back of my knuckles. Her skin was like warm milk.

"Maybe we'll meet again someday."

She grinned.

"If we don't, we always have the afterlife."

"Yeah."

My thoughts went to Scarla and the familiar ache dredged my heart.

Stargazer won't you kick with me (again).

18

FULL MOON RENDEZVOUS

*H*ands shook me violently from a deep sleep.

"Jett, wake up!" Leandra's voice was frantic. I struggled to get my bearings. "We overslept. They're here!"

Whaat?

She leapt to her feet and rushed to the window of the room where we had chosen to rest, and yanked back the thick curtains to reveal the night sky. I sat up and swung my legs from the bed, catching sight of the full moon shining from an inky canvas. My stomach curled as a long predatory growl sounded from the level below.

"Shane."

My nostrils flared with the distinct odor of a base human scent mixed with wolf. It was that strong, I could smell him even from beneath the gap of the closed bedroom door. My thoughts stormed like a whirlwind. The Lystalkers had transformed and were on the prowl.

Obviously, Clio hadn't found the great sorcerer Alvin in time to stop the change.

Avila.

I had to get to her. My chest constricted as I stood up and Leandra gasped. Her eyes flashed neon red through the dark.

"We have to leave – now!"

I wasn't going to argue that point. "The window."

It was our only option. A fierce snarl chilled my bones. The sound of heavy paw prints bounded on the stairs. He wasn't alone and they were coming. I swallowed the rising bile in my throat and dashed to the window and scanned the lawn below to see a dozen werewolves stalking along the clearing perimeter. My arteries felt like mortar as I saw the creatures for the first time.

Wolves on steroids. That was the prevailing thought as I fixed my stare on them. They were about three times the size of a normal wolf with accentuated features – eyes like the arctic gleamed from bristling black skulls while sharp canines extended over fleshy gums. Their ears were tipped with silver and pointed slightly back, and their snouts cringed. I couldn't help but be slightly captivated as I watched them move purposely and with stealth. The way their massive joints appeared disembodied beneath thick fur was enthralling.

And unsettling.

I shuddered and my pulse raced as I unlatched the

window and pushed it open. I turned to Leandra. She looked like death. "Go!"

Her eyes widened. "Are you mad? They'll eat us alive if we go out there!"

A series of loud growls tore through the house. My heart was an explosion as a deafening crash followed. They were breaking through the closed bedroom doors along the hall of the upper floor. I gave Leandra a shove.

"They'll eat us alive if we stay here."

She shrieked. A lusty howl rang out from below and she went to climb over the windowsill. She clung to the timber frame and froze as the door to our room splintered apart with a sonorous bang. The hairs on my arms spiked with the sound of a deadly snarl.

"J … Jett."

I barely heard her as I whirled around to face a pair of tapering eyes. Hackles rose from the wolf's forehead, it snarled, exposing large ivory fangs. I could hear his pack moving through the cabin somewhere behind him. My breath slowed with the passing moments as I caught my reflection in the gold of his eyes.

Exhale.

He was a glorious looking beast, but he was no puppy. He growled and crouched low before his legs uncoiled in one rapid movement toward me. Saliva dribbled from his fangs as he sprang. Speed was my friend as I vaulted over him to land on top of the bed. Leandra made a loud noise as he charged at her. She leapt from the windowsill and onto the slanting roof as he slammed into the window opening. His jaws snapped on air. The timber window frame began to crack beneath his force. Howls like sirens cut through the night and Leandra screeched. Thunderous thumps shook the house as the werewolves outside began scouring the walls of the cabin to get to her.

"Jett!"

The cabin echoed to the thuds of canine feet. *Cavernous.* The others were coming, but there was no time to think. Seconds felt like forever. I let out a hiss and extended my talons. I sprung from the bed to ensnare the werewolf's neck. The impact was rough. My jaw slammed against wolf skull and I immediately went for his face, sinking my nails into his eyes.

I knew it to be their weakness. His big head writhed. My hands loosened and he managed to catch one between his jaws. The crunch was agony. I roared as my bones fractured and my skin ripped beneath the force of his jaws. I roared and plummeted a fist between his eyes. The blow gave me enough time to yank my other arm free. I clung on hard and shredded his ears with my fangs while hooking my talons deep into his nostrils. *Vice.* I had him caught. A blanket of red filled my vision. Violence surged. He was a solid mass of muscle. I gritted my teeth and sunk my talons deeper as the beast began moving backward.

My blood boiled with the coppery taste of wolf blood. His wiry hair stuck in my gums. A throaty snarl reverberated as he began to rise up on his hind legs. His body thrashed violently and the next thing I knew, I was winded and catapulting across the room at an alarming speed.

Boom.

I hit the wall hard and slid to the floor as he turned to regard me. *Breathe.* I gasped for air as he stretched to his full height of about eight feet. Black fur glistened as he arched his neck to growl so loud it hurt my ears. My heart stammered. I stood up as three more wolves burst into the room, and my legs almost buckled.

Dog meat.

We were goners. Leandra screamed. My ears buzzed as she scrambled back into the room. Twisting werewolf's jaws filled the window frame behind her. She dashed toward me and clung to my arm. I didn't notice her talons cutting into my skin as I looked at the alpha wolf who hovered dangerously close.

Shane.

It had to be him. More wolves spilled into the room like slinking shadows. Their eyes were a menacing glow over slobbering fangs as they surrounded us and waited for his cue. They appeared unearthly and sinister, yet they carried a certain magnificence. However, that was the last thing on my mind as Leandra trembled next to me. The alpha rolled his head and growled before he dropped to all fours and skulked closer.

Is this how it ends for us? Butchered by a primitive breed of Lygarou?

I think I'd rather starve in a filthy cell mocked by our food.

The air in the room was full of tension. I held the alpha's cold stare. It was Avila and Sun who filled my head as he snarled. His hot breath was rancid in my face. Leandra yelped as he growled roughly before lowering his head and adopting a strike pose.

I glanced at her. "Don't stop fighting until you have to."

Her eyes were wild when she nodded a reply. Her dark hair whirled as she faced the wolves and crouched lower, thrashing her talons through the air with a monstrous hiss. I mimicked her moves as the alpha went to leap at us. The other wolves took his cue and began to advance. I surged forward and braced myself for impact.

Silence. The room spun and my head tingled. I was still alive, and the wolves had vanished. *What the hell?* I frowned. There was a strange whimpering at my feet. My eyes darted to see a group of men and women writhing naked on the floor. Leandra's voice was a distant noise in my ear.

"W … what just happened?"

I gaped and respite rippled.

"Clio, she came through after all."

Exhale.

19

VAMPIRES & WOLVES

*S*hane wore a pair of dirty jeans and nothing else. Tawny locks framed heavy-lidded eyes and weathered skin. His chest was broad, tattooed and flexed beneath a thick spread of matted hair as he approached me. The scent of wolf still lingered fresh on his skin.

"What the hell happened?" His dark eyes bulged. "What did you do to us and where the fuck is my family, blood-sap?"

We stood in the cabin living room. Leandra stayed close. The lighting was dim, but I saw them clearly. A handful of disgruntled Lystalkers stared with a dozen more outside with their wolf cousins. I was keen to get out of here and back to Avila. There was no way for me to know if she was still alive.

I gestured toward Blade and Athan whose remains

still lay where they had perished. "I was sent here to kill your family. I killed them instead."

Ragged nails fingered a long goatee over a squared jaw. He barely looked at them. He took a step closer, fists clenched. Three of his men came up behind him. They each clutched a stake and all of them were shirtless, and they stunk like day-old urine. I tried not to grimace as he spat words in my face.

"What have you done with my daughter?"

"I've done nothing with her."

Frustration brewed like a red stain. He waved a fist.

"I'm gonna rearrange your smug vampire features if you don't tell me what I want to know." He flicked a wrist above him and one of his crew pushed a stake into his hand. He pointed the stake at my heart. "Where is she?"

"She is safe with her mother in Sweetwater Valley." I pushed the stake aside. "You don't want to go there, my friend. Trust me."

He had a nose like a Roman; strong and prominent.

"I don't trust vampires, or humans for that matter. You found a way to cloak her, didn't you? You found a way to stop the Lystalker change."

"Not me. A friendly neighborhood witch helped out. It was either that or risk you and your kind eradicating humans altogether."

"Human survival is the least of my concerns after what they did to me." His voice was acidic. "Keeping me locked up for decades and using my blood to cause abomination. They're just all evil at heart … There's no hope left for humanity now."

"You're wrong, and your daughter is the key to undoing the damage caused by the use of your blood." I paused and my eyes bored into his. "Just not now."

"Why would you even care, vampire? You lost your heart the moment you turned kindred."

I nodded. "Maybe I did. Maybe I am the first of my kind to remember his heart and realize the power that lies in that space." I balled my fist and thumped my chest lightly. "Maybe, this is what the apocalypse was all about – something good must give rise from the ashes … from the bloodshed and violence. Something worth fighting for."

He gnawed at his bottom lip. His voice was gruff. "It's a loveless world."

"Not if we can find a way back to it."

His eyes flickered before he glanced at the men behind him.

"We will no longer turn on the full moon – you made sure of that. My pack isn't safe. When the vampire masters discover what you've done, they will hunt us relentlessly."

"If you remain elusive, they'll never know. Take your pack and go to Sweetwater Valley to be with your family. Bide your time and wait for the generations to produce the Blood Legend, then you will have your turn to take

KIM PETERSEN

back the city with *heart* behind you." I smiled. "Surely the evolved Lygarou can co-exist with humans and vampires in the future?"

He laughed.

"You might well be the last of the dreamers." He paused and his eyes narrowed. "If we go, what will you do? My sources tell me that the clan have already begun constructing a dome over one half of the city. They will use humans as blood cows and slaves in their new world. Will you join them?"

"My place is with my daughter and the Mysticus clan. The plans for the future may not appear humane, but it will keep the Leavings generations alive long enough to see the Blood Legend come into fruition. Until then, I will remain as one of them."

"And after?"

It was my turn to laugh. "When the time comes, I will search for my woman in the afterlife. I won't stop until I find your daughter's grandmother again."

His jaw dropped as realization dawned. "Now I understand."

"Yes. It was written in the stars with Scarla."

Leandra gave an exaggerated sigh. Her glossy lips pouted. "I have no idea what you guys are going on about, but I think it's best we leave while the night permits us to travel."

Ah, yes. Ignorance is bliss.

I grinned and silently thanked Clio. Leandra's

memory of this fiasco was already fading with the cloaking spell. It was utterly superb.

She clasped her hips and tossed her hair. "What are you smirking about?"

I shook my head. "You're right, we must leave now."

I exchanged one last look with Shane. We had reached an understanding and there were no more words left to say. I gave a fast nod before making for the cabin door with Leandra. We paused at the top of the veranda stairs to see a pack of wolves patrolling the cabin clearing accompanied by about a dozen men and women in various forms of undress.

"What about them?" Leandra said.

The wolves gathered at the foot of stairs and peered at us. Pale blue eyes and crimping snouts. A series of high-pitched screeches broke the silence as bats soared across the night sky and the full moon hung like a cryptic illusion.

I fingered the vial of Shana's blood safely tucked away in my jacket pocket before reaching for Leandra's hand.

"Can you run with the bats?"

She nodded.

"Shall we?"

"Yes."

I wound my fingers around hers. We descended the stairs and the wolves parted to allow us through, and we became part of the night.

Dreamers were now for all the tomorrows. Whatever awaited us back in the city, I would always carry my stargazer, *my woman*, in my heart. It was her love that would be my strength and my salvation.

BLOOD LEGENDS
ASCENSION
USA Today Bestselling Author
KIM PETERSEN

1

DISTRICT HUMAN

They call it Bloodfaye. I call it a perpetual fire on earth where the wicked are punished after death. That might sound like an exaggeration on my part. It wasn't. It was a forged existence. Nothing shone other than the silver egg that hovered above us like a deceptive halo. Imitation did nothing to appease a restless soul. It was the new kindred way of life.

I rubbed the back of my neck. My muscles ached from endless days working the laboratory. Today was no different. Bloodfaye was open for business. Humans had to pass a blood test before they were permitted into the dome city where they were promised a better life.

It was a sham. We took their blood for two reasons:

1. Contaminated blood could potentially kill a vampire if consumed.

2. The search for the invincible and elusive AB
   positive blood was as eternal as life after
   death.

The fact that I possessed a vial of gold mixed with Lygarou blood was a delicate situation, but I wasn't losing any sleep over it. As it was, Melissa was currently taking care of all matters sleep deprivation. The woman was haunting me. She had been my wife and Avila's mom. The last time I'd seen her was the morning she had left the house to go for her usual run. It was the same day she had died.

I frowned and pushed those thoughts aside as the beginnings of a commotion erupted from across the lab. It was the usual lab set-up – lengthy benchtops, glassed cubicles and an array of scientific machines. Marius was a resourceful overlord. I peered through the white coats skimming the room. They stunk like self-importance, and dotted between them were the Leavings who were ushered through the lab faster than a Sushi conveyer belt.

"Hold still, Leaving!"

The brash order was issued by some vampire kid they'd dumped in the laboratory and called a Mysticus scientist. There were dozens of them. Most of them couldn't distinguish a fart from a turd, let alone competently take the blood of incoming Leavings. I had no choice but to deal with it.

Mongrel blood.

I cursed and stood up from my workstation. Some

vampires were like foul gutters. This one was poking a Leaving woman in a rather offensive fashion. Time to intervene. I'd been here before. It was the barbaric vampire guttersnipes who lost their shit often. An event that inevitably resulted in a dead human.

"I said, stop fricken squirming bitch!"

I picked up my pace. The woman whimpered. I had a zero-dead human policy on my watch. They all knew it but not all of them had the ability to care when confronted by human blood and frustration.

The woman cried out as I approached. Her limp hair hung over grotty features like rotten seaweed. Her stench resembled the muck too. They seriously needed to do something about the hygiene of Leavings, preferably before they reached the lab for their mandatory blood testing.

I stopped behind him. His name was lost on me. They should consider issuing name tags too.

"Easy, kid. She's not a dartboard."

"Her veins are rolling or something!"

I peered at the underside of her arm. Her skin was angry-red and swollen.

"Small veins. Perhaps we should choose a butterfly needle and attempt on her other arm."

The dumbass didn't even look me as he gave a frustrated hiss before tightening his grip on her wrist. The syringe poised briefly. Her dull eyes glanced at me; her pasty lips trembled as he jabbed the needle into her flesh. He didn't appear to be aiming for anything. She shrieked and jerked her arm. *Blood fountain.* He hit it and it was suddenly spurting everywhere. She wailed louder. I groaned. His lips stretched to bare his fangs. A growl followed before he went to lunge for her. I stopped him by grabbing a fistful of his ginger hair in the nick of time. *Mongrel. Blood.*

"How bestial of you." I gave a growl of my own and yanked him clear off his chair. He landed on the floor and promptly scrambled to his haunches. His eyes flashed and he hissed at me. *Life just gets better ... and better.* I gave him a twisted grin and studied my talons. "Ah, and so he challenges me to a dual-dance ... vampire trout must be in the mood for a second death today, hmm?"

His brows instantly lowered as he started to back away. I expected as much, but my problems were far from over. I had a lab teaming with vampires and a Leaving who may as well have had an *"all you can eat"* sign plastered on her head. The air was now thick with the scent of hunger. They were stalking all around. Eyes like neon beads. Breath like hot alley cats.

"Back away, vampires!" The warning went unheard. I grabbed the nearest roll of cotton and pressed it against the woman's now overactive vein. He butchered her good for a rooky armed with only a thin needle. A low hiss emanated from behind. The woman screamed.

Shit. Fear elevated a vampire's insatiable desire for blood.

"Keep still and shut up." I gripped her wrist and scrambled among the empty vials, packages of syringes and antiseptic bottles splayed over the benchtop for some tape. It remained unfound and my heart thundered. The crusniks were closing in.

The woman skittered closer to me. I shoved her behind me, and she grappled at my lab coat as a female vampire with pink bangs and studded nostrils displayed her fangs. Talons twisted at the ends of her hair. Nostrils like a flame. Others inched closer, transfixed by the promise of fresh blood for the taking. Jaws salivated as they sought out the woman. *Meat market fair.* I needed backup.

Luckily there were guards and Shadow Guardians stationed in the lab for incidents like this. *Where the hell are they when you need them?* I gave the blood-lusting creatures my most hideous growl as some guards began pushing through the growing mob. *Finally.* Relief was in sight. It was Michal's shrill voice rising above pulsating hisses that caught my attention next.

"Coming through! Coming through!"

He emerged from among the throng of vamps with a few guards at his side, stopping abruptly when he copped sight of me and the woman nearly pushed up against the benchtop. Brown eyes blinked rapidly over her splattered blood as he made tittering noises. His fidgety thumbs probed his glasses.

"What in the name is this mess?"

The guards began ushering the predators away. Some of them resisted. They hissed and growled like feral animals. I ignored them and gazed toward the blood that doused the benchtop and floor.

"It's called blood, Michal. It's what we do here, remember?"

He gave me a filthy look. "How they expect us to work like this is beyond me!"

"Understatement of the century." I pushed the woman toward him. "Wrap her up properly and give her a pass."

His jaw dropped. Guards began shouting. A few of the mongrel bloods were getting feistier. The tension was brewing – just perfect

"A pass? B ... but, master ... she hasn't been cleared for District H."

I gave a tight smile. "She has now. Shall we use this current turn of events and escort the Leaving out of here?"

His lips parted. Spittle dribbled out of his mouth before he clamped his mouth shut and nodded. *Ding, ding.* He understood.

"Grab what you can," I said.

It was tedious smuggling items from the laboratory. Marius had guards assigned around the clock which had forced us to set up our own makeshift lab to work the hybrid blood. We'd chosen a discreet hub in the underground subway located along the wall that separated the districts in the far reaches of District H. It was better than nothing.

Michal fussed over the Leaving woman; he secured her wound tight while offering a running rant. "It's going to be okay, Leaving woman. We just have to ensure the bloodsuckers on the other side won't detect your fresh wound so easily... This will help you avoid the soowoo tooth fairy if you know what I mean."

"H - huh?"

She was terrified. I had to look away. Her life wasn't about to improve any time soon, but that was out my hands. I didn't run the joint.

Humans had become our bona fide blood-cows. If they passed their bloods, they were allocated quarters in District H – the human section of Bloodfaye. They were enslaved after that. Bloodfaye had a no free-loader policy, a fact I found ironic considering each Leaving was eloquently drained of blood every eight weeks to appease the clan's thirst. Most of them survived the periodic bloodletting.

Life beneath the dome was a far cry from the vision Marius had painted. Granted, the entire process was still in its infancy. There was much to establish as far as procedures and regulations were concerned. No time to think about that right now. Michal and I were just about ready to begin a process of our own.

I glanced at the guards on crowd control. The baking coven were still restless, but I knew the distraction wouldn't last.

"Hurry up!" It was a grunt issued at Michal as he carefully wrapped a few basic laboratory apparatuses in a white cloth – things like test tubes, tongs and funnels. I stuffed a pair of goggles, clamps and a few droppers into my pockets before encircling an arm around the trembling woman.

"Come on, love. Let's get you through to District H."

A handful of Shadow Guardians stood around the exit door. One of them was Lena – the tall leathery Latino who had accompanied me part the way into wolf-mission wilderness some time ago. She had taken to me since my return. I was reluctant to admit that the feeling was mutual. Her dark roots dipped with her curt nod.

"Master Jett." Chaffed lips grinned as she moved away from her peers and pushed open the door. "I see you're leaving at just the right moment this afternoon."

I gently shoved the Leaving woman across the threshold after Michal. "Hello Lena. As usual, your observation skills impress and delight."

Her eyes scanned my bulging pockets before flitting up to me. She flicked her chin and stepped closer. "Master Zaros was spotted wandering through District H earlier."

"And?"

Zaros was a fluctuating version of Marius; an overlord vampire. He was erratic and conniving. His desire for power made him extremely dangerous. I liked him as much as the vile aftertaste of a lowlife hawker.

"I saw him heading toward the old subway. He wasn't alone."

I squared my jaw. "Thank you, Lena."

She smiled and stepped back, sweeping her arm toward the door. "Good day, master Jett."

"And to you."

I walked from the lab with my pockets intact. The sounds of hyped hisses and growling guards were muffled beyond the closing door. I possessed many things of value in my pockets these days. None so much as the few members of my own secret sector.

2

STREETS WITH NO NAMES

*G*raphene and silicon wafers. The brittle crystalline solid filled many of the latticed gaps in the world's strongest most pliable material to create a humongous solar panel. *Lifeforce.* It was one big breathable UV protective heating pad; a fact I found pleasing considering my blood ran like the Arctic ocean. It was shaded like the moon and flexed slightly over the city like a futuristic hub generating Bloodfaye's power. I didn't know how Marius had managed to score so much of the innovative material that made the dome. It was damned genius.

Michal's feet did double time beside me as we strode through District H. We'd left the Leaving woman in the capable hands of Sun. She was one of the very few I trusted in the new world and happened to be handling the Leavings' lodgings that afternoon. The District reeked like rotten vegetables, human waste and stale sweat. They were still ironing out the ventilation and sewerage systems. They'd tapped into the city's main water supply. The water was clean and drinkable for our captives, albeit sewage was another matter altogether. I wasn't a plumber but I looked forward to cleaner air when visiting District H. Although, the district's living conditions weren't high on Marius' to-do list. He currently had more pressing matters to occupy his mind. Like establishing the reign of vampires in the new world.

The thought caused my gut to clench. I refocused. We were headed for the subway at the back of the city. I walked briskly through the dirty streets, barely seeing the small groups of Leavings lingering in the entrances of old brownstones and aging apartment buildings. They appeared desperate and somber. The vibe was desolate; the sky a silver moon promising nothing but a wasteland. Soon, it would become black with nightfall and the promise of death.

I caught sight of an elderly man sprawling on the dead grass along the sidewalk. His brown patched sweater swallowed his frail frame and he was motionless. He was barely alive and he was guard bait. Michal voiced my thoughts.

"Deplorable."

"Agreed."

"Then why don't you make a suggestion to Marius about the treatment of these Leavings?" He waved an arm toward the old man. "Surely his affection for Avila puts you in a position of influence? Elderly people are in no shape to undergo the bloodletting cycles."

I grimaced. "An overlord's affection for my daughter does not influence make, particularly when such suggestions serve no purpose in his agenda for power."

"Good point, though someone once said it was wise to keep your friends close and your enemies closer."

"Now we're using old-world clichés?" The thought of keeping close council with Marius made my skin crawl. "Look around, Michal, our overlord is too busy thriving on his own reflection, let alone his love for vampirism. There is no place for old-world thinking here. It wouldn't take a vampire genius to sniff out the wolf among the sheep when he comes calling."

He smirked. "Nice one." He was referring to my wolf pun. We were, after all, the keepers of such precious hybrid blood. He swallowed hard and glanced at me. "You know that you are in a position of power to help improve the living conditions in District H, at least until we can restore humanity with a cure for the V-virus."

"I know nothing of the sort. Besides, Marius listens to no one but himself, that I do know."

He huffed. "Takes one to know one."

I ignored his remark and glanced at him. He clutched the lab supplies against his chest and blinked rapidly. He did that a lot lately. His features were pinched beneath a layer of beaded sweat. He looked like a flushed ferret on a mouse wheel.

He looked back at me with annoyance. "What?"

"Nothing."

I looked away and deliberately picked up my pace. He knew how I felt about Marius favoring the affections of Avila. It bothered me to no end. There were hundreds of female vampires who occupied space in District V, and the shrewd overlord had a thing for *my* daughter. I didn't want to think about it.

Michal panted. He was falling behind. "Can we go any faster, *master*?"

I grinned. "I can go *a lot* faster, how about you?"

"I could if you'd turn me."

"Not happening today."

"When then?"

Never.

Michal was the only human other than the Shadow Guardians to remain off limits to vampires and the bloodletting program. He was fortunate and yet he wanted nothing more than to be kindred. Go figure. Marius refused to turn him and had forbid others to initiate the transition. Perhaps it was his fondness for the neurotic little man that compelled his reasoning. I didn't know, but his eternal death wasn't going to be on my hands.

I avoided an answer and gestured toward a group of Mysticus guards up ahead. "Let's just focus on the matter at hand, shall we?"

"Y ... yep!"

Arrogance. It was a pungent fume and one I'd grown accustomed to since my passage into vampirism. Most kindred naturally adopted a superior attitude upon turning. Even the greatest of egotists in the old world had nothing on this lot. Supernatural ability bred conceit. They thought they were invincible. I longed for the day to prove them otherwise.

My eyes narrowed on four male guards as we approached. They all wore the same getup – white leather and chunky black boots adorned with silver buckles. Thin white gloves concealed bony hands while dark glasses shaded their eyes as they bantered back and forth.

Impudence.

I had it nailed and adopted my most courtly pose as I gave them a nod. I could play the game. Decorum was second trait. As a master, it was expected of me. "Good day, gentlemen."

They gave a hasty greeting. Pale skin gleamed as luminous as their lustrous hair. Vampires were glazed and polished creatures. Even the most gnarly variety. One of them stopped walking and eyed the bundle Michal clenched against his chest possessively. He gestured toward the bulky wrap.

"What have you there, Leaving?"

Michal stiffened.

"N … nothing."

"Na … na … nothing?" He laughed as his goons halted beside him. "Looks like something to me."

Wizpire lightbulbs ensued.

"Yeah, what's with the parcel? Have the contents been cleared?"

Cowboys. My nerves bristled. I groaned inwardly as one of them moved closer to Michal. Hair like liquorice contrasted against white-leathered shoulders. Lips like gills twisted. "Answer the question Leaving."

Michal jerked. His eyes widened beneath his spectacles; tremulous fingers tightened around the bundle as I stepped in front of him. I tilted my head and deadpanned the guard. "You dare question a Leaving accompanying a master?"

Golden eyes penetrated dark shades. "As Mysticus guards it is our business to investigate all suspicious behavior in District H."

Calm. My temples throbbed. "He carries supplies requested by Zaros who is currently in the district awaiting our special delivery." I forced a smile and motioned behind me. "We are here in service to our overlord. Is our behavior more suspicious than the Leaving I spotted rolling on the street back there?"

He was silent for a beat and his gaze followed my gesture. "A sponge?"

"It would seem."

He nodded. "Thank you, master Jett. Our apologies for disrupting your path."

"Apology accepted." I moved closer. "You'd do well to remember that this Leaving plays an important role in the progression of Bloodfaye's scientific arena. He is vital to your masters and as such, you will treat him respectfully at all times. Do you understand, vampire?"

His goon peeps cackled behind him as they started to move away.

"Come on, Ty, let's go investigate the *real* suspicious behavior."

The cowboy said nothing more. His eyes flashed and the veins beneath his chin became magenta vines as he gave a fast nod and walked away. The cords in my neck twanged. I didn't dwell. Michal gasped loudly as we set off again.

"I … I cannot believe you!"

We took the final corner. The road stretched along the tall iron-meshed wall separating the districts. Brownstone dwellings gave way to an industrial scene. Broken windows and patchwork doors garnished the worn exterior of warehouses and outlet buildings. The streets were quieter in this section of the city.

I kept my gaze ahead. "What?"

His voice was fretful. "Pointing out that poor Leaving man back there. They'll cause him more harm and enjoy every moment. You should be ashamed!"

"Ashamed is allowing your cover to be blown, Michal." I glanced at him. "That man was already dead; you are not. Do you realize what they will do to you should they discover your part in our little running experiment?"

"Y … yes, they'll kill me."

"Not before they tie you to a post and slowly remove bits of skin and limbs one by one. Death by a thousand cuts – sound appealing?"

"N … nope!"

"I didn't think so." I slowed down as we approached the subway. The hairs on my arms stiffened as my gaze settled on the overhanging sign above the entrance. *Crata Village* – the smoke-stacked stop in the old world. The air stifled against my lungs and my ears pricked with the sound of a dull scream emanating from below street level.

Zaros. He and his crew must be in the underground tunnels. A rarity. Those subway passages were usually barren of life and the reason we had selected the site as our science hub in the first place. I motioned toward the doorway of the building near us. The dwelling appeared uninhabited and would provide a suitable space to stow Michal while I checked it out. "Stay here until I return."

He didn't argue. I ushered him through the door, briefly scanning a vast room filled with timber work benches, half-dressed mannequins and other unusual props. Rolls of fabric and industrial sewing machines covered in thick dust occupied the tables. I emptied my pockets.

His snuff-colored eyes blinked at me. "What if they discovered the lab?"

"Unlikely."

We'd chosen to set up shop in a control room in the most discreet part of the underground infrastructure. I'd spent many hours walking the metro before finally settling on a small powered room buried deep within the chute. If they found it, we were done for.

Michal placed the wrapped lab items on a table. His

fingers shook when he looked back at me. "The ... then what are they doing down there?"

I shrugged. "How should I know? Maybe they've taken to riding the subway to hell."

"Not amusing."

"Tell me about it." I shook my head and gave him a reassuring smile. "Listen, if I'm not back before a quarter till sunset, leave the stuff here and go back to the lab."

He nodded. "Okay. Just try and be quick and safe."

"Story of the new life, huh?"

I ignored the fear in his eyes and left him alone in the deserted warehouse. Despite the protection offered to the human citizens of Bloodfaye, we both knew District H was rife with dangers come nightfall. He would be a sitting duck. I wouldn't let him get plucked by some fangsta mongrel blood.

Adrenaline burned like fire as I descended the subway and emerged into the dark passageways. The air felt dank and cold against my skin, and a high-pitched scream chilled my bones. My breath was static and my boots light on grotty tiles as I moved forward. Putrid walls arched over me. *Flesh.* It was fresh and distinct, and it carried on the gust from the platform below. I stood at the top of the stairs and peered into the shadows. Laughter erupted. Everything was on high alert as I began taking the stairs and tried not to think about the danger I had forced upon my lifelong friend.

It was I who had collected the wolf-hybrid blood with plans to re-establish researching a cure for the Vampiric virus. And despite the supernatural blood running in my veins, it was I who breathed for nothing but the eradication of vampires from this world. The survival of humanity was stake enough. None so much as Michal's life. If he didn't survive, I'd never forgive myself.

3
HORROR IN THE SUBWAY

"*P* ... please! No more!"

I stiffened. The woman's plea was met with laughter. My ears pricked and my blood stirred. The promise of violence called me as my veins yearned for blood. It was instinctual. I bit back and halted midway along the staircase, gripping the steel balustrade before taking a deliberate breath. The shadows seeped into my lungs like a felony. Footsteps echoed from the platform below. I focused on her breath. It was warm, erratic and sharp, and it was combined with another. Two humans. A hiss borrowed from a snake's vocal repertoire. *Silence*. An insinuating voice followed.

"But my dear, are you not having fun today?"

Zaros. The sound of him made me want to pull out his heart. My thoughts whirled. I knew the best thing to do was to return to Michal and wait for the cadaverous dimwits to complete their heinous amusement. Revealing my presence would be a daft move and may warrant unwanted curiosity. We did not need that. I went to turn around, but I stopped dead when I heard a horrendous growl and tearing flesh.

Shit. I palmed my dark hair. The woman gave a blood curdling scream and my brain began to split. I was no superhero. I had enough to deal with what with weird dreams, a vial of certain blood and Avila's disturbing relationship with overlord arrogance. A conversation intruded my inner world.

"Argh … easy, vampire! I wish to have my pleasure with her."

A snarling voice responded. "Take her, then."

The woman whimpered and yelped.

"The hawker skank has little pleasure to offer. She's already been used up good by the looks of her."

Chortles ensued but I barely heard them. No other thought materialized after that. I was pure focus. I started to move down the stairs toward the platform. *Damn.* Kindred or human, some things never changed – the best thing to do was not always the best thing to do.

A heavy thud sounded as I took the final step onto the subway platform. *Body dump.* I knew the sound well. Fluorescent tubes flickered sporadically along the upper ridges of the tunnel walls. The stale shaft air carried the stench of urine, sludge and blood. I scanned the stretch of tiled concrete edging along tracks that disappeared into a black abyss ahead. A strangled scream and more laughter. I collected my thoughts and dashed forward.

Liquidation. It aroused my senses as I stopped near a pillar and leaned against the worn poster that plastered chipped tiles. Zaros pinned a Leaving man against a wall and toyed with him. The man's face was shredded and bloody. Bits of flesh hung from beneath his eyes and his legs buckled as Zaros etched another vicious pattern across his brow. He laughed as his victim gave a distorted wail.

Loathing was vile in my gut. I stared at the three vampires standing over the woman slumped at their feet. Her blood flowed freely. Her body was slack. Black leather gleamed under the volatile lights. Kindred eyes shone like death as one of them gave her a few kicks with his boots.

The jackass voiced his thoughts. "She's fucking dead, stupid." His dark eyes blazed below straw-colored hair. He kicked the woman again. "So much for our afternoon entertainment."

A lofty creature with emeralds for eyes chuckled. His lips were swollen cherries. "She's still warm enough for you to get it on with her, stud."

"Do I look like Ricky? I'm not into necrophilia."

"Who are you kidding? I saw you giving it to that sweet little blondie vamp the other night – you think that's not necrophilia?"

"She was breathing, dipshit."

"Yeah, a breathing corpse."

They broke into laughter just as the man gave an agonizing scream. My eyes darted to Zaros as he growled and dug his fangs into his throat. The man's head lolled back and the sound of his fading pulse caught my ears as Zaros siphoned his blood. He would be dead in a matter of seconds.

To live or to die?

I did not wait to ponder the question any further. I pushed off the pillar to interrupt the sickening scene. In a flash of a movement, I was breathing down Zaros' neck. His odor was a mix of pungent blood and fleshy delight. "Release the Leaving, Zaros."

Surprise.

His jerky movement was executed gracefully. It was remarkable. He tore his fangs from the man's throat and snapped around to look at me. His talons sunk into the Leaving's shoulder and his black eyes beaded. Blood stuck on his twisting lips and clung to his chin. The others slinked up behind me as Zaros roared and flung the man across the platform. He landed like a ragdoll.

I grinned but it was tight. "Rather dramatic welcoming."

His black leathered shoulders curled forward, and he rolled his head. He let out a deep growl. His breath was right in my face and offensive, but that was the last thing on my mind. He was a tall and solid negro vampire with a hot temper. I packed a pretty decent build for a white-collared academic, but he was a force I could not ignore.

My grin dissolved and I steeled myself. I quickly sized up the situation – two goons behind and to my right and one on my left. I kept Zaros in sight. He hissed between bloodied lips and fangs. My temples throbbed but I did not flinch.

"What the fuck are you doing in the subway, *master J*? Shouldn't you be busy solving the meaning of life?"

The goons cracked up. I ignored them.

"Clearly you're busy destroying it."

"What?" He wiped blood from his chin before gesturing toward the Leavings. "You mean these scuzbucket hawker Leavings? Their lives are worthless."

"Marius would disagree. Bloodfaye was created as a haven for all Leavings with principles based on mutual faith. They agree to participate in the bloodletting cycle in exchange for protection from outside threats."

I paused and flicked my chin toward the man. He was still but moaned slightly. "This treatment is not in the interest of conserving our blood supply."

Zaros gave a cold laugh.

"Marius isn't the only vampire to overlord the city. If I wish to explore the occasional indulgence, I will do so at my own discretion." He moved closer and I stood my ground. "You may have won Marius' trust by returning to the city a victorious baby-wolf killer, but you don't fool me, Dr. Weird."

His crew edged up behind me.

"Trust is overrated in the new world." I glanced at the vampires who now leered with menace on all sides. "You may want to consider calling off the lost boys."

"Why would I do a silly thing like that?"

I gave a half laugh. "Because it is vital that an

overlord possess the characteristics of a wise leader if he is to succeed in his quest to influence his clan."

He skimmed a bejeweled hand over his afro. "Like what?"

My lord, where do we begin?

"Like self-control and visions." I shrugged "Learning agility amid a changing landscape."

"You're suggesting I lack these qualities?"

I knew I was on dangerous ground but … I could not resist. "I'm suggesting you become more aware of these qualities."

He sucked in a breath and lunged at me. His fist slammed into my jaw and I stumbled against one of his cronies who promptly gripped my hair and yanked my head back.

Zaros' grisly image filled my vision. "You are one pretentious prick, lab rat." Razor talons seized my jaw. "I possess leadership qualities worse than any nightmare you've ever known."

Arrogance overload.

The one gripping my hair clenched his knuckles tighter. My pulse exploded with venom. "I don't doubt that … but violence is not always the way to go."

The lost boys laughed. Zaros growled, his fangs dripping with saliva as he closed in on me. I flinched and swallowed, bracing myself. A sharp jab stabbed my side. I flinched but impact was minimal. I thrust back my elbow, digging into the inflexible ribs behind me. He jerked back enough for me to get free. I spun around with fangs bared.

The damned on the damned.

Stony eyes gleamed at me and the lofty vampire flicked his hair. "He is unappreciative. I want to see your nightmare leadership qualities, master."

Zaros grinned like a demonic idiot. "Right on."

He began to prowl forward. *Fuck.* My eyes flitted between them. Four to one. The odds were clearly against me. Adrenaline rushed. Zaros crouched for a strike. The others mimicked their master. A fire burst in my mind. I was ready.

A shrill voice reverberated through the tunnel and stung my ears.

"Zaros, stop!"

I glanced beyond the vamps as Sun strode across the platform. Her eyes narrowed but she was a pleasant vision. Her leather boots clanked noisily as her breasts protruded beneath white fabric. She looked pissed.

Zaros and his gang whirled to look at her. Sassy female vampire. She had come into her own. Her lips crimped as her gaze trailed to me before noting the Leavings on the platform beyond me. "What's going on down here?"

Zaros was all cheese. His fangs almost blinded me as he squared his shoulders. "Sun, always a pleasure to see you."

"Master Zaros." She gave him a cool stare and

moistened her lips. "District H curfew is almost upon us. Marius has half of the city out searching for you."

"Is that so?"

"Yes."

He regarded her silently. A moment passed. "This scene was getting old anyways. We're done here for now."

Sun nodded and he moved closer to her. "I will be seeing *you* later."

She did not reply as he motioned for his crew and strode from the platform without looking back at me. The exchange perked my interest, but it fast faded when emerald eyes moved in front of me and hissed in my face. *Buffoon.* My upper lip lifted as he spun around and followed the others.

Sun came up beside me. "You okay?"

"Yeah. Thanks. Michal filled you in?"

"He was concerned." She gestured toward the Leavings. "One still lives."

"He won't make it."

Her eyes glowed like honey "He needs to; he's perfect. You're going to need him."

"Huh? Why?"

"Obviously he hasn't been processed into the district, yet."

"And?"

"For a smart guy, you can be awfully dumb, Jett. You will eventually need a loyal vampire to complete your experiment. Who better than a sired?"

My mouth fell open. "You want me to sire him?"

"Yes." Her voice was gentle and she reached for my hand. "Come on."

I said nothing more and allowed her to guide me. *The best thing to do is not always the best thing to do.* But who ever really knew what that was? A million thoughts erupted. None could comprehend the woman next to me. She was half angel, half minx, and she was a thief of the expected.

4

DEATH IS COMING

"Am I alive?"

"You're not dead."

"I'm not alive either."

I looked toward the sea. The water glistened like gothic black and the air was motionless. *Am I breathing?* I knew nothing in that moment and yet I felt a strange sense of tranquility. It was her presence. *Melissa.* The tips of her fingers found my nape and her voice was melodic.

"There are no accidents, Jett."

She smiled. I missed her smile.

"You're dead," I said. Her touch felt like a remedy. "We're both dead."

Coffee-colored eyes grew turbulent as she looked beyond me. Her lips thinned. A crow's call rang out across the shoreline followed by a hideous laugh. My skin crawled. The atrocious sound was familiar. Avila's shriek was the next thing I heard as I spun around to face a pair of beaded eyes on weathered skin. I sucked in a breath. I *was* breathing.

Ginger-beard – the hawker responsible for Scarla's death and the darkness that had claimed my daughter. I had ripped his ugly head from his neck some time ago and yet here he stood with his skull intact and his filthy arms ensnaring Avila. His scruffy boots dug into the sand. Crows hovered above him like a bad omen as he grinned with grisly intent. "I'm taking her with me to hell, blood-hustler!"

Avila appeared stoic as the earth parted beneath them and they began to sink into the grainy terrain. *Landslide.* Horror was an affliction. My lungs burned and I went to move but stopped short when Melissa's fingers clawed my arm. I barely heard her speak over my pounding heart.

"There are no accidents, Jett. My death … your death."

"Huh?" I frowned and twisted my arm from her grasp as Ginger-beard laughed before he began whistling a raspy tune.

The Doors: *This is the End.*

"This is the end, beautiful friend."

His barbed tone stung my psyche. I roared and bolted toward their submerging figures, lunging for Avila just as the sand edged beneath her chin. She peered at me silently and her eyes began to pool with blood as I desperately burrowed into the sand threatening to swallow her entirely. The suction was relentless. She sunk deeper into the cool sand without so much as a whimper. Ginger-beard paused his song to cackle some more as the beach devoured him like a noiseless vacuum.

My throat constricted. "No!"

The crows cawed louder above the rhythmic sound of the waves colliding against the seashore. The salty air caved in around me. Blood tears blistered across my daughter's pale face as I worked franticly to scoop the sand away from her. It was useless – I couldn't stop the incessant force.

"Avila!" I grasped at her dark hair as her face disappeared. *Fuck!* My grip tightened around strands of the black silk slipping through my fingers as the beach ingested her whole.

"A ... Avila!"

A stupefied moment. The distinct sound of a black wing. A haunting voice of the long dead.

"No accidents, Jett."

A wicked laugh and Ginger-beard spluttered as the beach closed in around his throat. His dark eyes gleamed and he crooned. "I'll never look into your eyes again."

"Motherfucker!" I cried.

I growled and repeatedly slammed my fist into his face. The sound of his crunching bones did nothing to satisfy the madness. Blood like artwork over gleaming sand. I knew nothing. *Nothing.* The sandy grains fell into his gaping mouth and he gurgled as I smashed his head further into the earth. Then he was gone and so was my baby girl. I remained, trembling.

There was a gentle touch on my shoulder. Melissa. Her sound was unwelcome as I began to extract myself from the disturbing nightmare.

"She has a secret, Jett."

"She's gone."

"Death is coming."

I forced my eyes open and focused on the ceiling. My head felt somewhat clammy and my fingers tingled. Night terrors. Who would have thought the undead could dream? If you could call it that. Melissa was coming to me more often and the messages were growing in intensity. Vampires can't dream the dreams of the spirited. We were denied such pleasures. We didn't deserve them.

I studied my palms and noticed they appeared to shimmer in the dark. I looked like the flipside of a dark star. I shimmied in black. A moonlit forest drenched in rain. *Interesting*. This is what sweat looked like to a vampire. It was one of our more appealing characteristics that I found fascinating. I sweat chocolate twinkies but I'm no delight.

I stretched out over my bed. Yes, I owned a bed and a big-ass brownstone on a quaint little street in District V. We even had trees lining the curbs – big green maples with luscious leaves that gathered above the street like a canopy. It added a slice of normalcy in a completely abnormal world. It wasn't always such a bad thing to try to forget every now and then. Not that Melissa was letting me do much of that lately.

Death is coming.

I think she was off a good two years on that score. I gave a half laugh and rose from my bed. Death had long ago arrived in the form of biological warfare experiments gone wrong which resulted in the incurable V-virus but I knew the woman meant to deliver an ominous message. Something was up. I couldn't remember the last time I'd dreamed of her – five, maybe seven years? Whatever the time, she had now managed to forge a real connection to my dream world and I wasn't digging it.

"Melissa, Melissa – can't you just be a little clearer about your messages?"

It was like trying to solve a cryptic puzzle and with everything else going on – prepping to begin viral cultures with the hybrid blood while at the same time upholding the 'good vampire citizen' image, as well as dealing with egotistical overlords and trying to keep incoming Leavings alive – I didn't possess enough time or energy to decipher her riddles.

I padded into the bathroom to douse myself with cold water, pausing to peer at my reflection. My eyes appeared as icy as the water below my thick brows and my ageless features were strange to me. Vampires were simulated creatures. There was nothing real in the unfamiliar sight staring back at me. Nothing but unearthly death and the remnants of a scrupulous heart.

It was hanging on by a thread.

Ha. What would Clio say about my "pure heart" planning to overthrow the kindred? Clio was the witch who helped to cover up the truth about the wolf-baby, Shana. The first generation of Blood Legend who Marius believed I had killed. As far as I knew, Clio remained hidden in the mountains with Shana and her mother. She had been adamant that we must wait for the hybrid blood to mature through the generations before vampires could be eradicated, but patience was never my strongest suit. I wanted them gone now. I wanted to be human again.

Would Clio think I was on a death wish? I frowned at the mirror. Why did I even care what the witch would think?

Hmm...

I'd be lying if I said my thoughts didn't often dwell on her, Sienna and Shana, but I wasn't about to mention those names out loud in the blood city. It was tedious enough that I had Shana's secrets tucked away in a vial of her blood, much less speak of my deception to the clan. Avila didn't even know. It's not that I didn't trust her, it was just too risky considering her connection with Marius.

The wolf-mother and her Blood Legend baby still breathed, but I sure as hell wouldn't be if that little piece of intel spilled into the wrong ears. That's why I wished to keep digging to cure the V-virus – to further protect what was left of Scarla's family and my own. Besides, imagine all the human lives spared in a world without bloodsuckers.

Action was required. I tried to shrug off the ghastly images of Avila's dream-death but I couldn't stop the sense of urgency rippling through me. If I could still pee, I'd be pissing a fountain right now. As it was, my innards were a dried-up wasteland that absorbed blood like a rapacious sponge. There were never any leftovers to warrant a good piss. Nostalgia was fleeting as I glanced at the toilet. I think I missed pissing as much as eating real food.

Get a grip, Jett. Pissing and food paled in comparison to the prospect of Avila's death. Michal and I had to get to work on the hybrid blood promptly. We had gathered enough supplies to start and now we even had a test-dummy in the form of Draven, the subway kid I'd regenerated, to test the experimental vaccines. He was currently holed up with Sun and I was eager to get to him. I had sired him and knew making a firm connection was necessary in gaining his trust if we were to use him in our little covert venture.

Ah, the things we must do to invoke change.

The faint sounds of Avila tramping around downstairs drifted through the crack of my bedroom door as I pulled on a blazer. I didn't bother to gaze out of the window at the pre-dawn light. The dome always misconstrued the time of day anyway and I knew it was still early.

Nocturnal creatures attempting to sleep at night as if they were still human was somewhat amusing, but the dome made it possible and it worked well for managing the Leavings. They were our lifeforce. It had been an adjustment, but my body clock was finally catching up to the new routine.

As I made for the stairs, I toyed with the idea of slipping from the house undetected. Things were proving a tad dicey on the home front of late. It was my fault. I called it realism, but I knew that I wasn't making it easy for Avila by withholding my approval of her relationship with Marius. She called it pigheaded genes.

I hit the bottom of the stairs and stopped briefly near an antique mahogany side table in the tiled entrance hall. Although not overly large, the high ceilings gave the area an open vibe. I looked up toward the delicate crystal chandelier overhead and listened. Avila loved that elaborate fixture but it did nothing for me. I kept it for her.

All was quiet. I detected no movement coming from the other parts of the house but for the monotonous ticking of the stately grandfather clock in the sitting room. I strode toward the door, freezing like the guilty when her voice sounded behind me.

"Dad?"

"Yup?" I spun on my heels with a sheepish grin that fast dissolved when I saw her face. She leaned against the wall in a pair of white pajamas, twisting the ends of her long dark hair. Her azure eyes flashed. I frowned. "Are you okay?"

She gave an abrupt sob before rushing to me. I pulled

her in tightly as she buried her chin against my chest and cried. It was a sight I hadn't witnessed for the longest of times.

"What is it, Avila?"

"It … it's mom."

5
WHIP-HAPPY

*I*t was late afternoon when I marched along the District H streets after spending the day working the laboratory. Sun was going to take me back to her place so that I could meet the kid from the subway. It was important that I establish a bond with my sired. I knew it instinctively. I was also instinctively acquainted with the ache in my shoulders from hours hunched over benchtops and processing dozens of Leavings through District H. It was times like these that I was grateful for my rejuvenation gifts.

I couldn't say the same about my current surroundings. The stale air was a pungent combo of food waste and human excrement. I kept my mouth shut and my eye on the endgame. I had agreed with Michal that something had to be done about the living conditions here. Perhaps I could figure out a way to improve the situation if I pushed past my deep resistance to converse with Marius. *Who knew how long it could take for us to cultivate a working cure? – Months? Years?* Our Leavings deserved to exist in some version of dignity in the meantime.

Marius. My hackles rose at the thought of him. It was the hold he had on Avila. She inexplicably adored him. I cracked my knuckles and increased my pace. I had to believe that whatever was going on between them would run its course. After all, I had raised her to use her smarts when it came to the opposite sex. I had to trust that intuitive instincts would prevail. The alternative was not up for contemplation when there was a kindred-less future to think about.

I took the final corner to the street that would take me back into vampire territory. Also known as District V. The usual hustle near the iron-meshed gates that intersected along the great wall was in full swing. The gates were heavily guarded around the clock and provided the sole pathway between the districts. It was a popular area since the implementation of the slavery program because those gates transitioned us between worlds – vampire masters and their human slaves.

The fictitious cliché involving humans serving vampires had outsmarted reality. Generation V had arrived to revolutionize real-world beliefs and it was a riot of the irony. Nevertheless, Leavings were strictly prohibited to wander District V without the accompaniment of their master. It was one of our most scrupulous rules that gave me no end of amusement.

Show me a Leaving stupid enough to venture a vampire-infested district alone and I'll show you a chicken with lips.

The smirk was wiped from my face when I heard a series of hollering ahead as four cackling Mysticus guards came into view. They stood in front of the Norbury City Library jeering at the group of Leavings scouring the hundreds of books that lay scattered and torn among broken desks, chairs, and lamps at the building's entrance. My approach went unnoticed, and I stopped behind the guards to assess the scene.

About ten Leavings were loading the debris into a large dumpster while two others stood at the library threshold heaving furniture through the doors and chucking books onto the mounting pile. The entire staircase leading toward the library entrance was a chaotic wreckage. Even though I was aware of Marius' plans to gut the building to make way for a communal food hall for the Leavings, witnessing our literature discarded in such a flippant manner was deeply disturbing. More alarming was that the task at hand appeared to have discharged the mounting frustration in the Leavings. They roamed, picked, and tore through the disarray in their ragged clothes and spilt boots, and they were all making a ruckus. I could sense their brusque disdain in the stuffy air as one crazy guard cracked a whip against the sidewalk while he and his pals cheered on the vandals.

"Shred 'em good, shitbags!" The brawny guard

sniggered. "That's right, fuck with ya history. You won't live long enough for it to matter, anyway."

The guards cackled before another waved a fist. "Come on, Leavings, show us what you've got – my bitches 'vag' gives more destruction than you lot!"

If this quartet had a brain between them, they'd be deadly dangerous. As it was, they were unpredictably risky. The vibe among the Leavings was beginning to border on rage, and it was sickening. I couldn't just walk on and leave these humans under the precarious watch of these vampires. Things took a dark turn when one Leaving man bent to his knees amid the carnage and raised a book above his head. The tarnished lettering that embellished the worn leather caught my eye right away, while tears broke through the layer of grime on his face as he looked at the bible balancing overhead. His quivering voice was faint.

"This is for Christ our Savior who failed us." He released a wrangled sob before he began mauling the scripture like a madman. Torn pages hung askew as he cursed God.

The guards in front of me laughed and nudged each other.

"It's book week in downtown District Hell, dirtwads!" The whip-happy guard hissed and cracked the leathers. The scuffed straps split a timber chair like a buttersnap cookie and narrowly missed a Leaving woman. He laughed as the woman screeched and whirled around, spitting dirty orange hair from her face, and waving a splintered table leg. *If looks could kill.*

"Back off, leech. You almost did kill me!" Her nimble fingers gripped the fractured pale of wood aimed at his heart as he stepped closer to her. She gave a loud snort. "Just try it, clot-buster, and you'll find out what happens next."

Had she totally lost her mind?

In the next moment, the whip was on the gravel and the guard had the woman ensnared between his claws and her head pushed back with her throat fully exposed. The splintered stake she held clanked to the ground. He gave a vicious hiss and grinned at his cronies as she screamed. The other three guards watched on, stupefied, while every Leaving stopped their pickings.

Surely this jackass guard knew better than to feed directly from a dome Leaving. One could only hope that he was savvy enough to avoid the harsh penalties involved in such a violation. He would face countless weeks holed up in the roach-infested cells beneath the city with only stray rats for feed. But hope was lost on the undead soul whose heavy-lidded eyes beheld his captive. My nerves tingled as I contemplated the situation, watching as the vampire rolled back his neck and bared his fangs.

Time was up. I took off like the wind, charging toward him as he gnawed into the woman's throat. The fragrance of the woman's blood dominated my senses as I slammed my palm into the guard's forehead. Bone collision. I felt his skull fracture before his head recoiled with the brutal impact. He snarled and stumbled backward, stomping heavily onto the debris underfoot. He leapt back to his feet and growled at me with his razor nails poised.

"Game over, blood-mongrel. Do you really want to dance with the devil today?" I said.

I stared him down as he considered his options, daring him to make the next move as the moment gave way to a whimper and a faint heartbeat. *Ba-boom. Ba-boom.* The vampire withdrew his claws to smear the back of a hand across his mouth. *Ba-boom. Ba-boom.* He smirked and began to slink away as the woman's eyes rolled up as she started to collapse. I caught her as the sound of Sun's voice called from behind.

"Jett! What the hell?"

I glanced around as she strutted forth clad in a white leather mini-dress and matching knee-high boots. Her platinum hair was piled atop her crown and the silver hoops adorning her lobes caught the afternoon glow offered by the dome canopy. She appeared angelic until she halted beside the guards and glared.

"Baboons! Treating Leavings in this way is completely unacceptable. Shame on all of you!"

They reacted with a shrug before seeking solace in the dirt at their feet. I lowered the woman and tore the fabric of my undershirt so that I could wrap her throat wound. A skittish Leaving man rushed to her side as she groaned. She would survive the vampire attack and I was thankful.

I adjusted my jacket sleeves and joined Sun. "Just an ordinary day in Bloodfaye city."

"Who the hell is in charge of this shit-show, anyway?"

"I am!"

Zaros. I groaned inwardly as his voice carried from the library threshold. "Surprise, surprise."

He grinned and started for the stairs as Sun gave him a death stare. He stopped short of us and regarded his crew before he glanced between Sun and me.

"What did I miss?"

"These vampires are mishandling our Leavings." I gestured toward the whip-happy guard. "That one attacked and fed from a Leaving woman."

Zaros' eyes flashed. "Thank you, master J. I'll take it from here and deal with them accordingly."

"Yes, right after Marius' announcement," Sun said. "He has summoned all Mysticus members for an audience in the Crypt courtyard at once."

"What for?"

"Nobody knows."

I ignored Zaros as he barked an order at his guards, instructing them to take the offender away. I frowned. "Charming. Another surprise, surprise."

6

MERCY

"How's the kid doing?"

"Fine. The kid has a name, you realize."

"You just saw our historical literature destroyed like yesterday's news. Names mean nothing now."

"Does to him." Sun glanced at me as we walked toward the Crypt. The streets were almost barren. "You should try to remember his name considering that he is to play host to your cure thingy."

"Thingy? That's one way of putting it."

"Forgive me if I'm not up to speed on clinical jargon."

I grinned. "Forgiven."

She did have a point. The kid from the subway was vital to me, but our prearranged meeting would have to wait. We were en route to hear Marius' big surprise announcement. The kid's name was the last thing on my mind as I scanned the District V streets. This side of the wall was the opposite to the slums that our Leavings were forced to endure. Everything was clean, shiny, and proper, and apart from a few strays, the usual freak-fair hive was lost on the bogus shopfronts and blood cafes. I liked it. Fake-faced vampire society had momentarily ceased, and the peaceful vibe somehow echoed my resolve behind forming the secret sector. A world where people didn't turn into blood-lust creatures was all I wanted for Avila and the rest of humanity.

Sun gestured toward the dome shell that blazed above us in an orange haze. "Always my favorite time of day – dusk."

"I know what you mean."

It was another reason to find the cure. I would give anything to again witness those breaking hours between night and day with my naked eye. I looked heavenward with longing. Dawn and dusk had always kept me grounded, reminding me what it meant to be alive. Now, I was nothing but a walking corpse who may never again know the revelation of a new day, much less the striking secrets of sunset. I didn't want to think about that prospect. Not when there was hope.

I jammed my hands in my pockets as the sound of the crowd gathering in the Crypt courtyard thrummed in my ears. *Busy bees swarming a honey jar.* We were about a block away from the laughter and chattering that carried along the treetops and brownstones. My stomach tightened. I was having trouble aligning with the fact that this was the first time Marius had summoned the entire clan on a whim to make an announcement. Obviously, something was up. Sun encroached my thoughts.

"Any idea about all this?"

"Nope." We rounded a corner, and the crowded Crypt courtyard came into view. "Maybe he's discovered a cure before me and wishes to free us from hell and damnation."

"Fat chance. You know how much he loves vampirism hell and damnation of new world order."

I did indeed. As did the few hundred vampires congregating in front of a timber stage that stood in the courtyard like an oiled oasis beneath an elaborate maze of wrought iron. I paused to take in the black iron twisting into glyphs and symbols that represented vampire folklore. A chill passed through me as my gaze settled on the brass candelabras wafting the scent of roses all around, pungently seductive above the four indigenous vampires who stood like stoic statues along the back of the stage, drums poised. The scene was dramatic, mystical, and deeply disturbing. It was all I could do as I looked at the dozens of fresh, scarlet flowers that gracefully entwined the iron.

"Some kind of set-up," I said.

Marius had transformed the Crypt courtyard into a public arena of sorts, but it wasn't the newly furbished courtyard that got under my skin as much as the underlying hint of romance in the air. *Smokescreens and deceit*. It was a biting stench that rose the hairs on my neck, reminding me why I avoided the Crypt as much as possible. The Crypt itself had been a place of worship in the old world. The lofty sandstone building was a majestic temple with a historical soul that Marius had claimed as his own. There was nothing holy about the place now. It reeked like stale blood and bullshit.

"Our overlord flirts with passion. He sure knows how to make a hellish impression for the nameless." Sun grinned before flicking her chin toward the fanged crowd. "Come on, let's crash the mosh pit."

"Don't you mean death pit?"

The death pit defied all universal laws in that it resembled a posse of waking dead extortionists overloaded with glitzy glares, florid lips, and an unmistakable sense of entitlement. All set firmly on pallid faces. I could have been amid the crazy bizarre on Bourbon Street during Mardi Gras. And I was one of the freaks.

Mercy.

I'd be lying if I said that a part of me was not dark, blood-hungry, and primitive. Even the purest of hearts is drawn to the allure of darkness. The urge to succumb to my preternatural instincts was my greatest pleasure and adversary. I was a walking contradiction battling my demons at the best of times. It's amazing what deep hatred could do to a man. It was almost as strong as love.

I followed Sun through the strange throng, making our way closer to the stage. A thousand snippets of disembodied voices trailed me.

"Oh, this is so exciting! I just love surprises!"

Ha. That makes one of us.

"Where is Marius? Do you see him?"

"No but check out the—"

Black locks flicked in my face as I passed.

"Heaven on earth, maybe we're going to get a taste of new blood!"

"That ain't gonna happen in the blood dome, baby."

A drawn-out hiss was swallowed by the crowd behind me.

"Who're ya calling baby, anal-ant?"

I weaved my way forward. Marius was encouraging an aristocratic lifestyle in District V. Some of us embraced it, others still secretly longed to feed as their kindred nature intended. But none of that mattered in this moment as every conversation gave way to a collective gasp followed by the smooth tempo of drums. I stopped dead in my tracks as Marius strode onto the stage suited up in white leather and gold and sporting a huge grin alongside Avila.

Huh?

The mob applauded and cheered all around me while I scratched my chin in the stupid hope the action might unclog my thoughts as I watched my daughter on stage. She appeared to glide along the timber boards in the full-length black dress that swept in her wake as she clutched Marius' hand, stopping front center on the stage. Her usually milky-white cheeks flushed and her eyes flared violet in the candlelight, contrasting against her dark hair. The beating drums subsided, and the crowd hushed.

I had never seen that dress nor had I seen her look so happy since before the apocalypse shredded our lives to madness. *What the hell is going on here?* I couldn't quite piece together the unfolding events, nor could I stop the wrenching in my gut when Marius combed a hand through his jet locks and laughed before addressing the audience.

"Dear Mysticus vampires, it pleases me to see you here. Thank you for allowing me to intrude upon your dusk hour, and with little warning no less. Your presence is much cherished."

Cherished? What a schmuck.

The crowd broke into the expected round of applause while Marius swept his arms in a grandeur fashion, gracefully receiving their reverence. Always the artful snake in the grass. He may have the majority fooled, but my knuckles ached as much the sly look on his face and I longed to rearrange those perfectly chiseled features. I focused back on Avila as Marius shushed the crowd before continuing to charm and seduce by offering a velvety slab of verbal vomit.

He gestured around the stage. "I can sense your growing curiosity. I bet you are wondering what this lovely optic spitball is all about, hmm?"

"Yes! Tell us!"

"It's the new Vampire's Ball!"

"Marius, I adore you!"

An eruption of laughter.

"I adore you too, my lovely! I adore all of you!"

Marius pointed at the crowd. "Welcome to the new Vampire's Ball!"

The pack cheered, clapped and cooed at our lordship while my kid remained silent. I wanted to rush up there and collect her. I wanted to take her some place far away from these poisonous people and stop the darkness from consuming her world, but I couldn't move as Marius waited for the crowd to quieten before finally getting to the point of it all.

"Of course, I'm only half-kidding about the Vampire's Ball."

He reached for Avila's hand before he looked at the audience. Sun glanced at me and frowned, and my boots anchored deeper into the lawn as I watched my daughter.

"I've said it before and I'll say it again – the path toward ascension for the Mysticus clan is undoubtedly paved with alignment, awakening and union. We do have cause for much celebration. As your overlord, I have kept my word and provided you the freedom to safely enjoy daylight hours once again. I have equipped you with an endless supply of blood in our Bloodfaye Leavings. You all dwell in comfortable homes with all the pleasures of the old world – I think suffice it to say that I have given you a quality of life that you never would have found outside of the dome."

He paused as the crowd applauded, then his voice rose over the cheering. "I give you all of these comforts away from outside threats. Now, it is time to initiate the next component in the quest for us to become the world's most powerful clan – union."

Marius glanced at Avila before he raised her hand in the air. "When next month's full moon appears in five weeks' time, I will claim my divine feminine as my own in the first Mysticus Claiming Ceremony! The two of us will merge our supernatural gifts into one loving dynamic as we revolutionize the world toward ascension. Ladies and gentlemen, I give you the future Vampire Queen – Lady Avila!"

Lady what?

The crowd exploded into a joyous roar and Sun looked at me. Her pale face was a vague impression as my world shattered.

7

ACRIMONY

*T*he beating drums became a distinct timbre of grief. My hands shook uncontrollably. *My girl!* I swallowed my pain along with the goblets of blood on offer as the crowd moved as if in a trance. The courtyard had fast transformed into a primitive dance of passion and erotica. Hips grinded and swayed. Euphoric moaning morphed into hissing and biting. This is what celebration looked like to the kindred. Their glossy hair gleamed beneath the inky dome shell as they groped, danced, and clawed while I stood frozen amid the psychedelic orgy. Each moment was like death as I faced the prospect of losing my little girl all over again.

Sun grabbed my arm. Her voice seemed distant. "Jett?"

I stared ahead. "She didn't tell me."

A Claiming Ceremony? I peered past the freakshow toward the stage in time to see Marius and Avila slip between the side curtains. *Impossible.* There was no way that Avila could become the Vampire Queen. Not my kid. It was obvious that such a stature carried dire consequences. A Vampire Queen of a powerful clan would make a primary target for every mongrel blood with half a backbone. And even more disturbing was that I feared the powerful position would rob her of what was left of her humanity. She would mirror her king and turn off her "humanity" switch. That was unacceptable. Marius must be influencing her. He *was* the one who had sired her. I felt a thunderous rush of rage hit me.

"I'm sorry," Sun said.

"About what?"

"That she didn't—"

The rest of her words were a mystery as I raced through the twilight weird-fest fueled by the rage within me. I broke from the crowd and paused at the edge of the courtyard. My nocturnal vision kicked in as I peered around and homed in on his smug masculine scent. Sunset was over and the dusky glow blazing across the dome had long sunk into night. I planted my feet wide, scanning the stretch of manicured lawns, cobbled pathways, and rows of rose bushes that studded the Crypt grounds before my sights settled on the Crypt itself. The domed cathedral appeared elegantly opaque with its leadlight windows and angelic statues but I saw none of it as I tuned out the celebratory background noise and into the muffled laughter drifting from around the back of the stage.

Marius and Avila. Their intimate conversation was daggers to my mind and fueled the dark energy within. Destruction beckoned. It was as gritty as dirt and it smothered my chest to reveal the agonizing truth: I was a vampire. *I am death.*

The emotions ruled me, and clarity was an illusion. Each moment I spent resisting my instincts to kill was nullified. I was the nameless creature of nightmares with a bloodthirsty heart. The compulsion for violence surged through me and I almost wanted to explode. Everything is nothing without her. She was all I had left in the post V-virus world. I bolted toward the sound of their conversation as my feet scorched the earth. I was going to shred Marius alive.

I found him leaning against the trunk of a tree with Avila in his arms. He was caressing her hips and speaking in a lover's tongue as she leaned in close and teased him. *Voodoo-born mind games.* Vampires exceled at trickery and seduction. They were among our greatest assets. Avila knew it. I lingered in the shadows near the backstage framework as I surveyed the area. A few guards were watching the outer grounds but none were in our immediate location. My shoulders were back in fine form as I snarled and prowled forward.

Avila gasped and spun around to face me. "Dad?"

I splayed my fingers and approached while two guards appeared like magic from the shadows. They were skulking the lawn like ancient warmongers, and stunk like day-old semen. Their white leather glimmered in my peripheral vision as Marius lifted a palm to stop them. They made no noise when they slid back into the shadows a few feet away while Marius stared back at me. *Insentient.* His eyes were a fossilized relic as I closed in before Avila stepped between us.

"Dad, stop!"

She gripped my arms and I halted abruptly. My vision blurred as her eyes became dewy and I tried to focus on her. "I should have told you, I'm sorry."

Her touch was almost anecdotal.

"Told me what exactly?"

"About our plans for the Claiming Ceremony. I should have given you a heads up."

"Heads up? Interesting choice of words, Avila."

"How so?"

"My *head* is throbbing mad because I just discovered that the only thing getting up and into your head of late is an alarming case of vampire brainwashing! No thanks to your overlord here." I glared at Marius. It was all I could do to tame my seething appetite. "You are *not* going to be the Vampire Queen."

Her jaw dropped and Marius sniggered behind her.

"Get a grip, Dad. This is *my* life and *my* decision, not yours. Do I have to remind you that Marius is your overlord too?" She gave a nervous laugh. "I know you are upset, but you're looking at this in the wrong way. No one here is your enemy. I am sorry that I didn't tell you, but I knew how you'd react."

"And how's that, Avila?"

"Like a hot-headed, stuffy-ass control freak. Must we do this here?"

"You didn't leave me much choice."

"No, I was the one left with little choice because of your fixed mindset about the new world."

What? Fixed mindset? Ludicrous.

I was about to respond when the definition of fixed mindset spoke up.

"She's right, Jett." Marius pushed off the trunk and approached. "We're all in this together. The new world, the Mysticus, and creating a new way of being. The transition has been difficult but I can now see the light at the end of the tunnel. Can you not see how this union is exactly what the clan needs to bring a sense of hope for the future?"

"Hope for the future? The future is as deceptive as the sky overhead. Nobody can foresee a favorable future in a virus-riddled world. You will bring her misery and death. It is too dangerous. I forbid it."

"Forbid it? Unbelievable! Dad, I can—"

Marius drowned her voice when he laughed.

"Come now, no need to be so dramatic. We've come a long way already in this virus-riddled world, as you so eloquently put it." He gestured around him. "Open your eyes, Jett. I have flipped a chaotic city on its head to create a controlled and safe environment for vampires and humans to coexist. Avila is safe with me. Surely the noble principles behind Bloodfaye satisfies your urban warrior heart?"

"Are you kidding me?"

I stepped into his personal space. The guards were breathing down my neck in an instant as my words minced on old hate.

"You dare to mock my *urban warrior heart* after stealing my daughter's humanity and then persuading her to agree to this bullshit ceremony business?"

I barely felt Avila pull at my arm as she said my name. Marius responded with a tight grin. His face was like an ambiguous mask before he glanced between the guards and waved them away. They retreated slightly as Marius licked his lips and leaned in close.

"Let us not forget that I have been gracious enough to allow you to live after you betrayed my trust and discarded the only known vial of AB positive blood known to exist."

He reached for Avila's hand and I tried to control my vampiric cravings as he continued. "Whether you give us your consent or not, I *am* going to take your daughter as the first Mysticus Vampire Queen because it is what she wants of me. Obviously, we would prefer to have your support in our shared vision to achieve ascension as the most powerful clan in the world ...." His voice trailed and he shrugged. "If you cannot bring yourself to the table, for Avila's sake, I will continue to allow you to live in your own misery so long as you obey Mysticus rules. Do we understand each other?"

Incineration.

I went to tell him that he could shove his rules right

up his pompous backside when I looked at Avila. She gnawed her bottom lip and her eyes appeared like sea-glass gems pleading with me. I squeezed my eyes shut and collected the rage at the tip of my tongue, taking a deliberate breath before looking back at her.

"This is what you want?"

"With all my heart."

Her reply was enough to finish what was left of my urban warrior heart. I was losing her to a power-hungry slavedriver and there was nothing I could do to stop it. All at once, Marius' sordid words fell at my feet and I saw the baby girl who I had adored and protected since birth. I had set this wheel in motion the day I had left her with Marius in favor of saving humanity.

It was reliving my failure all over again.

8

I WANT TO SHOW YOU SOMETHING

"*I* can barely remember her. I mean, I know what she looks like but it's hard to recall the way she was as a woman and a mother."

Avila stopped and looked up. One half of the dome was illuminated like rustic gold with the rising sun but that wasn't her focus. I followed her gaze to see a handful of sparrows in flight.

She frowned. "Birds?"

I grinned. "They've found a way in."

She laughed. "I like it."

"Me too."

She fell quiet as we walked the sleepy District V streets. This section of the dome was a far cry from the crud on the other side of the wall. Marius was sprucing up the place. Everything from shopfronts and buildings to every brownstone on every block. He was committed to ensuring a high living standard for the Mysticus clan and took great measures to create a sense of belonging and purpose for us. Naturally, they celebrated his generosity. There was nothing selfless about his benevolence, though. That much I knew.

The fact was currency was no longer an issue in the new world where the kindred reigned supreme. Now, all things were available to us on a whim. Most Mysticus members had never lived a better life before this one. Marius knew it. They were easy to appease. It will be interesting to see what happens when familiarity sets in. *Contempt.* They'll be expecting a mile soon enough.

"What was she really like, dad?"

"She was … like you; beautiful inside and out." We paused on the sidewalk at a crossroad. Golf carts were parked along the curb on the street ahead. Marius was slowly introducing a means of transport to the citizens of District V. I had to admit that it was a great perk. Vampires were a snobby bunch at heart. We'd rather catch a ride than to waste precious supernatural energy where possible. It made us feel civilized. I wanted one.

Avila watched me. "Why did you love her?"

The streets ahead were livening up. It was the main thoroughfare. I gestured toward the opposite direction where the avenues remained subdued. Inner-city vampire suburbia resembled the old world beneath a sleek sky canopy. We could almost pretend to be human that way. It was ironic.

"This way," I said.

She fell into step beside me as we took a corner to a

street that led nowhere. I took a moment to relish the first real conversation I'd managed with Avila since my emotional outburst over Marius' big announcement. "Why does anyone love anyone?"

She stuffed her hands in her pockets. Her nose scrunched. "What do you mean?"

I shrugged. "There were billions of people on earth before the virus struck, Avila, and most of them loved someone. Yet, no one who has ever fully abandoned themselves to deep love can ever articulate the experience enough to justify the feelings."

"Sounds intense."

"Love is intense." I pulled her close, squeezing an arm around her shoulder like I did when she was a little girl. "I love *you* intense."

"Hmm … that's a different kind of love. You're my father."

"Doesn't make it any less significant. There are all kinds of love – not everyone is capable of giving and receiving deep love, least of all the kindred."

Her eyes flickered up at me. "You haven't answered my question."

"Oh, you think I'm deflecting?" I smiled and nodded toward a tall vampire dressed in a beetroot-red suit as he passed. It was frightful attire, but I was growing accustomed to the odd sense of fashion favored by the kindred. Personally, I preferred a more reserved look. I now owned an impressive collection of suits. Most of them were black. "Let me see … I loved your mother for her unusual quirks and quiet habits. Her passion for biomedical genetics and cracking genetic codes was admirable. She loved her work, though she was unable to share most of what snared her attention away from us due to company privacy policies. It was extremely alluring nonetheless."

"Ha!" She nudged her shoulder into me. Her voice was feathery. "Only a scientist nerd would consider genetic code-cracking attractive."

"You've got that right – but only those who love bloodwork and DNA analysis could actually understand what I mean." I laughed. "Which, of course, is now just about the majority of the population."

Avila snorted. "Not so much. We just love to ingest blood by default. Not study the stuff."

"Well, I loved your mom by default. Couldn't help myself. She kept a secret smile just for me and no one else. I loved that about her. She had a knack for driving me crazy too, but I loved every moment of our life together."

She gave a soft laugh. "She used to play music."

"Hip Hop was her weakness. Go figure."

Avila stiffened and pulled away. "I miss her, dad. More than ever; as if we've just lost her."

"We never stop missing someone we have loved."

She groaned. "Why do you always have to be so philosophical about everything?"

The question had some interest, but she wasn't looking for a reply. She followed up rather quickly.

"It gets old … fast."

"Well, I'm just …"

"I don't need your philosophy to know that I am getting married soon and she isn't here to share it with me." Her arms flailed. "No one is around to tell me how to love a man or how to be a wife or help me choose the right dress while we laugh over silly secrets about men."

"Silly secrets about men?"

"Dad!"

"Come on, Avila, you're overreacting. I'd hardly call a vampire Claiming Ceremony a marriage."

Her face darkened as she turned on me. "And to make matters worse, you're being a total douche about the whole thing."

Douche?

I was charmed to the point that my feet stopped moving. "This entire city is brimming with vampire douchebags and you're choosing to give yourself to douche-blood-bag supreme himself. How do you expect me to respond?"

She gave a low hiss. "Geez, I don't know, dad. How about inserting a dose of support in your stuffy vamp suit?"

Her hair almost hit my face as she spun around and began stalking ahead of me. I took a sharp breath. *Since when was I stuffy?*

I wasn't sure that I wanted to know. I started after her. "For the record, philosophy doesn't necessarily equate with stuffiness."

"No, but the word 'master' might."

I stayed quiet for a moment, keeping her pace as we passed a few kindred. As if it were bad enough that we were having this conversation in public, now we had a few spectators to boot. Two female vampires, pale arms wound around each other, stood smirking on the stairs of a brownstone. *Twilight syndrome*. They were an entitled bunch. I looked ahead.

"This isn't the time or place, Avila."

She said nothing though I tuned into her silent message. We gave each other access to our thoughts occasionally. That was usually when there was something important to share when in the company of the more amusing members of our community. I had to admit that it was a cool gift to possess, though right now, her frustrated plea felt anything but that.

She turned the last corner and entered a narrow laneway that ran along the back of a building. My pace slowed momentarily as she walked ahead. The image of her strutting ahead reminded me of when she was five-years old and I had just told her that her mother was never coming home again.

"Where are you going?" I called.

She spun around and the muted morning light caught her crown. She bit her bottom lip and gestured with her chin to follow her. I resumed walking and saw the little girl who had bit her lip and silently trembled after hearing the words that would change her life. *My little tough nugget.* That was the moment she was reborn into a different kid. Blood would stain her chin before she had finally allowed herself to cry in my arms.

She stopped next to a tacky timber door and looked at me. I glanced at the building that had clearly seen better days. It appeared to be a sporting arena undergoing repair. Scaffolding stretched along the outside.

She began to fidget with the sleeves of her sweater. "I want to show you something."

I nodded and went to follow her inside the building, but my senses snapped before I even crossed the threshold. I frowned as the beginnings of what looked to be an internal barnyard complete with livestock came into view.

What the hell?

The place wafted with the smell of spelt combined with the faint odor of animal waste. The vast space had been gutted and refurbished into a makeshift farm. On the far side of the arena stood a replica of a timber barn house with huge double doors and a pitched roof. There were stables with sheep and horses, as well as chook pens and goats. It all spilled into an outdoor grazing area via an enormous roller door. A wheat-colored hen closely tailed by her chicks waddled by as Avila turned to look at me. She tossed her head and folded her arms. Her eyes homed in on me.

"It's for the Leavings. Fresh produce all the way." She gestured beyond. "He even has plans to grow crops along the outside perimeter of the dome so he can feed them the best. He's sending out men each night to begin sanctioning and securing the fields off."

I stepped closer to her. "And why do you think that is, Avila?"

She frowned. "He's not as bad as you think. He wants to find his heart again and I'm the way. I make him *feel* something, Dad. Don't you see that I can make a difference as the vampire queen?"

I held her gaze and my stomach churned. *She believed in him.* I shifted my gaze on a wiry goat chewing on a stick of hay. "Do you love him?"

Her reply was everything I didn't want to hear.

"I do."

9

CRYPTIC LOOKING GAME

"Thank you for joining me, Jett."

Marius leaned back on his French Provincial chair across the table and grinned. *Game.* It was written all over his face. His thick hair was as glossy as the black satin sleeves slipping down to his elbow as he motioned toward a woman who lingered in the shadows on the far side of the saloon. "We have much to discuss."

News to me.

Discussion with Marius in the Crypt was the last thing I desired but I had no choice. The overlord had summoned me. I gave a brief nod and looked away. We sat in a large room that Marius called his saloon. It was a stately affair with a sophisticated vibe. The elaborately framed artwork and sculptured furnishings created elegance. Too bad the charm didn't extend to my host.

"What do you think?"

I looked back at him. "About…?"

He gestured around. "The Crypt, of course."

"Of course."

The Crypt was really an old stone cathedral created by our ancestors. It had been a famous icon of the old world. He was currently transforming it to make it more homely. If that was possible. I focused on the woman as she busied herself with a crystal decanter and two silver goblets.

"The renovations are coming along superbly. You must be pleased."

"Yes I am. Anything to appease my beloved. She certainly has an interesting and strong mind." He laughed. "I admire her very much."

It hurt to nod. *Avila.* She was to live here. I tried not to grimace.

"She's been encouraged to be herself."

"I am forever indebted to you."

I held his gaze. "You love her?"

"She lights me up on the inside. Everything I do is for her." He leaned forward. "Does that surprise you?"

"No."

The woman approached us. She wore next to nothing and carried a polished tray. Her skin was milky and deliciously smooth, and her long hair blazed red over a boob tube. I couldn't help but notice how her legs paraded beneath a tiny white skirt. All thoughts momentarily evaporated. *Desire.* The animal within ignited.

Marius called them his chamber ladies. He claimed that their presence here supported the new community. A vampire overlord required serving in his private abode. I wondered if my strong-minded daughter shared the same views on his barely clothed servants. I also wondered how far their services extended. Vampires excelled at indulging.

She neared us with a sultry smile. "Gentlemen."

"Thank you, Dana." Marius barely glanced at her as she placed a goblet in front of each of us before filling them with blood. She smelled like a field of lilies and wild sex. I caught the slight shift in her eyes when she looked at me.

"May I get you something else, master?"

I shook my head and looked away. Vampire desires were something to be acknowledged before you could fully master their influence. I wasn't about to indulge. Least of all with one of Marius' chamber ladies. He waited for Dana to leave before speaking again.

"Above all else, it is my desire to keep your daughter safe." His talons wound around his goblet. "That is why I summoned you here."

"Then we are on the same page in that regard, though I find it odd that we're sitting over silver goblets to speak of your love for my daughter." I took a sip of blood. It had been warmed and it was heavenly sweet. This was the new way to feed in Bloodfaye. Marius pushed for a cultivated society. It was better than the alternative. I drummed my talons against the silver stem. "Why am I really here, Marius?"

"Always direct."

"Life's too short not to be."

"Good one." He laughed but I didn't. He set the goblet down. "Are you happy with your living arrangements?"

Game. Here we go.

We both knew that I had been given special privileges since my return from wolf-hunt wilderness. Marius had ensured that I was able to select my preferred dwelling. He claimed it was because I had proved my loyalty to him after my betrayal but we both knew the truth. He needed me on his side for two reasons. We'd just discussed the first.

I shrugged. "Happy is something that belongs in the past. I am satisfied with my living arrangements, thank you."

"You are quite welcome." He gave a stiff smile. "And I trust that you have had time to adjust to the news of the upcoming Claiming Ceremony?"

"Did I have a choice?"

"We all have a choice."

I laughed. "Well, it seems that choice *and* trust are overrated in the new world."

"Perhaps you are right on that score. Though, from one man to another, I can assure you that I have the clan's best interests at heart."

"And what of my daughter's heart?"

He was quiet for a moment. The sound of laughter faintly drifted from other parts of the Crypt. He traced a finger across his brow and switched the subject. "How are things progressing in the lab with the incoming Leavings?"

"If you're referring to testing an AB positive blood type – zero success. However, it is important that the conditions be improved for the Leavings."

"How so?"

"The goal is to offer them a safe place to exist in a vampire-infested world. Their experience here should be somewhat humane from the moment they arrive, especially if you wish for others to seek refuge here by their own freewill … word has a way of leaking." I raised the goblet. "They are, after all, sustaining us."

"Hmm…" He looped his hands around the back of his head. The move was casual yet conveyed a certain amount of power. My senses bristled.

"This *is* something to be considered. You are aware that the Leaving intake process is still developing along with District H living conditions. I will ensure your suggestions are integrated, however, I am about to begin fostering another division of Leavings. I will, of course, require your full co-operation."

Ah, and here comes the meat.

I said nothing and waited for him to elaborate. Though nothing could have prepared me for his next words.

"From this moment on, all present and future Leaving

children are to be separated from their parents and taken to District X where they will remain until they reach maturity."

"Say what?" I could feel my face straining. "Since when did Bloodfaye have a District X?"

"Since the beginning. I do not inform you of everything, Jett."

"Apparently. Why?"

His look of self-gratification made my fingertips tingle.

"You haven't figured it out? For a smart guy you can be incredibly dumb."

"So I've been told. What are you going to do with the Leaving children?"

His eyes lit up. "I'm preparing for the future survival of the Mysticus Clan and ensuring the safety of your daughter. That's about all you need to know at this stage."

"You're protecting the Mysticus by taking children from their parents?"

"Yes."

"You can't possibly expect them to survive such an ordeal after everything they've already endured at the hands of the virus. The children *need* their parents."

"And we *need* to survive. The children will die if they remain in District H. You know they will eventually be taken. Even I cannot always control the supernatural urges of the kindred as much as they cannot control themselves. District X offers them protection and security."

"It offers them an orphanage and a loveless existence!"

He slammed his palms on the table. The oiled timber splintered as he dug in. "This *will* be done, and not only will you comply but one day you will thank me for it and so will Avila."

I regarded the man who had taken my daughter from me and delivered her to hell. He was about to claim her forever. *Hollow hate.* It filled me like dark beauty. I'd rather die than thank him. Of course, now wasn't the time to say as much.

He sat back in his chair. His features were unreadable. I was staring at death. "I'm certain we can get on the same page in regards to this situation too." He paused to ensure he had my full attention. "Of course, we cannot have Zaros discovering this little side project for now, not until I am satisfied with his allegiance to the clan. We both know he presents a risk."

That was true. But Zaros and his unpredictable ways were the last thing on my mind in that moment. As were the children. I nodded. Marius was right about irresistible supernatural urges. Mine was looking game and it felt like a renewed purpose.

I would do whatever it took to stop the Claiming Ceremony.

10

CRAZY SCIENCE

I clicked my talons against the bench surface as the sound of Michal's voice droned in my ear. He was going on about developing cell culture and cellular layers. It was clear that he was displeased. My nostrils burned. Ethanol stunk like spirited rotting garbage at the best of times and the confined space in our inoculation chamber made the stench almost unbearable.

"Crazy, crazy!" Michal's scrawny shoulders hunched over a set of measuring equipment. He pushed on buttons and scowled before squinting at me. "The voltage across the cellular layers is unstable. I can't determine the correct pathways. In one moment, the junction formations appear tight and confluent, and in the next, they are leaky. I'm going to need more time."

"Which we don't have."

I had already spent hours studying the cell development and realized that we may have been somewhat ambitious in our presumed timeline. The hybrid blood was composed of many interconnected parts. It was complex and extraordinary. I knew it could take months, if not years, to reach the next step in the process. It was an obstacle I refused to acknowledge out loud. We *did* exist in a new world comprised of new rules.

Michal pushed his glasses up along his damp nose. "But if we are to develop a working recombinant vaccine, we're...."

"Going to have to improvise." I ignored his gaping jaw and gestured toward the series of cell cultures growing in dishes along the benchtop. They sat among analytical instruments, balancing equipment and titrators. "Must I remind you that this is no ordinary vaccine research?"

"N – no, but it *is* perhaps the most vital research we've undertaken."

I leaned against the bench and eyed him. The sleeves of his lab coat were stained like rust and he appeared more erratic than usual. "What's vital is that this happens before Avila is claimed by our overlord to become a pawn in his dirty power-play games."

"Y – you don't know that that is the case, I'm sure Marius has noble intentions for Avila, as for the future of the clan.."

"Ha." His response was all it took to run hard in my blood. "If you believe that bullshit then you are as sly as the blood on your sleeves." He was about to speak when I grabbed his collar and wrenched it. "Who the fuck is feeding from you, hmm?"

He trembled and began to stutter. "I – I – I can't stop him."

"Who can't you stop, Michal?"

His eyes twitched as he met my glare. "Z – Zaros."

"Zaros?"

"Yes."

Crafty motherfucker.

I released him and stepped back. He squirmed awkwardly as I regarded him. "Since when?"

"Since whenever he felt like it." He stuffed his hands in his pockets. "I've been their 'pet' from the start; you know this."

Indeed. Yet those kinds of arrangements were meant to cease when we migrated into Bloodfaye. It was the whole point of the bloodletting program. I shoved a palm through my hair. My scalp felt clammy.

"I don't like it."

"What's to like?" he shrugged. "Enduring the bite of the kindred doesn't exactly tickle, you know. B – but there is a way to stop him."

"I'm listening."

"Turn me."

"Now who's crazy, crazy?" I gave a half laugh and started for the antechamber. It was the sheeted off section we had constructed between the room entrance and inoculation chamber which served as an airlock. It wasn't perfect but it served its purpose to create a sterile environment. I paused and looked back at him. "To turn you is defeating the purpose of everything we are trying to accomplish here. Once we have a vaccine to the V-virus, there will be no vampires around to feed on you and call you 'pet'. You'll be free again."

He yelped and flapped his arms in the air. I tried not to smirk. He looked like a cross between a dog and a penguin.

"But that could take too long! We don't know if it will work or if someone will discover our deception before we can even begin to embark on the plasmid construction." He was referring to the next step in the vaccine development – the one I was reluctant to acknowledge. I watched as he paused to gulp some air. "And the vampire gods know we can't do that until the epithelium indicates the presence of tight junctions."

I grinned. "Like I said, we will improvise."

"But even improvisation can't determine the immunogenicity and safety of the vaccine for our candidate. It could be dangerous for him."

"More dangerous than a vampire?" I laughed. "The kid is supernatural now, Michal. We can't damage him any more than I already have."

He looked away. I could tell he was biting back the words. He knew better than to argue with a vampire. His gaze appeared lucid when it finally met mine. "Where are you going?"

"I'm going to find Zaros."

"Oh."

I contemplated him for a moment and saw a man whose heart was filled with fear. "Everything will be okay."

"Okay."

I gave a stiff nod and gripped the flap of the plastic sheeting wall. "Good. I want a trial viral vector ready to transfer to our rat subjects by tomorrow night. Make it happen."

He nodded fast. "Yes master."

"And stop calling me master, would you," I said as I stepped into the antechamber. The thick plastic folded closed behind me and my next breath was ethanol free. My lungs silently rejoiced.

11

BLOODPLAY AT THE MUSEUM

*I*t was white, moved slower than I could run and stunk like rotten eggs. But I couldn't refuse the shiny golf cart parked out front of my brownstone on my return to District V. It was a gift from our lord and master. I knew he meant to butter me up somewhat, but I wasn't feeling overly special because just about every vampire in the city was queued up to get one. I noticed that my cart was swankier than most. It had built-in heated seats. I figured if I sat here long enough, my cold-blooded ass might have a chance of thawing. One could only hope.

I shifted my butt against the warm seat as I set off toward downtown Bloodfaye. It was a delightfully indulgent sensation. I smiled. I'm certain that someone once said it was better to let our hopes and not our hurts shape our future. Well, my ass was full of hope alright, but I knew it was short-lived – I was on my way to see Zaros.

For reasons beyond my comprehension, Zaros and his crew had taken a fancy to the Norbury museum and slept among artifacts and other things formerly preserved for public exhibition. I was familiar with the building as it had been one of Avila's favorite places to visit as a child. We'd spent many hours wandering the halls discussing ancient species and extinct reptiles. She had particularly favored the Smilodon exhibition for their long, curved saber-shaped teeth. *Ha.* It's no wonder she had taken to the new world like a duck to water. Long teeth are all the fashion nowadays.

I focused on the road as I steered the cart through District V's main artery. Vampire folk were out in droves, with the latest fashion trend on display as they pranced around like glow-in-the-dark fireflies. Freak show psychics. Faceless blondes. Wicked civilians. Laughter abounded and irritated the crap out of me. Marius was fast achieving his objective for the Mysticus. It was clear they felt at ease and protected in the dome city.

I swallowed hard and pinched my lips shut. I wasn't sure if I was more disgusted with myself or this entire nice, law-abiding urban affair. As if we hadn't become the definition of demonic force existing comfortably while enslaving humans for their blood. And I was an active participant. I could only hope that respite from this damnation would arrive in the form of tomorrow night's viral vector.

A gangly looking vampire waved me down as I stopped in front of the museum. He was clad in dull worn leather. His hands resembled chopsticks and his face raw sewage and partially hidden beneath dark glasses. He was quick to cramp up my personal space as soon as I alighted from the cart. I backed away. I hated people getting too close and he emitted like a postman's sock.

"Master Jett." He planted his feet wide but his pockmarked jaw slackened. "Err... do you have business with ... um ... Lord Zaros?"

What is this – the evacuated Twilight security clan?

"Clearly I didn't come here for my health."

He went to say something, but I ignored him and started for the wide set of stairs leading toward the museum entrance. I tried not to flinch when he fell into step beside me.

"The Lord isn't ... err ... taking unsolicited guests right now."

"Unsolicited? That's a big word." I took the stairs two at a time and kept my eyes on the twin glass doors of the museum. *Awesome.* It was security clan free. "Not to worry; I'm sure Zaros is expecting me."

"He – he didn't say as much." He side-stepped in front of me as we reached the landing. His lofty figure blocked the entrance as he adopted a business-like expression. "I'm going to have to ask you to wait here so I can get the lowdown from Zaros."

I shrugged. "You've got to do what you've got to, huh?"

Saliva pooled on his bottom lip. "Err … yeah … I guess."

He interpreted my comment as cooperation and gave a nod before bony fingers hooked over the brass handle and pushed open the door. I didn't give him the chance to make good on his word and shoved past him and into the lobby, my boots squeaking on the tiles when I paused to sniff out Zaros.

"Oi!" The dweeb-guy rushed up behind and grabbed my elbow. "What the fuck do ya think ya doing?" he hissed.

Spoiled innards. Vampires had foul breath at the best of times.

"Back off, dweeb."

I shoved a palm into his chest, snapping his ribs like crispy sugar peas. He stumbled back and I returned his hiss in the most vicious way possible.

"Touch me again and I'm looking for your heart."

He slurped back the running drool from his lip and clawed his palms but said nothing as a chorus of laughter erupted from unseen corridors to reverberate all around. *Bloodplay.* It was just the beginning. My nerves chilled as I looked around the lobby. The walls stretched with shadows in the wake of a few discreet downlights, barely illuminating the pterodactyl bones that suspended from the highly slanted ceiling. The skeleton appeared grotesque, hollow, and chalky. To my left was the patently vacant counter.

"Ha. You really do have a heart fetish, master J."

Zaros strode into the lobby like a slinking panther and he was wearing a pair of chrome buckled leathers that hung loosely above his groin. Some of his crew trailed behind him. My nose swelled. He smelled like a cocktail of sweat and semen and wore nothing else but the ink staining his bare chest.

He stopped short of me. "Losing your own love-Gucci so soon?"

Chutzpah.

"The devil wears Prada these days."

The two blood-gangers lingering behind Zaros laughed. I recognized them from our recent subway rendezvous – the green-eyed schmuck and the straw-haired scarecrow. Throw them in an exhibit and call it human evolution turned vile.

"Iconic," Zaros said. His black stare zeroed in on dweeb-guy. "Really, Isaac?"

"I …. err …. um …. he got inside, master."

"Clearly."

Isaac wiped his leaky mouth with the back of his hand. "I'm sorry. I …."

Zaros held up a palm to silence him. His voice was like knives. "Get back out there and try putting in some big dick energy in ya fucking job, yes?"

"Yeah – B. D. E. M." Green-eyes grabbed his balls and gave a thrust for good measure. "Moron."

Scarecrow laughed. Isaac sneered. Zaros dismissed the scene with a flick of his wrist. "Leave us!"

He was silent as the three vampires left then he turned and glared at me. "Why are you here?"

"Michal."

"*Your* pet?" His fangs glinted like the bones hovering above us. "Now, that is a surprise."

"He is not my pet nor is he yours."

He gave a wide gesture with his arms and laughed. "Ah, but the world is now full of devils who wear Prada and human blood-smooches, don't you agree?"

"No."

"Marius has created the perfect conditions for such a package and from where I'm standing, you be shipping with it, *doc*."

"I'd be shipping better when you give me your word to leave Michal well alone."

He laughed. "Ludicrous!" His skin appeared darkly fluid as he started to ramble. "A vampire's word is not gospel, but it might suffice to hold if you are willing to stand beside me." He paused. "I know your undead heart still pumps for humanity. You resent the way the Leavings are being treated in Bloodfaye."

Ugh. Incoming vampire verbal diarrhea.

My forehead began to throb. I gave him a look that must have encouraged him to continue. The shit factor didn't disappoint.

"Listen doc, I'm with you. This vampire master is outraged about Marius' plans to enforce slavery on our Leavings. Is it not enough that we drain their blood every couple of months to satisfy our thirst?" He paused and thumped his chest. "History and white men were never kind to my people. The world has changed, and we've been given a clean slate, but Marius wishes to recreate treacherous old pathways in the form of fascism and subjugation. Damn! The dick wants to bring back slavery! It isn't right."

"And you're suggesting ....?"

"Freedom for all."

I laughed. "Delusional."

"Why?"

"Because the world is blood-driven and as much as I reject human slavery, those Leavings are safer in the dome than out in the wild."

It was true. We might be the only vampires currently dominating this town but it was foolish to believe that other clans would not eventually try to stake our territory and our humans. And it wasn't as if humans were currently in large supply.

Zaros' nostrils flared so wide that I almost caught a glimpse of his brain. He placed a talon over his belt and studied me. "There is another way."

"Enlighten me."

"Help me overthrow Marius and ensure my place as Bloodfaye's sole overlord, and I will make sure all Leavings are given a real choice – they can come and go as they please so long as they agree to take part in the bloodletting program."

"Sounds ideal but you're forgetting one vital thing – their freedom will bring anarchy and more death. We're dealing with a horde of carnivorous creatures whose dead hearts live to hunt and kill humans. As it is, Marius has succeeded in establishing civility to the clan – at least for those beneath the dome. Freedom for the Leavings will stoke the primal urges of every vampire in Norbury city. They won't be safe; they'll become prey again."

Zaros stepped closer. His breath crept over my face like a rancid cockroach.

"These are the times to be thinking hard about which direction you and your *pet* be shipping." His eyes drilled into me. "Especially considering that your girl is, by default, about to become a prime target as the vampire queen."

I clenched. "Is that a threat, *master*?"

His upper lip curled to reveal pearly tusks. "Call it what you want blood-sap, but if I were you, I'd be calling it the right way."

Bloodplay. He had delivered and it was violence I felt calling me in that moment. I took a deliberate breath and forced myself to think about bananas. I didn't come here for brutality, and I sure as hell couldn't eat a banana. Not for one moment did I believe his intentions for the Leavings to be noble, particularly when accompanied with dirty intimidation. He sought supremacy and nothing more.

I was about to say as much when the familiar, sweet sound of angel-minx filled the room. My jaw felt like led when I saw Sun striding toward us. Her pale skin revealed more color than usual, and I noticed a distinct sensual sway to her hips.

What the hell is she doing here?

"Jett." She stopped next to Zaros. They exchanged a lingering look before her eyes settled on me. Her hair shone like golden vine. "How very unusual to see you here."

I gave a half laugh and looked at Zaros. "Love-Gucci found."

DREAMING OF YOU

"*D*addy, I've got a secret!" Avila rushed toward me and flung herself in my arms. Giggles like popping corn muffled against my sweater. I stroked the back of her head. The dewy air clung to her after having just returned home from an outing with her mother. Bright eyes peered up at me. "Do you want to see?"

"Of course, I want to see."

"Avila." Melissa appeared at the threshold of my office. She tried to smile as she leaned against the door frame. "Daddy is working right now. Let's show him your secret later."

Avila wriggled free. Her nose crinkled as she began to pull off her coat. "But I want to show him now."

"It's okay, little nugget, you *can* show me now." I looked at Melissa and mouthed a "Hey you".

She normally responded to our love language but not today. She frowned before going to our daughter. I leaned into my chair and watched as she helped Avila remove her woolen coat. The distraction was welcome. Blood diagnostics and mineral content graphs were clogging my brain like sloppy discharge.

Avila's undershirt momentarily stretched and slipped from her shoulder as she shrugged off her coat. The scene slowed down long enough for me to spot the plaster fixed on Avila's upper arm as Melissa readjusted her sleeves and softly chided: "Remember what we talked about when it comes to secrets?"

"Yes Momma."

Melissa dropped her head to the side and gave me a coy smile. Her upper lip lifted, and her face flickered. *Bones.* Her skull blinked at me. Then it was gone when she turned to whisper in Avila's ear. The vibe was like an echo. I tried to speak but couldn't. It was then that Avila spun around. Her vibrant skirt cut through my brain with her fast twirl as she bolted from the room.

"Be right back!"

It took all my will to speak. "What was that all about?"

"What?"

"Secrets."

A dark grin and my tiny hairs raised.

"She's got a secret."

"Yeah, so she said."

Melissa's face glitched. "She's got a *special* secret, Jett."

"Melissa?" I managed to stand up. "Is everything okay?"

"Nothing is okay."

Avila came back into the room. "Daddy, meet Shana!"

"Sha–" I was looking at a wolf.

I tried to refocus. The wolf's gray gaze was like a moment of serenity amid a twine of sterling fur. Her coat glossed in the waning sunlight offered by the window behind me. Peculiarity just hit its stride. I collected my bottom lip as Avila clawed her fingers through the wolf's mane and laughed.

"Mommy said that I could keep her, but I must keep her a secret because she's super, super special."

Melissa stroked Avila's forehead. "*Our* super special secret."

"A very special secret."

"Between you and me," Melissa said.

"And Daddy!"

I shuddered. My two girls felt like strangers and there was a wolf in my office called Shana whose eyes spoke secrets of their own. *Shana.* The name circled my head like a lazy siesta. I was grasping at straws.

"Wait – a wolf?"

"Remember what I told you? There are no accidents, Jett." Melissa turned abruptly. Her thin arms flailed like a mad woman. "Secrets become death and death becomes poison!"

Hello.

Nothing made sense, and yet, everything made sense. Realism set in my bones even as I became aware of my lucid dream state. Messages from the dead kept me on my toes. Shana was the half breed Lygarou whose blood I was working with Michal. Melissa had brought her into my dream. *Why?* Nothing was normal about the new normal.

I tried to regain balance. It *was* my dream. Control was within reach. I fingered my chin to help harness clarity. An odd sense of time warp snapped my awareness as I held Melissa's stare.

"What secrets are you talking about? Shana's blood?"

"No."

It was strange talking to the dead in your dreams. She was real but not. The next real thing I knew was Avila's scream as she was lifted off her feet. Her legs kicked wildly as an unseen force held her suspended in the air.

"Daddy!"

"Avila!"

So much for dream control. Some dreams felt more real than what we call reality. Avila's screams escalated. I let out a frenetic growl and went to move but my boots were nailed to the floor.

What the?

Delusion was control. The room shrouded into darkness. The enemy wasn't in sight, but it was present and powerfully demonic. Every one of my nerve endings stood on end. Fear provoked hostility. My calf muscles squeezed as I strained to move. I knew evil like second skin, but this invisible entity was Satan. Every part of me knew it.

Avila called out. My name sounded like a chilling crossword clue. Melissa reached for Avila. Primitive instinct overdrive and a wrangled snarl. *Nightmare.* It was as wicked as the bright flash in the corner of my eye. Avila's back teeth ground like needles in my ear as a shadow above her began to take form and the air was suffused with the vile and eerie.

Wayward genies and perverted ogres. Everything went askew. A hellion eye hung like the sullied. *Succubus.* Melissa screamed and Avila was gone. *Gone.* Shana's doleful howl filled the hollow before silence.

Melissa's haunting voice followed me into wakefulness. *"She has a secret, Jett; a special secret."*

DRAVEN SANGUISA

a usual laboratory work day of blood-hype hustle and foul mouths was beginning to wind down with no dead Leavings to report. It would count as a good day if they still existed. A few Mysticus scientists and guards remained scattered throughout the workshop. Bleach and solvent vapors irritated my senses as I glanced at the Leaving man sitting next to me before pricking a syringe into his flesh. He was among the last bloods scheduled for the day, and honestly, I barely noticed him.

I was almost immune to the fresh heartbeats cruising through bloodwork central. Humans appeared the same of late – skin and bone, and fermented hatred that reeked of saline. At least their bodily stench had been eradicated. Marius had made good on his word and implemented a cleansing process prior to giving all Leavings a bed in what was called the Segregation Hall.

The Segregation Hall was an old school gym transformed into a giant dormitory where they secured Leavings before scheduling them for bloodwork. They were then assigned quarters in District H provided their blood was clean. Diseased Leavings were denied entry into Bloodfaye. We had no use for contaminated blood. The Mysticus avoided sickness at all costs and had learned the hard way. Greedy kindred peeling from the inside out had paved the way for us. Diseased blood was a potential vampire killer.

Aside from taking the blood of Leavings, Marius was also commissioning another pass for the incomings in the form of a physical assessment which was set to take place in the Diversion Yard. Basically, we would be able to determine their slave-value factor and thus assign them to suitable jobs. I figured those Leavings who were out of shape would be thrown back into the ruined city with the diseased humans and outcast kindred. Yes, not every Norbury city vampire had made it into Bloodfaye. Some kindred proved too weak in the face of their supernatural cravings and desires. Their rebellious nature could not be controlled even by the vindictive likes of Marius. We called them the Cruentus.

Rebellion was a long-running theme nowadays. The Segregation Hall had become the pulse for Leaving gang bangers and hawkers to wreak havoc over their weaker counterparts. Even a vampire apocalypse couldn't snub man's deep-seated need for power and coercion. Humans. Vampires. Lygarou. Witches. It didn't matter which skin we now wore. The feeble were always going to be abused and monopolized.

The Leaving man jolted me from my idle thoughts when he cleared his throat. I didn't look at him when I replaced the puncture wound with a cotton pad and instructed him to apply pressure. His voice croaked as I went for some white tape.

"So, what's it like on the other side, doc?"

"It's heaven on earth."

"Really?"

"No." I tore a piece of tape and stuck it over the cotton pad. I looked at him and saw a young man with a lost future whose copper eyes flecked blue over deep shadows. I shrugged. "But if you play it smart and follow the rules, you've got a better chance at survival than out there."

"Any chance they'll turn me?"

"No."

He chuckled. "Didn't think so."

"You can make it in the new world if you keep your head down and wait it out."

"Nice advice coming from the top of the food chain."

I grinned. "Depends on how you look at it. Our survival depends on yours. So, who *really* tops the food chain, hmm?"

He looked beyond me as the distinct sound of heels tapped on the tiles from some place behind. "Now, vamps like her can top my food chain anytime."

Feline rabbit holes. Man's everlasting mystery that

the apocalypse couldn't annihilate either. Such is the nature of the supernatural alike. I didn't need to turn around to know her identity. I could detect Sun's angel-minx scent a mile away. Particularly now that she burned with Zaros' sex between her thighs.

Her touch on my shoulder was electric. "Master Jett, are you ready for our meeting?"

"Just about."

I copped an eyeful of blazing amber and my heart almost seared to ashes. I deliberately avoided looking at her tight blouse and dropped my gaze to take in the black shiny knee-highs skimming up her calves. She was more distracting than usual. Feline rabbit holes indeed. I wasn't jumping in. I turned to dismiss the human.

"Close your mouth and move on, Leaving."

His pulse throbbed in my ear as I motioned for a nearby Mysticus guard to escort him away. A white leather clad guard stepped up pronto. He was unusually tall and barrel chested for an Asian man-cum-vampire, and his skin showed fading pitted scars.

The Leaving man grazed a hand over his scalp and laughed as he stood up. "Nah. She be my Desdemona."

"Ha." Sun gripped her hips as the guard grabbed the Leaving's elbow and gave a good yank. He stumbled back, but he kept his eyes on Sun and grinned. She shook her head. "You are no Othello, Leaving."

"I can be any kind of Shakespeare that you want me to be; just name it, honeypot."

Sun burst out laughing. The guard scowled and

shoved the Leaving with a snarl. "Watch your mouth, cockbag."

"Alright, alright! I'm watching." The Leaving man flailed his arms and moved forward with the guard shadowing him until they reached an exit door a little way along the aisle. It didn't stop him from sneaking a quick wink at Sun before he was pushed from the lab entirely.

Sun's laugh was all breath and no sound.

"It's nice to see some of them are still spirited." She smoothed her skirt. "He should have gone with Juliet."

I shut down the workstation computer and stood. "Don't tell me you are a sucker for dying love?"

We started walking the aisle between the long stretches of pristine white benchtops that were our workstations. The lab was empty now, allowing us to talk in private. I had a few things to say.

"I think all of us are suckers for dying love these days."

"Perhaps more of us than others."

She curled a lock of hair over her ear and glanced at me. "It's not what you think, Jett."

"What do I think?"

"That I am making a mistake with Zaros."

I glanced up at the square oyster lights mounted flush against the ceiling. "He's catfishing you without the social media part, Sun. He's deceptive and dangerous. You need to stop sleeping with him."

"Excuse me?" She scowled. "You're getting way too

big for your vampire boots. I don't answer to you or anyone, *Master J*."

"Dumbest thing I ever heard you say."

There was someone I was eager to meet waiting on the other side of the door at the end of the aisle. That's why she'd come here. "None of us are free in the new world. You know this."

Her boots clicked behind me like the passion in her voice.

"They can't take away our freedom to love."

I fixed my stare on the large chrome door a few meters from me. "You love him?"

"N – no!"

She smelled like a woman in love. And if there was anything that I knew about a woman in love, it was that she was loyal to her heart. I turned to meet her fiery eyes.

"You're a part of the resistance, Sun. Screwing the enemy compromises your allegiance to our cause." I gestured toward the door. "You are risking everything that we have been doing to reverse the damage inflicted by the V-Virus – and for what? A supercharged orgasm?"

"My allegiance to the secret sector is as solid as ever. For you to even question my loyalty to you is barbarous." She paused and inhaled sharply. "It's just sex and nothing more."

"Then make it nothing more." I ignored whatever response she was about to throw at me and strode toward the door, briefly looking back at her as I gripped the handle. She swallowed visibly beneath my stare. "Is he informed and prepared for his part in the viral transfer?"

"Yes."

"Good."

I pulled on the door handle to reveal the image of a male vampire sprawled across the bench seat that butted against the wall of the building's entrance. Long hair the color of mud contrasted against the white of his shirt, while his knees rested bent against the wall and appeared swamped in a pair of baggy jeans. He jerked to his feet in an instant, scraping a hand through his hair and bounding toward me with a twitchy grin. His voice was unsteady.

"Master Jett?" His shoulders lifted with his sudden laugh. "Sire, I have been waiting to meet you."

"And I you. Let me apologize for our delayed introduction, things have been a little hectic of late."

"Oh, totally fine, dude – I – I mean, sire." He started to pull at the hem of his T-shirt. His eyes darted between me and Sun as she came up next to me. "I want to thank you for saving my life back in the subway."

God. Is that what he thought I did?

I didn't know that I agreed, but I wasn't letting him in on that piece of intel. "You are very welcome. Sun tells me that you are all set to undergo your transition back to humanity in the coming days. I am pleased that you have accepted your vital role in bringing normality back to the world and thereby saving many lives. You are to be commended for your courage."

He nodded rapidly. "I am at your service, sire. Whatever you want."

"Hmm – Sun tells me you have a name?"

"Draven Sanguisa."

"Sanguisa?"

"Yeah, my Pop was Latino."

"Well." I clasped a hand on his shoulder and smiled. "I am certain that all who remain in the world will soon come to know of a kid who goes by the Latino name Sanguisa."

His dark eyes glittered like a night sky. "Whoa! That is totally cool."

Yeah. Totally.

14

BY MY SIDE

"*In the dark of night. Those small hours, I'm uncertain and anxious. I need to call you.*"

I whispered the song lyrics and a part of me wanted to break. Avila's voice drifted from another room along with the haunting strains of the old INXS track *By My Side*. She had her Bluetooth speaker connected. We were thriving on electricity in the blood-dome as some kindred were skilled tradespeople. I often wondered if they'd ever achieve lighting up the web again. It wasn't in the foreseeable future.

I wish you were so close to me.

The song had been one of Scarla's favorites. I sank back into the living room sofa and inhaled. I whiffed the charred woody remnants of Palo Santo and tangy furniture polish. The scent of Avila's incense sticks clung to every nook and cranny in our home. She said it was to cleanse our space of negative influences and bad energy.

She said it provided spiritual protection. I didn't resist her reasonings and rituals – were vampires capable of connecting to anything remotely spiritual? The wicked didn't deserve protection from an omnipresent higher being. But my girl still needed to believe in something good. Her life overflowed with dark nasties and I was one of them.

Scarla never was.

By my side. I wish you were. I wish you were.

Soul-stealer. I still thought of my lover every day. My soul yearned to be closer to her and even though I felt her essence within me, it was never enough. I vaguely looked at the reading nook across the way. The stained white timber panels were reminiscent of Louisiana French flair with their arched French windows and overstuffed cushions that scattered over the broad padded seat below the bookshelves. I saw none of it. I only saw Scarla – the part of me that wanted to break.

Breathe Jett.

It was all I could do to keep from losing my mind over her absence from my life. That and focusing on dispelling the plague that had inevitably taken her from me. At least in my humanity I would escape an eternal life without her. Maybe I deserved this everlasting hell. I wasn't always an angel in my mortality.

Was I doing the right thing?

I knew the repercussions were high enough to claim my life sooner rather than later. If the viral vector reversed the effects of the V-Virus tonight, I planned on reproducing the strain and slipping it into the clan's blood supply. Marius would have my heart for sure. Let him have it.

"Hello, earth to Dad?"

I startled as Avila laughed and walked into the room. "Where were you just now?"

She wore an ivory satin gown like second skin and high strappy sandals. Her toenails were painted scarlet. I had to take a second to collect my jaw. "Right here, baby girl." She looked so …. womanly. I was disturbed. "Wh-what are you wearing?"

Her eyes dropped to the floor and she smiled before looking back at me. "What do you think?"

My mind raced and my gut turned to vinegar. Obviously, the revealing outfit was for the Claiming Ceremony.

"Isn't it a bit…." I gnawed back my words when her vulnerability hit me hard. I forced a smile. "You look beautiful."

"Really?"

"Yes. You look your mom."

She pushed a hand through her dark hair. "That can't be a bad thing."

"Your mom was a stunning woman. You couldn't go wrong with genes like that."

She grinned and performed a slow pirouette. "Do you think she'd like it?"

I cleared my throat and thought about last night's

dream scene. It was better than thinking about her wearing that gown.

"I have no doubt. Listen, odd question – do you remember the time when your mom took you out for the day not long before she died?"

She stopped moving. "She took me places all the time."

"Yes, but this particular time you may have come home with a plaster on your arm. Did you get hurt? Do you recall?"

"I was only young, Dad. I don't know. How come?"

"No reason."

She snorted. "Liar."

I was silent for a moment. Avila didn't know about my secretive activities and alternative plans for the impending extinction of the Mysticus clan, and I wanted to keep it that way. Knowledge like that meant risk and I wasn't jeopardizing her safety for all the blood in the world. Nor did I wish to cause her alarm.

She sat down on the coffee table in front of me. Her skin was like ice when she reached for my hand. "What's going on, Dad?"

"I've been having strange dreams."

"Of Mom?"

"Yeah."

She frowned. "Me too. I didn't want to mention because they have been—"

"Disturbing?"

"Yeah."

Interesting. Extremely.

I leaned forward. "Do you remember the details?"

"As if it happened for real. She shows me death and mayhem, and she keeps repeating the same messages." Avila pulled her hand away and began fidgeting. "She says that I have a secret and there are no—"

"Accidents."

"Exactly! I don't know what she means or what she wants. I mean, I can sense this desperation and then I think it's just me experiencing the pre-wedding jitters, you know?"

I scowled. "I don't know, because you're not getting married."

"What?" She stood with hands on hips.

I groaned inwardly. *Big mouth.* Like I needed to address this battle right before a deceptive life changing and potentially life threatening event.

"I thought we cleared this up?"

"Give me a break. Old habits die hard."

"Well you better find a way to bury them because the ceremony date has been changed to the next full moon."

"Huh?" I blanked out for a second. Her face was a puzzle before I seized back my thoughts. "But that's in a few days. Why the sudden push forward?"

"Four to be exact. Marius doesn't want to wait for the following full moon. We've waited long enough."

"B-but, what's with the full moon deal? We're not werewolves or witches."

"And we're not human either, Dad. Haven't you

noticed the power that accompanies each full moon?" She chuckled. "It creeps under your skin and merges with our blood. We are an ancient species, mythical creatures of the night now. Immortals."

No shit. Not for long, baby girl.

"I can feel it, though I don't see why the Claiming Ceremony needs to take place on a full moon night. It's not like it will make a difference."

I could play ignorant when it suited. Resistance did it every time.

She blew back a strand of hair that had fallen over her lips. "It makes all the difference and you know it. We're linked with the earth's elements like never before! It's like discovering and connecting to an incredible version of our existence. You have to honor it, Dad."

"You're passionate like your mom too."

She gave a halfhearted laugh. "You once said that we can't stop change. Don't you think it's about time you stopped fighting this?"

"We should never stop fighting for what we want."

"And what do you want, Dad?"

I wanted my little girl back. I needed my soul lover in my arms again.

Avila's eyes homed in on me like crystallized darts. I looked away. *Was I doing the right thing? Could I change it for the better?* The inner conflict was a wrangle between old and new worlds. It was also torment. My neck was stiff when I looked back at her.

"I want you to be happy."

"That's the easy part. You've just got to let it go and deal with the reality. You are a vampire and I am going to be the vampire queen. Embrace your gifts and your part in it."

I stood up and stroked her cheek with the backs of my fingers. Her smooth white skin reminded me of a geisha. A phantom geisha.

"It's important that you try very hard to remember what happened that day when you came home with a plaster on your arm when you were little." I nodded as she frowned. "Do you think you can do that?"

"You think it matters?"

"Yes."

"Okay, I can try."

"Good." I turned and made for the door, stopping at the threshold when she called after me.

"Where are you going?"

I shrugged. "I'm going to do what you suggested."

"And what's that?"

"Embrace my part in the new world."

She half laughed. "Whatever."

I smirked. "You do look beautiful in that gown."

She nodded and I left the room with my insides churning with quiet desperation.

Well, I wish you were so close to me.

No wishes could bring Scarla into my arms again, but I could do something about my daughter. My nerves were on fire as time slipped away from me. I was on my way to the subway lab to kick V-Virus ass. I didn't want immortality.

Was I doing the right thing?

The choice was out of my hands. This was the path that was notched deep in my undead bones. I couldn't acquiesce to a vampire who had stolen my daughter's humanity and screws with humans for his own power-hungry vampire agenda. Avila's future was worth fighting for. And so was my return to a human heart that could break.

In the dark of night, these faces they haunt me.

15

STEEL DUST PROMISES

"*A*re you sure this is what you want to do?"

Sun's talons were needles in my arm as we stopped short of the inoculation chamber. We were as deep in the subway as the old steel dust clinging in my nose. I met her stare.

"Second thoughts?"

"It's not my call."

"Not true. You are just as much a part of this as me." I pried her fingers from my arm. Her hand felt jittery. "Or are you?"

"What is that supposed to mean?"

I shrugged. "I'm not the one sleeping with the enemy."

"Who I go to bed with is my business. What you need to think about is the fact that what we're about to do cannot be undone. Marius forgave us once; he won't overlook this if it goes to shit." She shook her head. "He

320

will kill us."

I laughed. "Is shit such a bad thing?"

She was about to reply when the sound of footsteps carried along the subway shaft. She looked away as Lena and one of her crew came into view. They were here to keep watch over the door while the so-called 'shit' was going down.

Hello, Latino Shadow Guardian.

She almost made it all better. I think it was her stark human *in-your-face* qualities. She reminded me of spirit. I watched as Lena stalked toward us in a pair of dirty denims and a matching jacket. Her chunky boots were scuffed, and a worn leather whip was slung at her waist.

"Master Jett. Reporting for rebel duty." She flipped her canary colored ponytail as she stopped in front of me and poked a thumb toward the man beside her. "You know Jamie?"

"Lena." She smelled of summer spunk and the spearmint gum between her jaws. It was nothing new. I acknowledged Jamie with a nod. She was right in that I was familiar with the buff middle aged man with a hot score on his back. I knew his past enough to know that vampires had wiped out his family. He was good for the resistance. His eyes spoke of war and hatred.

I motioned to the lab door behind me. "If anyone comes down here, knock on the door but under no circumstances enter the room beyond. Got it?"

Lena's expression dimmed. "How come?"

"It's a contamination thing. The same applies if you

hear anything going down on the other side – don't open up."

"Hear anything like what?"

I laughed. "You know, wrangled screams—beasty, contorted growls, mystical chanting."

"Why do I feel like I'm a part of a screwed-up version of a horror movie?"

I grinned and grabbed the door handle. "Because you're now living the Hollywood dream, sweetheart."

"Ha. Some dream."

Her retort followed me and Sun into the inoculation chamber, though it was just as fast out of my mind as I pulled on my lab coat and offered Sun a disposable blue smock. We stood between the lengths of sheet plastic that constituted a makeshift airlock chamber. I regarded her as she fastened the smock at her waist.

"You didn't answer my question before."

"You didn't answer mine."

"I'm here, aren't I?"

"Same."

She looked at the flipside of the plastic wall separating us from the lab. Draven's lofty figure slouched on a stool while Michal whizzed around him, taking his vitals. Their images appeared fluid through the plastic.

"I just want you to be sure that this is the right thing."

Am I doing the right thing?

I had made a choice to push tonight's planned trial viral vector to the real deal. Draven would now be receiving the injection in replace of a lab rat. The changed Claiming Ceremony date meant that I was out of time and hope had never looked so crucial. I took a breath and reached for the plastic flap. "I don't know what's right or wrong anymore. I just know that I have to try."

I parted the flap and walked into the chamber before she could answer. The stringent vapors of ethanol greeted me along with Michal's skitzy glance from his position in front of Draven, stethoscope ear tubes jammed in his ears as he pressed the chest piece against Draven's skin.

"Game on. Are we all set?" I said as I approached.

Draven scratched his ear and laughed. Michal scrunched his nose in concentration. I examined the viral cultures and microbial strains that sat in glass dishes along the benchtop as I waited for him to finish.

Michal pulled the tubes from his ears and looked at me. His eyes appeared as big as Garfield's through his thick glasses. "We're as set as the unstable cellular layers; how's that for you?"

"We're dealing with blood that originated from witchcraft. I doubt we'll ever achieve confluence and formation of tight junctions – Works just fine for me. Do you have the viral vector ready for transfer?"

"I've developed a working recombinant and loaded it into the microprocessor controlled injector. Bu-but—"

I interjected. "Good," and gestured toward the tidy cot we had managed to bring in undetected. It wasn't exactly the ideal medical style of bed to suit our needs given the circumstances, but it was a bed nonetheless.

"Draven, why don't you go take a load off?"

Draven rubbed his chin and glanced at the bed. The mattress was covered with white cotton topped with a stained lumpy pillow. It was butted up against the far side of the plastic wall of the room. Not that it was that far considering the room resembled a miasma matchbox.

His throat rolled as he swallowed visibly. "Wh-what's going to happen to me tonight?"

Sun moved between us before I could reply. She looked at me as she spoke to him. "It's just like we talked about, remember?"

"Yeah, but what if it doesn't work?"

I smiled. "The worst that could happen is nothing. You are much stronger than your human self. I mean, you are an immortal being for crying out loud. Our vaccine formula is essentially a reproduction of the same properties that already flow in your blood, with an added twist of a developed version of the V-Virus."

"The wolf bloods?"

"Yeah, the wolf bloods. Which means you will not die tonight, promise."

He nodded. "Alright, I trust you, doc."

"Gratitude."

The word barely formed as he slinked from the stool and followed Sun to the cot while I sucked in a breath. I'd just delivered a promise knowing that promises made by the undead remained undead. I let out a long breath and watched Sun stroke his forehead and offer soothing words.

Why did I do that?

It was the part of me that believed in the path. This little shindig had to pay off. I palmed my throbbing head as Michal's discomforting words thumped against my temples.

He gripped the stethoscope tube that hung around his neck. "Ho-how can you be so certain that we'll do him no harm when we're working like blind mice running up to the farmer's wife? I-I-I think we should wait until we know it's the right thing to do."

"It *is* the right thing to do." I grabbed the microprocessor injector from the bench. "His vitals?"

"Sta-stable. How do you know?"

This question made my headache worse. Did no one else get it?

"Listen, my daughter is about to belong to a blood-sucking fiend who can't see past his supernatural inflated ego; humans are being treated as blood-cow slaves and innocent children are currently being removed from their parents to one day become soulless immortal puppets to soulless king puppeteer himself – we have in our hands the solution to stop all of this before it gets worse."

I paused and regarded his frigid expression before stepping closer. "That's how I know. Can we get this done now?"

"Yes master."

"Awesome."

The following moments played out like a scene from who knows what. Injecting a viral vector into someone's bloodstream was far from extraordinary and Draven was an ideal candidate. He was a young, healthy vampire who took the injection without incident then rested while we kept an eye on his vitals.

I expected his transformation back to humanity to be much like transitioning into vampirism – an uneventful transaction between life and death. He would have to die to reawaken in his human form. Too bad the atmosphere in the inoculation chamber couldn't die and be reborn along with him. It was that tense.

"What now?"

Sun and I exchanged glances as I leaned against the bench while Michal fussed over Draven, taking his vitals with various instruments. Sun perched on the stool fiddling with the hem of her smock.

"We wait."

She groaned. "This place gives me the creeps."

"What? You don't like what we've done with the joint?" I grinned. "That blue suits you."

She scowled. "Yeah well, don't get used to it. I don't plan to come back in here."

"You're too lovely to be a scientist anyway."

She laughed. "Is that what I am these days?"

"You're still like the sun when there's no sun, *Sun.*"

We both smiled and I went to touch her twilight skin when Michal gasped and whirled around to look at us.

"His heart has stopped! It's working!"

"Hello, hello."

I pushed off the bench and went to the bedside, with Sun close behind. I noticed Draven's talons recede and his skin become plump pink like the living as he slept. His breath kickstarted and then deepened.

Sun grabbed my arm. "He's human again!"

Yes!

I laughed as Michal squealed. The shindig *had* paid off and now we could begin the next phase of eradicating the V-Virus from the world. Humanity would be ours again. I felt like singing with angels and was about to say as much when Draven groaned. He convulsed violently for few a moments.

Sun grabbed my arm. "What's happening?"

Draven abruptly stilled. My nerves were like sharp knives. His eyes flew open to settle on me as I peered back into dark demon red. Realization dawned and Draven's skin turned to mottled yellow putrefaction. He opened his jaw and growled like a hungry beast as his beady eyes flicked toward Michal. Sun's gasp nipped at my ears as Draven sat up and grinned. His voice was gnarled and born from age-old steel dust and wilting promises.

"I'm back!"

16

THE NEWBORN SANGUISA

*M*ichal dropped the stethoscope and backed away from the bed. His fear was pungent. I didn't take my eyes off Draven as he stood up, rolled his head, and hissed. Hot breath like curdled innards went right in my face. I stood firm as I regarded him. He looked like something straight out of *The Night of the Living Dead,* only this deranged creature came with a nice set of lethal fangs. I went to move forward but Sun yanked on my arm and I stumbled back. Draven stretched his neck to sniff out fresh meat. His infrareds settled on Michal.

Holy shit.

Michal was a few feet away and about to become Draven's midnight snack if I didn't do something about it. I pulled my arm free from Sun's grip and called out.

"Draven."

It was enough to grab his attention. His spidery eyes darted between me and Michal. I glanced at Sun.

"Get him out of here now."

She went for Michal as I moved in front of them. Draven looked at me. My skin crawled at his grisly voice.

"Doc made good on his promise." He showed me his palms and laughed. "I'm still alive!"

Yeah. No kidding.

But I would have selected a different word to describe his moldy chowder-like complexion. His now blotchy skin was sallow and sagged in thick tucks at his throat. His hair hung stringy and thin over his scalp.

What have I done?

There was no time to dwell. "You're right, I did say that you wouldn't die tonight, and you didn't."

He gave a throaty chuckle and looked at Sun and Michal as they made a dash toward the lab door. I followed his gaze to see Sun usher Michal forward as she reached for the flaps of the plastic wall. When I glanced back at Draven, he ran his tongue over chaffed lips.

"But you didn't say the same for anyone else here, doc."

I could literally hear the whirl of my pulse a moment before Draven vanished from sight. *Damn.* He moved fast, and in the next moment, he was behind Sun and clawing at her shoulder. I went after him as Sun screeched and tried to shove Michal through the plastic flaps and into the airlock chamber, but Draven flung her across the room before the action could be completed. Michal yelped as he tripped forward and fell on his knees in front of Draven. He scurried across the floor as Draven laughed and moved in on him.

I barely heard the shattering glass and the scientific gadgets crashing all around as Sun landed on the benchtop somewhere behind me. I homed in on Draven who was now within arm's reach. I hurled myself onto his back as he reached for Michal. His leathery neck disappeared into his shoulders as I latched onto him and hooked my claws into his face. He struggled as the stench of his skin overwhelmed me. I dug my fingers into his face as hard as I could and roared. That was when his brute strength locked in. He was a vampire on steroids. I knew I couldn't contain him for long. I gripped his head with one hand and punched hard into his temple to restrain him long enough for Michal to get up and escape the room.

"Piss off, doc!"

Draven's massive knuckles pounded me square in the forehead. *Crack.* My skull almost split in half and at the same time he snarled and started to back up and thrash madly, breaking my flesh like a stinging laceration. I held on tight, locking my nails into his face and repeatedly smashing into his head. It was like pounding into a tenpin bowling ball. I roared again and squeezed my thighs around his torso, hanging on as we were flung backward.

He stilled for a transitory moment as his lofty frame inflated with a gulp of air before he twisted rapidly and struck my head. *Boom.* My nose snapped and bent with crabbed fingers peeling my skin like bloody floss. My own gore blinded me, and another blow flashed brilliant white behind my eyes. My teeth felt like mulch and my jaw shattered with the next incoming blow. Giddiness took hold as I began to lose my grip on him, barely managing to stop myself from slipping by hooking my fingers into his ear.

Draven growled as I glanced at Michal scrambling to his feet. His eyes bulged as he stood frozen on the spot.

"Go!"

For God's sake, go!

Next thing I knew, my ears were whistling, and I was hurtling toward the other side of the room. It was a fleeting experience, and so was the hard thwack against my face when I slammed into the wall. Everything throbbed. I sprung to my feet and darted for the cot, snapping a hollow steel leg from the bedframe as Sun moved in on Draven who was closing in on Michal. Her fangs glistened as she pushed herself between Michal and Draven, and plunged a shard of glass into Draven's chest.

It was only a second as she spread her arms to barricade Michal, backing away as Draven looked at her. His chest sunk with his wheezy breath.

"You—you stabbed me?"

Michal trembled behind her. I knew the poor sod wasn't game enough to make a move in this moment. I gripped the bed pole and edged toward them, sneaking up behind Draven as he peered down at the jagged glass protruding from his gut.

"Draven?" Sun's voice trembled as she glanced at me. "You're not yourself, we gave you to viral vector, remember?"

Draven shook his head. "I-I don't feel so good."

His corpselike fingers folded over the glass as I gripped the bed pole and crept closer.

"It's just the side effects of the vaccine. It's going to be okay." Sun stepped closer to him. "You just need to relax so that we can fix this, okay?"

Draven looked at Sun and my hairs prickled as he cackled a reply. "It's not going to be okay."

Draven tore the glass from his stomach and in one fluid motion stabbed it into her throat. Blood poured out in a flood. Michal screamed. Sun gurgled and grappled at the shard as she collapsed to the floor. Draven roared and lunged for Michal. I was right behind him, driving the pole through his back.

He let out a loud scream and hunched forward, gripping the pole as it pierced through to the other side of his body. I jammed it further into his back and released a growl of my own. He yanked the pole clean from his body and threw it aside. In the next moment, he was tearing at my torso in a frenzy.

The room sweltered. He turned into a killing machine. I caught the madness reflecting in his eyes and knew we were goners. My body burned as he hissed and slashed at me, shredding my arms. My insides were spilling freely from my gashed body as I tried to grab his heart. But as soon as I lunged my fist into his chest, he gripped my arm and snapped it. *Crunch.* My bones shattered and he held me fast and poised his other clawed hand above my heart. My legs almost buckled as he twisted my broken arm.

"It's too bad that I never got to know you, doc," Draven laughed. "I guess it was all just meant to go to shit."

Avila's face flashed behind my eyes. *Could I leave her behind to face this world alone? Did I have a choice?* Choice felt like the sinkhole of hopelessness that was about to become my chest. He snarled and started to move, and I braced myself for impact when he jerked, a sudden intake of air gushing from his mouth. His eyes widened and blood bubbled from his lips, dribbling down his chin as a shard of glass appeared in his throat.

Huh?

Sun came into view behind Draven. She was a ghoulish platinum demon as she twisted the glass deeper into his flesh. His fingers began to slip from my arm, enabling me to yank myself free as he spluttered and turned toward Sun. He roared and went to fling himself at her but Lena's Amazon-like figure appeared out of nowhere as she planted a roundhouse kick to the side of his head. It was enough to throw him off balance. He staggered, giving me the opportunity to follow up with a few sharp jabs to his gut with my good hand.

His blood drenched his chest as he stumbled backward. Lena and Jamie grabbed a sheet of the plastic wall and folded it around him. He made an unearthly screech and thrashed around before Lena booted his ankles hard and he fell to the ground in a tangle of plastic.

I launched myself on top of his squirming figure, holding him fast and gesturing at the plastic walls. "More! Hurry!"

They ripped plastic sheeting from the walls to secure the super vampire whose struggles lessened as we rolled him within resilient layers of suffocating fabric until he was finally restrained and out cold.

The fight was over, and we had survived. I took gulps of air and looked down at his wrapped body, feeling my own body begin to repair the injuries suffered by the monstrous creature I had created. Illness settled in my stomach as my thoughts collected over what I had just done. It was Lena's thick Latino accent that pulled me back to the present.

"What in the hell is that thing?"

I shrugged. "Draven Sanguisa. Worse than any horror movie."

"Ha. You created the first ever Sanguisa?"

"Seems to be the case."

She glanced around the tattered lab. Equipment, glass, and blood now replaced the working space we had created. "So, what's the next move?"

"Chains, and lots of them." I gestured at the Sanguisa. "This won't keep him down for long. He will revive and tear through this plastic within a few hours at most. We need to secure him properly so that I can figure out what to do with him."

She nodded. "I know where a bunch of them are stored down in the rail tunnels."

"Take Jamie and Sun and get them. I'll stay here with Michal; and Lena, the next time I tell you not to open a door, please listen. You could've got yourself killed."

She smirked as she started to back away. "So, could've you, *master*."

17

ILLUSIONARY PROMISES

*N*umbness born of calamity was a footslog pounding against the sidewalk. My head hurt as much as my heart as I stalked the District V streets while the Sanguisa vampire slumbered deep in the subway chutes beneath the city. *Abomination.* Lengths of plastic sheeting choked the air from his body along with the steel chains that wrapped and anchored him to the putrid underground walls. The beast was secure but I couldn't say the same about my current state of mind. Internal warfare trapped me in no-man's-land as I headed to nowhere in particular.

What an idiot. I pushed my hands deep in my pockets and buried my chin in my jacket collar, barely hearing the rain slamming against the dome above as I contemplated how far my desperation to hold onto my daughter boarded on stupidity. Michal had been right when he argued that the viral strain wasn't ready for transfer. Not only had I failed in my attempt to produce a cure before the ceremony, but I had made things a whole lot worse by creating a hellion vampire. Charity was nowhere in sight as I forged ahead, the pressure in my chest radiating like hot stones. I needed time to think my way out of this disaster.

As it was, time was impartial. It was there, lingering like an eternal emptiness. I couldn't turn back the clock to retrieve the last few hours as much as I couldn't alter the days between now and the Claiming Ceremony. Time was a double-edged sword that swallowed my hopes to revive humanity and would devour Avila's.

My girl would be lost to me.

I walked like a madman through the dark streets while the rest of the city remained desolate during the final hours before dawn. I had avoided returning home in District V after leaving the subway. Home felt like a farce that would provide little comfort given the circumstances. I was starkly aware that my real home was as unreachable as hamburgers and sunlight. *Home was wherever Scarla was*. It was her precious soul behind the amber eyes I had once known, and it was everything I had lost to immortality. I halted to press my head on a light pole. The cold steel was oddly pleasant against my forehead as I studied my boots. The light overhead flickered.

Keep your shit together, Jett.

Anxiety was the enemy that would bring me down

faster than any vampire. Only the strong and durable could survive in the new world. I may have royally screwed up, but my kid still needed me around even if I couldn't return her to humanity. I had to keep my big boy pants intact and figure out what to do about the monster vamp before his existence revealed our deception. Sun was right when she mentioned that the discovery-penalty would mean our death.

A series of distant hollering broke through my sordid self-indulgence. I looked up, realizing that I had wandered far beyond the Crypt grounds to venture off the usual city grid, ending up in the section of Norbury city formerly known as public squalor.

The precarious light pole supporting me intersected two dark alleys. I stood amid rundown buildings covered in faded graffiti, decades-long grime and creeping vines, and the sidewalk that stretched along the narrow laneways was filthier than any pavement on the other side of the great wall. It was evident that Marius' refurbishing plans for District V hadn't extended this far in the dome city. I frowned and pushed off the lamp post, scanning the slums and spotting a steel boom gate about midway along the alley. Several unambiguous "No Trespassing" signs plastered the gate.

Interesting.

My curiosity was piqued enough to investigate. If the current post-apocalyptic experience had taught me anything, it was that nothing was off-limits in the new world. Blame it on an acute version of cause and effect.

Nowadays, we all knew that certainty had always been an illusion. Still, I kept to the shadows as I prowled the alleyway, gathering momentum as I approached the boom gates before taking the steel structure in one fluid leap. I leaned back on my haunches when I hit the road on the far side of the gate, and my senses were on high alert as I tuned into my surroundings. A whiff of fertilizer strayed from the rear of the deteriorated apartment buildings at the bottom of the alley. I studied the perimeter of the eastern side of the dome city beyond the buildings. I had reached the dome city boundary where the pliable dome material was tethered to the earth with polypropylene woven tubing and layers of barbed wire. The dome wall itself glowed like the moon.

What must this be in the still of a Bloodfaye night?

Voices and laughter mingled with the background sound of rumbling machinery. Something more than my inner torment was rattling the still of the night. I set off again, keeping light-footed and closing in on the foul scent of horse manure and moonshine shenanigans. When I reached the end of the alley, I slowed my pace and slinked into the doorway cranny of an abandoned building to watch the showstopper. It was delivered via the spectacle of a field of crops droning with farming machinery and dozens of people working amid rows of corn, wheat, and other germinating delights beyond the dome wall.

A few floodlights offered synthetic daylight as I gauged the action beyond the parted meshed gates of the dome wall. I could just discern the massive series of barbed fences bordering the other side of the field while Leavings and vampires alike buzzed around the open field performing various tasks such as operating farm machinery, spraying the crops and bunching produce into containers. The entire area was heavily patrolled by a small legion of Mysticus guards and I could see evidence of progressive construction taking place in the surrounds.

I recalled when Avila had mentioned Marius' intentions to implement an agriculture program to provide fresh produce for our Leavings. It seems that I had stumbled upon its whereabouts. Admittedly, I was surprised to see how established this little set-up was. Production was in full swing and thriving but that wasn't what was dominating my interest at this moment. It was the highly secured compound sanctioned just beyond the gate threshold that seized all my attention. My gaze settled on the black bold letter "X" marking the high, iron-meshed wall of the compound. A chill went through me.

District X.

It had to be the place where Marius kept the stolen Leaving children. Devious sprite. It was plain to see that Marius had ensured an impenetrable form of security in and around the fields, and more so for his covert hidden district. The place was a heavy-duty fortress crawling with whip carrying guards, solid fencing and impassable walls. I even noticed the beginnings of a surveillance system being installed atop the walls. The strategically mounted cameras gave it away.

"Oi! You there!"

"We've got a violation!"

My observations were abruptly interrupted. I looked at the group of guards who were patrolling the dome gates as a few of them stopped to sneer at me. *Shit.* I'd been so preoccupied with the scene that I had failed to notice them noticing me. I exhaled slowly as their pallid faces scrutinized the shadows and appeared as brutish as their leather-clad boots stalking the terrain. I began to retreat as about five of the guards started for me.

"Don't move, asshole!"

Yeah, right. I wasn't about to give myself up to this foul-toothed lot. The guards growled and increased their pace to a sprint as I spun around and hot-footed it back down the alley.

"That was an order to stop, vampire!"

"Get him!"

I could sense the blood-hungry adrenaline stoking their energy as their boots stampeded behind me, but I had a good ten-meter head start on my side as I raced down the dark road with my pulse blazing along with my feet. I took the boom gate in a matter of seconds before ducking off the alleyway to cut through the narrow passages offered by the derelict apartment buildings studding the quarter. It wasn't long before the sound of their chase faded behind and I had appeared to have lost them. I emerged from the rundown section of the city minutes later to stroll the rest of the way back to my brownstone complete with yet another compelling revelation.

The new world had again made good on uncertainty and illusionary promises, but I had my own demons to deal with.

18

BACKFIRE BLUES

*P*lum and pineapple filtered into my senses as I gazed absently at the bouquet of frangipanis taking center stage on Marius' polished dining table. Or was it candy and spices that allured my transitory attention? The flowers had a unique scent and I almost had an urge to squish one of the fleshy white petals while Avila and I waited for *lord arrogance* to join us. We were here to discuss all things Claiming Ceremony and the like. The event would be held in three nights time and I guessed it was important to some. However, my mind was far from bogus vampire ceremonies; I had a bad case of backfire blues and I still needed to figure out what to do with the newborn Sanguisa.

Alive or dead?

That was the choice facing me. We could either keep working what remained of the cultivated bloods in an attempt to reach a viable solution or cut our losses and kill the kid before he caused more trouble than he was worth. Considering how difficult it was to contain his super-charged kindred strength, the latter option was looking rather appealing right now.

Avila's gentle laugh interrupted my thoughts. She sat across the table from me, reaching to fill a silver goblet with the blood offered in the large crystal decanter between us.

"Remember the scene when Louis discovered Lestat alone in that old house near the end of *Interview with a Vampire*?"

I frowned. "Vaguely."

"He was sitting in the dark, feeding on rats and looking as if he had died a thousand deaths and faced the devil more times than an ogre."

"So?"

"So, you look like Lestat and I'm wondering if it has something to do with why you didn't come home last night."

Hmm .... the things we say without uttering a word.

I forced a smile. "Keep wondering, kiddo. This isn't the time or place."

"It never is...."

She looked beyond me, grinning as Marius entered the room. My spine instantly chilled as I half turned to see him striding across the saloon in flowing black satin and shiny red boots. His expression was just shy of elation as he focused on Avila. I swallowed a groan when he plucked a frangipani and presented it to my daughter.

"For you, my beautiful queen."

She took the stem, bringing the flower to her nose and smiling coyly. "Why, thank you, sir."

I wanted to puke as he stroked her hair and fawned all over her. His voice shucked every nerve.

"In Hindu mythology, the frangipani flower is a symbol of devotion between two people, and Buddhism symbolized them as new life and a renewal of energy."

He paused and cupped a palm beneath her chin. "I couldn't think of a better flower to be present here, with you, today."

"And with you, my love," she murmured as he kissed her.

I cleared my throat and cramped my lips shut when Marius regarded me. He reminded me of a superficial smoothie, and he reeked like insincere slick. *Why could Avila not see this?*

"Jett! How rude of me." His face split with his grin and he reached for another flower, thrusting it toward me in a most elegant fashion. "To the new life!"

Give me a break.

"Yeah, thanks." I took the flower and promptly dropped it on the table next to my goblet. Honestly, I had no patience to endure this quaint meet-and-greet. More so with a new breed of souped-up vampire on my hands. I sighed inwardly. There was no choice but to suck it up for Avila. I preoccupied myself by gulping down my civilized blood-drink as Marius sat next to Avila and began to engage his audience.

"I assume Avila has told you about our plans to move the Claiming Ceremony forward?"

"Yep."

He reached for her hand and gave her his version of a smile that meant something special. My stomach constricted. I went for the crystal decanter to refill my goblet. I needed something to distract me from the strain his voice caused as he continued to speak.

"We may be eternal beings, though time is still precious. Why wait?"

"Indeed. What of me here then?" I laughed. "You want me to arrange a bachelor party? Perhaps take care of the hire cars or look for a wedding planner?"

I ignored Avila's scowl as Marius narrowed his black beacons on me before taking a long sip of blood. He licked his lips and gave a grisly smile.

"If only we could still enjoy wine and its heady effects. We may have cause to loosen you up a little, old man."

"Hey, I'm loose." I held his stare. "But I'd feel a whole lot more liberated if you would return the Leaving children to their parents and let them be."

"Impossible."

"Why? What's so impossible about letting human families be together?"

"Dad—" Avila's voice was cold enough to numb me as I realized that she was on board with this disturbing scheme. The cords in Marius' throat amplified.

"Because those children are pertinent to the future of

the clan and that is all I am willing to disclose on the matter at this time."

"You don't trust me?"

"Trust is overrated in the new world. You said so yourself."

"True. Though I assumed that we might be moving into curry favor territory, considering that I am here today."

He laughed. "Only time will reveal the extent of your loyalty, Jett. Until then, my interest in the Leaving children are none of your concern other than the fact that your work is vital to their destiny and that of the clan."

I said nothing and leaned back in my chair, realizing that it was as I had suspected – Marius planned on raising the children to one day transform them into the invincible vampires offered by the elusive AB Positive blood. Without the love of their parents chiseled in their psyche, they would make soulless killing machines.

Marius leaned on the table and pressed his fingertips together. "One of us has to think ahead if the Mysticus is to prevail as the dominant kindred bloodline. This is just the beginning of the new world. We don't know how many other clans exist or what's to come."

I immediately thought about Draven. His strength *was* incredible and who knew what other powers he possessed. It was enough to strike fear into my heart. What was I thinking? To allow such a dangerous creature to remain is a risk I wasn't willing to take. I shuddered at the thought of what might happen if he was to escape his subway confinement. Marius was right, the children were none of my concern when there were more pressing and dire matters to deal with, at least for the moment.

The atmosphere was tense. Marius watched me stiffly. I knew that he meant to pluck the thoughts from my mind as I treated him to a triumphant glare. Avila gave an exaggerated sigh. She shook her head and forced a half-hearted laugh.

"Seriously, we didn't come together today to discuss Mysticus politics; rather to talk about a joyous event which will further solidify and bring a sense of community to the clan." Her features thawed about an inch of my resolve. "Now, we just wanted you to be prepared, Dad."

"For—?"

"For the offering ritual prior to the Claiming hour which will take place at exactly midnight."

"Offering ritual?" I flinched. "As in a sacrifice?"

"A Leaving sacrifice, yes."

"What for?"

Avila's expression darkened. I knew these moments were critical to her. "A ritual is about moving out of our ordinary space and crossing the threshold into something more profound. It makes sense that we perform a sacrificial ritual to demonstrate to all Mysticus members that our union is essential to the evolution of the clan." She paused to ensure that her words caught my attention. "Spilling the blood of an innocent will assure purification to the Claiming."

"Where did you pull that garbage from?" I had to look away from her. "Lestat's personal diary?"

She snorted and went to reply when Marius intervened.

"The life of a Leaving symbolizes longevity and opulence and is to become a tradition in all future Mysticus Claiming Ceremonies." He grinned. "We do have to honor the primitive instincts driving us all from time to time and pay homage to the vampire gods. Livvy and I shall feast on the blood of a Leaving woman prior to the Claiming."

And the shit just keeps piling and piling.

I sunk my talons into my palms and stood up. I had enough of this bullshit. It was all I could do to survive the overwhelming urge to tear this Crypt joint to pieces along with its egotistical overlord.

"Vampires don't have gods." I looked at my daughter who was fast becoming a stranger to me. "Vampires have horrendous, crud-like demon deities who eat gods for breakfast and scour the sludge beneath the city. Would you care to meet one?"

"Ha. Good one, Dad!"

Avila glanced at Marius and they both laughed. That was when I turned away from them, striding from the room with a belly full of curdled blood and a major decision on my shoulders. Avila called out just as I reached the door.

"Dad, are you okay?"

I paused, etching a notch into the timber threshold

with my nails as I looked back at them. Avila's stare appeared as vivid as the wallpaper on my old cell, but I barely saw her pale face examining me. Backfire blues pushed my mind into a thousand pieces as I nodded.

"I'm fine."

Just fine.

19

SHIT-FED MONGRELS

The energy in District V was anything other than ordinary and I hated it as much as the walking dead parading along the sidewalk. Fraudulent grins arranged on fake plastic faces made my head spin. My fingers strained over the golf cart steering wheel as I made my way back home. As if it wasn't bad enough that my rejuvenating bones still ached from last night's unexpected fiasco, I was looking down the barrel of a hard choice, but the sickening sight of the festive ornaments made everything that much worse.

Ugh. Someone please shoot me right now.

But a bullet could not take away the vision disturbing me. It was difficult not to notice the silver and gold rattan balls that hung from trees and street posts amid strings of fairy lights and wrought iron vampire glyphs. Marius was fully embracing vampire folklore and traditions, bringing back ancient lore to instill a sense of ancestry and belonging to the clan. It was a smart move, but the entire concept made me feel as if caught in a bastardized version of a fictitious world that I couldn't escape.

As soon as I turned off the main thoroughfare and into the quieter parts of the city, my thoughts returned to the pressing matter at hand – killing Draven Sanguisa before he was discovered by the likes of Marius' crew. I wasn't fooling myself into believing that my background in hematology was enough to save me this time around, nor the fact that I fathered the soon-to-be Mysticus queen.

I had made Avila a promise to always protect her. Granted, she was in sync with her supernatural self and the lifestyle it offered, and she was free of the resentment and hatred responsible for the secret sector I had formed. *Life*. Who would have thought I'd ever be a dead man alive fighting against my own kind or having to decide what to do about a primitive breed of kindred I had created by accident.

I would have no doubts about Avila's ability to survive in the new world without me if it weren't that she was about to become queen and a prime target for power hungry vampires like Zaros. Marius was a calculating fiend at the best of times, but he was smart enough to implement a belief system that promoted a sense of self-control to the clan along with his other more unacceptable visions. It was Zaros and kindreds like him who made for unpredictable enemies.

I sucked in a breath when I copped an eyeful of the devil himself sprawled across the small patch of lawn that constituted my front yard. Zaros. *Terrific*. He appeared like a black leathered reptile lazing beneath the muted dome sun with his arms tucked beneath his head as he lay just shy of the set of stairs that led to my front door. He remained still as I stopped the cart and approached him.

"Zaros." His name bit my tongue.

"Hey doc!" He flashed a grin that reeked like sour lemons.

He stood up and began brushing imaginary grass from his leathers before he gestured toward the brownstone.

"Man, you've got some kind of cool crib going on here. I may have to rethink my own prehistoric flavored dwellings; become more domesticated like you."

"What do you want?"

"Always direct."

"Life's too short not to be."

"Always a comedy show too." He ran a bejeweled hand over his afro. "A shorter life-span can easily be arranged."

"Yeah, no shit." I was expecting Sun and Michal any minute. "Seriously, why the hell are you here, Zaros?"

"Hmm—do I detect a knot in your tightly woven white-boy knickers?" He laughed. "Is there someplace else you need to be other than in the moment with me?"

"Is that a trick question? Let's cut the bullshit; you're here to find out if I'm going to support you in your endeavors to overthrow Marius—" He went to say something but I kept talking. "Ah, yes, and not to forget the nice bonus threat hanging precariously over my head."

"I'd rather call it gentle persuasion."

"What planet are you on? You hit me sideways with threats to kill my daughter when she becomes queen and that's persuasion to you?"

Oddly enough, that sentence sounded rather normal.

"When you put it like that then I can see your point. I heard tell they pushed the Claiming Ceremony ahead."

"And?"

He made a sly gesture which resembled a shrug. "Come on, doc, for a smart guy you can be as dumb as a donkey on heat."

He paused and looked beyond me. My nostrils twitched as the distinct odor of blood fangsta blew my way. I ignored lofty emerald eyes and creature scarecrow as they sidled up next to Zaros.

He sneered. "Means you are going to have to let me know whose side you're on before your kid makes the choice for you."

The goon-vamps laughed, and white fire seared behind my eyes. I pushed it down with a sharp breath and stepped closer to him.

"Your shit-fed mongrels are stinking up my property."

Zaros said nothing but his eyes blazed while his mongrels hissed at me. I glanced at them before looking back at Zaros.

"Do I look like a shit-fed mongrel to you?"

He stiffened and clenched his fists. Sun and Michal

chose this time to appear in the golf cart steered toward the curb. Sun stopped in front of the brownstone and frowned at the scene on my front lawn.

I started to retreat from Zaros and his donkey crew.

"Time to leave, I have *invited* company to receive."

He glanced at Sun as she strutted toward us in her usual mini-skirt and knee-high get-up. The golden bracelets adorning her wrists shone like wine. Michal stayed put in the cart.

Her eyes narrowed as she gripped her hips. "What's going on?" She was all sass and femininity. She glanced between me and Zaros. *God help us*. The combo was alluring.

Zaros grinned at her. "We're all good, baby girl."

"We had better be."

He regarded her for a long moment before looking back at me with a grim expression. "Dumb as a donkey on heat."

The two goon vampires sneered at me as Zaros slinked closer to Sun. She held his gaze as he stroked the side of her jaw with the backs of his fingers. Her thumping heart drummed in my ear. I noticed her bottom lip tremble slightly. In the next moment, he was gone, leaving Sun as still as the dew at dawn.

"What was that all about?" She said.

She had secrets I would never know.

"Vampire power games are all the rage these days, didn't you know?"

She tossed her blond mane. "I wish I didn't know."

"Don't we all."

I gestured for Michal to get out of the cart. He was transfixed by something unfathomable. *Wait till he gets an earful of what's coming next.*

He nodded abruptly and made a move toward us. I glanced at Sun. "Things have changed. We have much to discuss."

"Okay."

I strode up the stairs thinking of sweet unspoken secrets and dewy dawns I'd never know again. I had failed in my quest to restore humanity. Let the world transform with the arrival of the future Blood Legend. I knew what I had to do.

20

BLACK TARGET DOWN

I gripped the machete handle and ignored the dank grit smothering me. The subway tunnel felt as if it was closing in on me. I paused as my eyes adjusted to the darkness broken sporadically by the flickering tube lights edging the ceiling. The faint sound of dripping water echoing along the shafts ignited my senses. I was moving with ghosts and striking irreversible deals with the devil as I moved in on Draven Sanguisa with the intent to kill.

Miscreant.

I felt lower than a slippery eel for all I had caused to befall the kid, but I couldn't immerse myself in the submerged guilt if I was going to make it through to the other side. Sun and Michal had agreed with my decision that he had to die. The alternative carried grim consequences both for our part in his creation, as well as for the clan – the deadly creature was an unpredictable liability we could ill afford to probe.

I opted to go it alone. This was my mess to clean up and there was no way in hell that I would allow Sun anywhere near the Sanguisa vampire even in my presence. I may be supernatural but I was no superman version of vampire. I had barely managed to survive my last encounter with the beast much less protect Sun. I was just glad that he would be somewhat debilitated from two days chained to the wall and sweating in a plastic cocoon.

Get in and get out. After a restless sleep, I had spent the day hamming out the oncoming scene in my head. The cold Japanese steel blade of the machete was sharp enough to slice through the plastic layers constraining the Sanguisa so that I could sever his head without having to break him out. I chose the method of execution for obvious reasons – efficient appeal. Anything to minimize the suffering for all involved. Draven might be a formidable miscreation on my part, but I didn't want to cause him any more pain than necessary.

Admittedly, that might be a tad ambitious on my part. I knew that the Sanguisa would kick my sorry ass all over Bloodfaye if given half the chance. Tonight, the machete was my Holy Grail. I would do what I had to do to snuff him so that I could determine my next moves. The Claiming Ceremony was looming the following night. When I took the final bend leading toward the subway lab, the madhouse flashbacks faded into obscurity as an acute rush of sensory overload hit my psyche. My hackles raised and I slinked back against the wall, peering ahead to where the tunnel narrowed. The lab door was slightly ajar. *What the hell?* The lab should have been secured but the florescent lights blinking through the small gap of the unlatched door proved otherwise. Chills hit me as the smell of unprocessed blood blew downwind. It was tangy, sweet, and crisp; and it was the classic hallmarks of the newly spilled. I tuned into what may lie beyond the door.

Death sounded like silence. I swallowed the moment and steeled myself before lunging for the door. My steps were fluid and purposeful, the machete blade glinting as I stole along the chipped tiled walls until I stopped short of the lab door. I dared not breathe as my eyes darted to the ground to see the blood seeping from beneath the door, slowly filling the cracks in the concrete. The blood flamed glossy, gaudy, and tasteless as it collected dirty steel dust particles. My whole body trembled as I eased the door open and beheld a dazzling pulp. The putrid lab walls were now exposed as the blackened husks they were prior to installing the makeshift inoculation chamber, and offset the chaos of scientific equipment and gadgets, stools and glass shards reminiscent of the Sanguisa creation. Everything was the same but for the Sanguisa himself where we had left him chained to the wall in a deep roll of plastic which now was strewn in pieces on the ground, the thick chains cast aside. Now fragmented parts of human anatomy lay in a sea of blood.

The Sanguisa was gone. I copped an eyeful of the vertebrae, stripped of muscle, and the tenderly deep pink sequence of a spine laying across the bench amid expelled innards. Blood infused red meat, spilled gore and discharged coils of rust-colored intestines. The ghastly image flashed to the beat of the flickering lights. *Blink.* A decapitated head, unrecognizable. *Blink.* One hollow eye socket, the other gleaming at me. *Blink.* A mouth cracked wide open, frozen in an endless scream.

Blink.

I scanned the room with my eyes but detected no movement. Whoever was responsible for this carnage appeared to be gone. My fingers tightened over the machete handle as I slowly crossed the threshold, pausing to choke back the urge to gag when the bitter odor of guts overcame me. My ears pricked at the sound of a raspy breath and my gaze darted toward the slight sound emanating from where the cot stood broken along the far wall, thin mattress askew. I gasped as I recognized Lena's peroxide-stained hair showing from beneath the mattress.

"Lena."

Her name clung to my lips as I rushed toward her, and the sound of the blinking lights clicked against my nerves as I threw the mattress aside and kneeled on the floor next to her. I flinched and almost recoiled when I saw that half of her face was a raw lump of meat without a trace of skin, one eye like liquefied roe. The flesh on her throat was exposed with bits of flesh pulled off, a splintered hole revealing her larynx as a mess of cartilage and veins. *No!* I opened my mouth to speak but I couldn't find words as the machete slipped from my hand and I reached to cradle her head, trembling when a piece of her scalp, stained with matted scarlet hair, flapped back. The rest of her body was perfect as she lay corpselike in a pool of her lukewarm blood. *Dead.* I had been too late.

"What have you done?" I said the words aloud but I wasn't sure if they were meant for me or her. Why was she even in here? "I—I'm so sorry, Lena."

I was unable to look away from her as I realized that the dismembered body was Jamie, Lena's friend and Shadow Guardian wingman. I exhaled as Lena's blood soaked through my pants while a mixture of fear, grief and repugnance took hold. Only a starved and primitively mutated vampire could do something this heinous to his prey. The Sanguisa. But where was he now?

So much for getting in and getting out. I had a dead friend and a psychotic new breed of vampire on the run who I needed to find and deal with before someone else did; preferably before a repeat of this scene had time to unfold. I went to stand up but froze when a barbed voice came from above.

"Sorry won't undo all that *you've* done, doctor crazy."

My blood went colder than usual as I looked up and scanned the ceiling, spying the Sanguisa' crabbed figure suspended and clinging to the notches above me. His neck twisted and appeared disjointed as his beaded eyes hunted me down and flashed crimson. Blood-tinged saliva foamed at his lips with his hiss.

Chingar.

The backsliding creature was here all along. He could burn with the old railway coal for all I cared. I met his stare and barely heard myself speak over the body rush. "Nice party trick."

"Thanks to you. Did you come here to kill me?"

I went to say something, but I blanked out as the sound of his laughter burrowed deep in my mind before he released himself from the notches to land gracefully on his feet near me. He snarled and I sprang for the machete that still lay on the ground next to Lena. I grabbed the handle but it was knocked back onto the concrete as the base of my skull caved in like a whoopie cushion.

Crack!

I fell forward over Lena and saw stars. Sanguisa launched himself on top of me and broke into a frenzied attack, tearing up my back with scalpel-like talons while he roared as my face jammed into Lena's open throat.

Boom!

The air was gone from my lungs as sanguine fluid, mashed up arteries and the like filled every crevice of my face. It was warm and gooey, but that was the last thing on my mind as the beast saddled me, screeching as he forced his fist through the flesh on my back. I gave a demented groan as he withdrew his palm, taking fistfuls of my bits with him. He beat me senseless as I braced myself against the relentless onslaught. My body became like iron as I homed in on my supernatural strength, summoning the violence in me.

Black.

I felt voltaic and raw as the Sanguisa screeched and tore at my shirt, peeling the skin on my back as I pulled my face from Lena's throat and growled loudly, with saliva trailing down my chin. I blacked out fear and fury as I embodied the knave, the *enfant terrible*. I screamed and moved like a bullet, repeatedly striking my elbows into the Sanguisa's chest before flinging him off me. I grabbed the machete and leapt to my feet, spinning to face him with the blade outstretched as he charged at me.

Black breath.

The steel went into his gut as if slicing through butter. His face contorted as he halted. A static moment and resounding heartbeat. *Ba-boom. Ba-boom.* My brain fizzled as he wrapped his claw-like fingers along the steel, grinning.

"You want me dead but I'm a nightmare you can't kill."

"We'll see about that."

Those were tough words, but they were meaningless and we both knew it despite following up with a hiss as I gripped down on the machete handle. Just as I was about to twist the blade further into him, he slid his torso along the edge of the knife. My boots skidded on gore as I started to back away. He menaced me with a deep growl before thrusting himself forward. The next thing I knew was the pressure of his fingers hooking into my flesh and the sensation of his fangs sinking into my throat, squeezing the blood from my veins. I tried to move but my legs started to give way as my vision tunneled and dizziness took hold. *Freefall.* My blood whooshed right out of me and my thoughts evaporated along with my energy; I was putty in his hands until I was gaunt and bloodless.

His ugly face was a convoluted picture as he withdrew and laughed. The last thing I heard was the snap of my neck before the room stopped blinking.

Black target down.

21

THE OTHER SIDE

$\mathcal{V}$iolet flames rose in the distance over a body of water that resembled a transparent blue gemstone. I stood overlooking a pristine beach, gazing ahead and feeling weightless. The smell of sea salt purified me. I lifted my chin toward the sky, inviting a renewed feeling of vitality as it surged through me. It was different here. Nothing made sense but everything was perfect. I had a strange sense that I could embody any version of myself that I wanted. It was an inner knowing that was as deep as marrow and forgotten in the next moment as I focused on the simulated stratosphere burning an amethyst wildfire. A sense of peace permeated.

Where am I?

"You're on the other side, Jett."

"Huh?"

A bearded man appeared beside me to pluck the

thoughts from my mind. He radiated a warm smile and wore a string of scarlet beads over a loose white shirt. His long brown hair fell in waves and glowed with the magenta aura. He looked familiar.

"Jesus?"

"Hell, no. My hair is so much better than Jesus." He laughed and offered me his palm. "The name's Alvin."

"Alvin ….?" My voice trailed as we shook hands and the penny dropped. "You're the all-powerful and elusive witch dude of Sweetwater Valley."

"Not so elusive now, huh?"

Guess not. Though I had no idea why he was the one to greet me here, the place he dubbed as the other side.

"We are strangers, you and me."

All I knew of Alvin was that Clio had sought his help when we needed to create a spell to cloak Shana, the half-bred wolf-baby. Marius had wanted her dead, but I had learned that her survival was vital as she carried the origins of the Blood Legend genes that needed to mature through the generations to produce "the one". Alvin began to loop his beads around nimble fingers. His silvery whiskers twitched.

"I wouldn't be taking time out from Eden's garden for a stranger, and F-Y-I: call me a sorcerer, an alchemist or even a conjurer if you must – but don't call me a 'witch dude'."

Okay. Witch dude has a sore spot.

"It's more of a preference." He shrugged. "The years have made me somewhat particular."

"I get it." A sense of mild frustration shimmered as I realized each of my thoughts were for the taking. I flicked my chin toward the dynamic horizon. "The years have made me dead for good this time, I can feel it."

"Perhaps you're right. Your body *is* currently a bloodless bag of bones lying in human guts and numbles on a filthy subway floor in the city of vampires."

"Thanks for the explicit recount."

"You're quite welcome."

"Are you dead, too?"

He shook his head. "Witch dude, remember?"

A bizarre feeling of euphoria flooded me as I watched him twist the beads around his fingers before releasing them to then repeat the process in the opposite direction. If this was death, it wasn't so bad. At least the pain was gone. "So, let me guess, you are here to escort me to the Pearly Gates or something?"

He laughed. "Nah. Clio sent me. I came here to remind you."

"Of what?"

He gestured toward the sea that moved to an ethereal tide. "In about thirty seconds, the greatest love of your life will appear to escort you to the hereafter if you so wish to join her."

"I have a choice, then?"

"We always have a choice."

A series of fragmented memories flashed into form as I peered toward where the grainy sand met the sea below a display of lights more vivid than the Aurora Borealis. I felt as if all my pieces were finally merging into completeness. As if there was nothing more left to do.

"Ah, but there is much more left for you, Jett," Alvin said. "That's why I'm here remember?"

I barely heard him as Scarla arose from nowhere to appear on the shoreline some few hundred meters from us. She wore a sheer white dress and rows of auric bracelets adorned her wrists. I couldn't hear her, but she laughed as she followed prints along the sand and toyed with the waves lapping at her feet. Her wild hair caught the breeze and cascaded like golden silk down her back. *Angel.* My soul lady was here for me.

"I'm going home."

"It's an option."

I kept my eyes trained on Scarla. She was the woman who had arrived in my life years before the apocalypse to steal my heart only to be brutally taken from me at the hands of a ginger bearded hawker. She was all that I had wanted in this world and I had been lost without her. I felt the familiar yearning swell in my soul when she turned to smile at me.

"It's an option that I want."

"Understood." Alvin thumbed his wiry whiskers. "I too have loved, but never have I been so fortunate to have shared such a deep connection with another the likes of which the two of you share."

I didn't look at him. "She showed me what it meant to really open my heart to pure love. She showed me who I was and the type of person I could be."

"The type of person who wouldn't turn his back on his true purpose to assist those in need—."

"No one needs me now. Avila is giving herself to Marius. She will never be the girl I raised after this. He will take every ounce of what's left of her humanity and empathy before long."

"You're wrong, Jett. The world has transformed with dark energy and now, more than ever, it needs those among the living who are pure in heart to keep the balance until the true Blood Legend arrives. You are still needed to play out your role in Avila's life, as well as for the greater good of humanity. Your daughter has a special secret."

"Riddles. You've been talking to Melissa."

"There are no riddles in truth. Melissa's messages were your cues to decipher and follow at will. Even in our higher-state positions, we are not permitted to hand you the information on a silver platter—. It must be given enough to help guide or warn. It's not how it works on this side."

"Like I said, riddles."

I was distracted when I noticed Scarla pushing strands of hair from her face and her dress clinging to her thighs as she started walking toward us. *Home*. Her energy expanded like an unfurling petal to connect with mine. I smiled. She felt more ardent and beautiful than any star in the universe and my heart almost burst with the love encapsulating me. I wanted to run to her, but Alvin's words bound me to the spot.

"Your presence on earth is vital to the unfolding Blood Legend legacy. The girl of tomorrow with the unique bloodline will need you to help her embrace and understand her greater purpose someday." He gestured toward Scarla. "You know that love is a powerful force. You can feel that truth deep in your soul, yes?"

"Yes."

"Then you will know that the love between you and your soul lady is a rare gift strong enough to last and flourish over time and space if you honor it. She will always be with you, Jett."

Illusions?

"No illusions, only truth. Allow the truth of what I say to seep into and affect you. *Then you will know, my friend.*"

He didn't say those last words out loud, but I heard them regardless. I frowned and looked at Scarla who was approaching ever closer. To reclaim and rebuild a home from yesterday. A sense of urgency formed at my spine and split my thoughts. I *needed* to be with her yet something powerful pulled me in the opposite direction as the desperate sound of my name called from another dimension.

"Jett! Stay with me, Jett, please!" A heart-wrenching sob stifled along an invisible barrier separating realms. I recognized the voice as Sun's. "Jett, don't go. You can't just leave me here in this world without you!"

"Sun?"

Alvin gave me a critical look. "It's time to choose now."

"Yes."

My pulse quickened as I beheld the violet lights blazing across the sky, deadlocking me with an impossible choice that I couldn't escape. *Scarla.* She halted midway between the space separating us. Her teeth grazed her bottom lip as amber eyes caught me in an intimate flame made for two. Her voice penetrated my soul like a gentle caress:

"I know it burns and that the distance between us hurts, my love. I miss you so much and love you even more. But your home is always inside of you, Jett. You take our love with you in your heart and soul. Our work together transcends through time and space, I'll always be here, with you."

"I love you."

"I know." Her smile was honey as she waved, and my insides screamed when her final words fell into my mind. *"Waiting for the day—."*

"Waiting for the day."

Her image began to fade and the constant dull ache her death had left behind returned as she disappeared from view. My neck started to throb like crazy and my mind whirled. I gulped air and spluttered as Sun's face doubled in my vision and the subway lab flashed into my awareness.

Blink.

"Jett! Thank God!"

Blink.

Sun threw her arms around me and I flinched. My throat felt like sandpaper as she thrust her wrist at my lips, offering me her vein. "Drink."

Blink.

It was all I could do as remnants of the other side and the feeling of Scarla's energy faded into reality and blood-soaked carnage, and the knowledge that a fierce vampire called Sanguisa was now on the run.

"Welcome back. I'd thought you were gone for good," Sun said.

I almost was.

"It is a curious thing, the death of a loved one. We all know that our time in this world is limited, and that eventually all of us will end up underneath some sheet, never to wake up. And yet it is always a surprise when it happens to someone we know. It is like walking up the stairs to your bedroom in the dark, and thinking there is one more stair than there is. Your foot falls down, through the air, and there is a sickly moment of dark surprise as you try and readjust the way you thought of things."

— Lemony Snicket

THE CLAIMING

*S*un pushed a thin, light rod into my palm as we stood on the sidelines of the Crypt courtyard. Pre-Claiming ceremony celebrations were in full swing. My feet felt tethered to the earth as I dealt with the hyped crowd and music. I strained to hear.

"It was my grandmother's. I think you could use it more than me tonight," Sun said.

I looked at the slim stave. It was about the length of my palm and crafted from rose quartz with a silver finish at the tip. A small chunk of raw crystal was mounted in delicate silver claws at its head.

"So—I'm going to use this to slay the enemy?"

"If only it were that easy." She folded my fingers over the stave and gave a half laugh. "It's a crystal energy wand. It's not much, but it might help you from going over the edge tonight. My grandmother believed in it."

"Do you?"

Her eyes glazed. "I believed in her."

I slipped the wand into my pocket. I didn't have the heart to tell Sun that it was a hopeless cause. A crystal energy wand was cute, but it wasn't going to fix the fact that I had royally screwed up. Lena was dead and there was a ruthless Sanguisa in the wild who ate vampires for breakfast.

Archfiend.

The definition of diabolically evil had gone lower than the empty pit in my stomach. I shuddered and tuned out to my surroundings. The feeling of Sanguisa fangs sinking into me and siphoning my blood was fresh enough to shoot daggers in my nerves. He had been long gone by the time I returned from the other side. The Sanguisa's whereabouts was a mystery but that wasn't the only sickening part. It was his calculated savagery that made me nauseous. I knew that I couldn't bring him down alone. Of course, that cheery prospect would have to get in line as I faced an even brighter failure – Avila's doomsday ceremony.

I flinched when Sun reached for my shoulder. The impetuous sound of drums beating against the rowdy crowd blasted me back to reality. It was quite unfortunate.

"Jett?"

"Huh?"

"The offering." She gestured toward the stage. "I think it's about to begin."

It took all I had to keep it together as I focused on the hedonistic vampires clustering on the courtyard lawn.

Fanged men and women frisked to the hypnotic beat of the drums. Hisses, mixed with the lingering scent of blood and rose oil, saturated the air with seduction. An array of retro-style threads created a colorful patchwork audience that shone as bright as their hair beneath the glowing lanterns and strings of fairy lights dangling above the courtyard.

I looked up. The dome illuminated white silver, reflecting the rising full moon denied to us on this side of the egg. I was part of an entombed burlesque saga. I was caught in a twisted version of *Queen of the Damned,* only my daughter was the one about to pledge to hell and damnation. This was life imitating art at its most sardonic. I tore my eyes from the mob and saw the stage. Things did not improve.

Smoking hot succubus.

The stage was scorched with fire and women. Dark goddesses danced among the flames offered by burning candelabras pulsing to the hypnotic beats produced by the drummers behind them. Their barely clad bodies gleamed like smooth velvet masked with smoke, rose embellished wrought iron and the dainty silver chains on their hips. They were intoxicating but their beauty was lost on me, despite the lashings of sheer fabric accentuating their femininity. The entire affair was flagrantly romantic, somewhat perverted, and loathsome. No wonder my head ached.

Sun's voice was the comfort I couldn't quite grasp. "What a circus."

I stared ahead. "The circus I couldn't prevent."

Her skin felt cold yet soft when she clasped my chin to command my attention. "Maybe you weren't meant to prevent it, Jett. Maybe you were just supposed to be there for the people you care about as we all adjust to the new life."

Her gilded eyes found my soul and I started to quiver on the inside. "Maybe you just had to find a way to accept what you cannot change."

Ouch.

She had a way of stirring deep truths but her honest perspective could not remove my mistakes nor could it fix them. The Sanguisa flashed through my mind. Being there for the people I loved did not equate to unleashing a demonic force on them. I was about to voice as much when the drumming stopped and the crowd hushed. The sound of Marius' silvery tones congealed in my veins.

"Welcome!"

He walked on stage sheathed in shiny white leather and chunky black boots. His jet hair slicked to his scalp like licorice. The vamp partygoers clapped as the on-stage dancers flocked to him, and he patted their behinds one by one as they each gave him a kiss before vanishing from the stage. His dark gaze lingered over the last sultry blond as she sashayed from view before he cast a smile at the audience.

"Mysticus vampires, greetings and welcome to the clan's first ever Claiming Ceremony!"

A round of applause accompanied a few melodious responses.

"Marius, I love you!"

"Hell yeah, baby!"

Laughter.

"Bring on the ascension!"

There was a loud ovation.

"Where's our vampire queen?"

Marius laughed. "Oh, I see you lot are as eager to get on with the ceremony as much as me. How very exciting! All of you are about to witness a crucial event that will be recorded along the vampiric timeline as an evolution of vampirism. You've got to realize that there is great power in love and connection, and that, my friends, will lead us toward ascension. Who knows what treasures lie in our future! It's a good time to be undead!"

Another generous helping of applause and exuberant praise ensued. I tuned out to the noise of the crowd and focused on the man who aroused hatred in me like no other. The blame consumed me. He was responsible for forcing my family into an irreversible life of death and now he was about to take the final victory – everything good still left in my girl. I didn't know how being around for that was going to do me or her any good.

I fingered Sun's wand in my pocket as Marius greedily lapped up the adoration lavished upon him by his minions, laughing and working the crowd like a pro. The man was in his element. It was clear that he was born to be a vampire overlord. I felt dirty on the inside just watching him. I knew that his devotion to darkness and his conniving manner would always be our greatest discrepancy. He laughed some more and hushed the mob.

"Ladies and gentlemen, shall we have ourselves a vampire Claiming Ceremony?"

"Yes!"

"Are you ready to greet your new queen?"

"Yeah!"

"Bring her out!"

Marius poked a finger at the audience.

"Who's as love-hungry as me?"

His final words sent the crowd wild. A sea of arms rose and shook as the horde shouted their approval. The energy peaked when one woman leapt onto the stage, skillfully landing next to Marius. She ripped open her flimsy silver tank top revealing salmon nipples on opaline skin that saluted the whistling audience. Her fangs glinted through the yellow hair clinging to her face as she flung herself at him.

"Take *me* as your queen, master!"

Marius flinched.

"Easy there, Lamia," he said as he pried her talons from his arms.

The crowd heckled, tootled and booed as two beefy guards appeared from nowhere to seize the rogue vampire. Their expressions remained stony as they gripped her arms.

Marius smirked. "Be a good vampire and run along now, darlin'."

The woman spat and cursed at the guards as they dragged her away. The crowd cackled louder as she issued a drawn-out hiss before she disappeared off stage.

Marius gave a dismissive wave. "It appears as though some of us are just a bit more love *ka-razy* than others. Alas, we all know that my heart belongs to one woman only – here she is, Lady Avila!"

Disintegration.

Everything inside me shattered as Avila appeared from between the curtains at the side of the stage. Her long dark locks contrasted against her pearly white dress that revealed too much for my liking, and her wrists shimmied with rows of silver bangles that matched the delicate crystal headpiece suspended on her crown. She paused briefly, scanning the audience with a wave before walking into Marius' embrace. A series of whistles and catcalls followed until she gave a coy smile and addressed her devout subjects.

"Hello my fellow Mysticus creatures! Your fervent greeting flatters me. I am supremely honored, and I thank you for being here with us tonight to commemorate our union. As your queen, I vow to always support and stand by your king—even when he gets too much to handle!" She stopped to laugh. "Seriously though, through our love and devotion to one another and to you, it will be my pleasure to help guide the Mysticus clan toward a prosperous and powerful tomorrow!"

Applause erupted along with a string of idolized praise.

"Simply stunning."

"Dark beauty. I know why she stole his heart."

"She just owns that dress!"

Please! I swallowed a snort and briefly contemplated leaving. Surely, Avila wouldn't miss my presence here. I could hardly stomach any more of this ghastly scene. Sun shot me a look and I groaned inwardly. I knew she sensed my inner turbulence. I went for the wand in my pocket and prayed for the balance she said it would produce. My fingers tingled. It was torturous to be here, but I couldn't leave Avila until the deed was done and she was safely tucked away in the Crypt. Her presence on stage made her vulnerable. That much I knew even as Marius prepared to initiate the ceremony.

My eyes rested on my girl as he took her hand. She looked giddy. Her milky complexion flushed under the subdued lighting and her lips were swollen scarlet. The girl who spoke wonder in my heart from the moment she was born looked happier than I had ever seen her. *My little nugget.* Perhaps Sun was right in that my role here was meant to support my loved ones in their choices instead of resisting them. Marius' voice rose over the courtyard to interrupt my introspective moment.

"Ladies and gentlemen, the Claiming hour is almost upon us. I urge you to practice your stealthy gifts of honorable silence as our chosen Leaving woman joins us for the offering ritual."

A collective gasp hung in the air before quiet befell the throng. The drummers began a gentle tempo as

Marius gave a discreet nod toward an obscured figure lurking in the shadows at the left of the stage. All eyes followed his unspoken cues as the curtains slowly parted. I exhaled, mentally preparing myself for the sight of a terrified human who was about to face her death but the sonorous tongue of Zaros struck cold in my heart instead.

"Surprise!" His brawny figure was a swathe of black leather striking against flashing onyx eyes as he paused at the curtains to plant his feet wide and grin at Marius.

"What? Not who you were expecting to see?"

"Hoped, more like it."

Zaros laughed before he flicked a bejeweled hand toward the back of the courtyard and strode onto the stage with the slick of a preternatural hunter. My senses were instantly on high alert as I went to move closer to Avila, weaving through knitted bodies and making my way toward the front of the stage. Sun stuck close behind me as the crowd gasped and huffed before a sudden screech sounded from the back of the courtyard. I turned around to see the crowd whirling and clustering together as a series of screams emanated from the rear.

"What's happening?"

"Argh – they're demons!"

"Wh-what is that thing?"

More ear-piercing screams and dreadful hissing chilled me to the bone as I tried to decipher the situation. Something terrible was going on at the rear of the courtyard but I couldn't see from my mosh pit position. Avila shrieked and Sun grabbed my arm. I looked at my daughter as the stage curtains flung open and about a dozen of Zaros' crew strode into view. They were armored in patchy brown leather and clutched wooden stakes but my attention was drawn to the creature who slinked alongside them – Draven Sanguisa.

Shit.

Marius' guards rushed onto the stage. Zaros and his crew stopped short of Marius and Avila, but my vision homed in on the Sanguisa who was now prowling the edge of the podium, growling and hissing at the audience. I didn't hear his gnarly laughter or the terrified gasps, nor did I notice the hysterical cries echoing in the night. Death had come calling. My miscreation had multiplied. I knew it even before Zaros' opened his mouth to impart what I most feared.

"Now that I have your full attention, I would like to introduce Bloodfaye's newest members who will assist me as your true overlord toward the ascension Marius here likes to shamelessly dangle in your face."

He paused and smiled, and that was when I glimpsed the Sanguisa stalking either side of the courtyard perimeter. I spotted four in total and they were accompanied by more members of Zaros' crew. Their deathlike features stole my breath to the point that I barely heard Zaros speak again.

"It is indeed a good time to be undead. Ladies and gentlemen, meet the Sanguisa!"

Panic rippled like a silent wave. Mine was an internal scream.

23

QUEEN AVILA

arius' eyes bulged. He gripped Avila's hand as Zaros stood like a vainglorious cock penetrating the crowd with his dark stare. The stage was brimming with white-leather muscle and dingy stake-carrying crew who sneered at one another. However, my eyes were trained on my girl who was stranded amid the macabre brew. The atmosphere hung rigid on the sounds of prowling Sanguisa and their hideous hissing as they harassed the crowd fringing the courtyard. I stole between the vampires who bunched at the foot of the stage.

Atrocious.

Now that Zaros had a dirty trump card to play, he was obviously here to use it to overthrow Marius in his quest for power. How he had happened upon and managed to tame the Sanguisa was a mystery. Even more astounding was how he discovered his ability to turn others like him. There was no time to dwell on the expositions. The tension in the courtyard was mounting and a sense of foreboding threatened. Zaros laughed as he stalked across the stage to where the Sanguisa stood at the ledge of the far corner glaring at the audience. Zaros threw an arm around the beast and smirked.

"Now, before we get into the nitty-gritty of why I've crashed this fancy shindig, let me reassure you of your safety. I may look like a terrible vampire, but I do have heart." He fisted his chest. "The Sanguisa, on the other hand, are every bit of the blood-craving bogeymen they appear to be. Any dodgy move will set them off. Believe me, you want to avoid risking their very unpleasant qualities."

"Hells bells and evil spells."

"Disturbing—h-how is this so?"

The crowd broke into a tumult of shrieks while the Sanguisa on stage threw open his arms and chortled. His dark stringy hair stuck to his scalp as he proceeded to bow. His spidery eyes darted as Zaros stepped back as if to give him the floor. As the commotion unfolded, I continued to slip between the last of those who occupied the space separating me and the stage.

"What just happened? Where's our blood-show?"

"What is that creature?"

"I don't—"

One woman clutched her heart.

"I-I can't look away. He's utterly repulsive!"

I stopped short of the stage. Avila was only meters from me. The jittery crowd pushed around me but she immediately saw me. Her slight figure was almost ingested by the burly guards surrounding her. She looked at me and shook her head. I knew she meant for me to stay put and I would for as long as bloodshed remained at bay. Besides, I was all too familiar of how Sanguisa responded to sudden moves. My blood rushed as Marius released her hand, shifting away from the grouped guards. His voice was thunderous.

"Threats, Zaros? You must be forgetting yourself. Allow me to remind you of your place by issuing a warning. Take your punk-villain freak show and get the fuck off my stage before I have you ass-whipped from here to China."

He swished a hand through the air, cuing his guards for action. "That isn't a request."

"Ha!"

White-leathered Mysticus guards went to move but were instantly sidestepped by Zaros' men. They exchanged a series of snarls as they showed their teeth, flexed muscle and assessed one another. I recognized Zaros' usual vermin accomplices in *emerald eyes* and *scarecrow* but they were the least of my concerns as the threat of violence fumed. A few of the guards nudged and thumped chests as they began to slowly circle the stage, moving between flaming candelabras and rose-studded twisted iron. With Avila's henchmen and adversaries playing hangman appetizer, she was free to move. Her gaze flitted to me and she bit her lip as I motioned her over to me. She started to edge closer, halting when Zaros gave a biting laugh.

"Requests, requests! If only I had a dime for every bid you ever ordered, sir."

He flailed his arms while the Sanguisa menaced beside him. "Oops, that's right—dimes are worthless in the new world where only blood and violence speak on the devil's tongue. Mysticus members, are you not as sick and tired of Marius' constant demands as much as me?"

A restless murmur spread among the people, but he talked over them. "Listen up vamps, I am here to present to you an alternative way of life. Marius never gave you a choice but that's about to change."

What a crock.

These guys were the definition of crazy comics, albeit dangerous ones. It was obvious that Marius was fighting a blowing gasket. His face was flushed red as he strutted like a mosquito bitten swindler out for blood.

"Outrageous! How dare you challenge my authority. My visions and actions have manifested Bloodfaye – the sanctuary *you* call home. It was I who created the dome city and, in the process, provided the security and freedom for us all as we move into a more empowered and civilized existence as we embrace our supernatural gifts together, for better or worse."

"I choose worse." Zaros smirked. "See what I'm saying? This guy's head is too far up his pompous ass to notice how *you* really feel."

The crowd's laugher bordered on hysterics, and bewilderment set in as Marius growled and the Sanguisa stalking the courtyard perimeters moved toward the front of the courtyard, closer to the stage. It was the unchecked gasps that arose from the people as they passed that revealed their whereabouts. I met Avila's stare. She inched a little closer as Marius' laugher stripped my nerves.

"Weak-minded fool. Do you really think your small posse of rabid vampires are enough to overthrow me? Where did you find them? Copulating with turds in the Norbury city sewer?" He jeered. "I have a legion of loyal guards and the most gifted Leaving scientist to remain in the world behind me to outwit any malformed vampire species you could ever conjure."

"Are you certain of that, home-boy?"

The stage curtains parted, and it took a few seconds for me to recognize Michal as he walked onto the podium. He was dressed in black leather, carried a wooden stake and his eyes gleamed like apache tears minus the usual spectacles he wore. His pasty complexion rested on contempt as he scrutinized Marius.

Hell, no. I did a triple take. *What did the schmuck do now?*

My eyes were glued on my friend even as the audience started spitting and hissing.

"You wouldn't happen to be talking about my main vamp-man here, Michal, would ya? Turns out, he was recently sired to me which means you are shit out of luck in the super-smarts scientist arena."

Marius's expression darkened as Zaros laughed and proceeded to deliver his proposition to the Mysticus crowd. His afro flickered violet in the light as he paraded the stage.

"With me as your overlord, I promise to give you and our Leavings the freedom to be who you are, follow your deepest desires and live your most fulfilling lives without the fascism and slavery offered by Marius. Would you not prefer the new world to be liberated from tyranny-flavored dictatorship and undemocratic rule? Would you not enjoy a society independent from the suppression and terror the likes of which Marius has shown us?"

"Enough!" Marius roared. His mouth contorted as he rose an arm to signal his guards to act. The bicker-barge show was over. Fangs were exposed to issue snarls. Talons flared at the ready as the corpse contingency party obliged their master's order.

My eyes flew to Avila as the guards began to go at it. Undead on undead. My heart imploded along with my ears. Leather and stakes. Bloodcurdling screams, and the other Sanguisa screeched as they pounced, shredding the violent mash-up of flesh ripping supernaturals.

"Dad!"

"Avila!"

My voice was swallowed by the horde on the lawn as the energy ignited to an uproar and they transformed into cats on hot bricks. Vicious hissing mingled with heated snarls as they started to flay, claw and thrash. *Jab.* A set of razored claws stabbed my back as the weight of a hundred bodies converged on me. I ground my teeth as anger overtook my body. The crowd pushed forward. It was death pit alley, and I was entangled. The ground disappeared from beneath my feet and unearthly Sanguisa roars rose above the chaos. I looked up to see Avila sprinting toward me.

"Dad!"

Avila!

I couldn't form her name for lack of air. My lungs caved as I shoved away the vampire hissing in my face before thrusting a fist into another mongrel who was shoulder-jamming me. The stage landscape blurred with head-to-head clashing. The distinct sound of crunching muscle and snapping bones impaled the courtyard. Zaros barked a command and Draven Sanguisa gave a horrendous growl before charging for my girl. He moved like tomorrow.

"Avila!"

I barged into the guy in front of me in desperation to attain the edge of the stage as her screams echoed in my brain. In seconds, the Sanguisa shadowed the space between us. Rawhide talons expanded from his decayed hands as he rolled his head and howled. Everything faded into oblivion as Avila trembled and stepped back. The Sanguisa sneered and hunched his shoulders before he charged at her. I screamed wildly in an attempt to snare his attention.

"Oi! You – Draven Sanguisa!"

The beast ignored me. I dug my talons into the timber

stage and my feet found the ground. I steadied myself against the untamed crowd and was about to propel myself onto the podium when the Sanguisa halted to sniff out the air, moving his neck like a rapacious wolf. Something dramatic shifted and I froze as every supernatural being in the courtyard suspended hostility, watching as the great demon vampire folded to his knees and bowed before Avila.

Silence.

Avila's gaze flew to me and she gave a half laugh. I tried to collect my jaw as the four other Sanguisa slinked across the stage to pay homage to my girl, each of them dropping to their knees. Draven Sanguisa then spoke the words that blew my mind.

"The Sanguisa are here to serve you, Queen Avila."

24

THE SECRET

The moments were surreal. Everything slowed down yet played out over a matter of seconds. I blinked rapidly as I watched the strange scene unfold on stage. *Queen Avila?* She stood with the grace of a lady and childlike candor. Her stare grazed over mine, but I was nothing but a patchy depiction of war-torn horror and astonishment as fragments of truth hit me. *Secrets and murder.* Clarity was a series of unbroken signals in my mind and I could barely breathe as memories collected over several days, weeks and even years became transparent, and a long-gone voice revisited.

"She's got a secret, Jett."

"Melissa."

Her name was barely a whisper on my tongue. *Secret genetic codes.* Dreamtime messages encrypted from a mother who dedicated her life's work to biomedical genetic exploration. She had worked for the same underground government agency as Michal, and during the period when they were conducting experiments on Shane's blood no less. Shane was the original Lygarou wolf whose genetics held the primordial werewolf secrets derived from sorcery. *How could I have missed this?* I exhaled slowly as I thought of the plaster on Avila's arm and a wolf called Shana.

"There are no accidents, Jett."

Bittersweet revelation found me and at once I knew that Melissa's death was no accident. She must have uncovered a genetic code in the Lygarou blood at the agency. The vital link to the cure they had wanted to keep under strict lock and key. So much so that they had her murdered. It was the same agency whose quest to transmute original Lygarou blood into a powerful biological weapon eventually infected the world with the V-virus. Those covert dirty experiments on Shane's blood were responsible for millions of deaths and the apocalypse.

The entire courtyard seemed as if entranced by the peculiar turn of events. All remained still but for Marius as he cleared his throat before walking to Avila. He spoke to her softly as my internal world exploded with the final piece of the puzzle unraveling through my mind. Melissa must have been starkly aware of the precarious nature of her discovery, enough to risk our daughter's life and take precautionary action. *Queen Avila.* I realized that my girl acted as a viral host by carrying the encoded wolf gene in her system since she was a child.

Holy shit.

I had created the Sanguisa with the blood taken from Shane's newborn baby girl, Shana. It was obvious that the wolf-cum-vampire creatures sniffed out the original Lygarou blood gene in Avila. My head spun as I began to understand that even as acting as a viral host, Avila was their Alpha. Even more jarring was the fact that her blood carries the encoded gene that will cure the V-virus – the missing link needed to eradicate the undead for good. The answer to rid the earth of vampires had been in my face the entire time.

Long before the apocalypse hit, Melissa had ensured we possessed the key to reverse the damage caused by magic and genetic mutation. I loved her even more in that moment, even as I lit up on the inside as much as broke on old truths. I had made so many mistakes that had cost the lives of innocent people. I had lived on the edge of desperation, hatred, and failure; mourned lost love and feared for my daughter. I had died and visited the other side only to return to discover that while I can't control change, I can still offer the world and my girl a chance at salvation.

My voice was almost a singsong as I started to laugh.

"Avila! You're their Alpha, girl!"

"Alpha? Huh?" The crowd broke into a chorus of gasps and chatter as I hauled myself up onto the stage and she started toward me. "How's that possible?"

"Your mother."

"Mom?" She halted. I could almost see the wheels

turning in her head as she began to figure it out. "The dream messages—and the plaster?"

"Yes!"

I laughed some more and vaguely heard Marius chuckle over the perplexing rumbles emanating from the vampires on stage as they looked at one another. Some of them slapped each other's backs, the blood caking their faces spilled with laughter. Others, those who showed up for violence and slaughter, gave lowly snarls and peered at Zaros who remained remarkably silent on the far side of the stage as a thrilling vibe raptured across the blood city.

Everything was going to be okay.

I could feel it in my bones as the five Sanguisa stood up, their spindly figures turned to cast eyes on Avila, watching for her cues. They each appeared the same in that their skin clumped rotted, gritty, and brindled beneath scarcely covered scalps, and there was a coldness in their eyes that superseded any vampire I had ever seen. I shivered in the knowledge that they belonged to Avila and not Zaros, and now, his play for power was over.

It seemed that every vampire in the Crypt courtyard started to get the gist of Avila's powerful status and the ramifications it represented. She was their vampire queen despite the Claiming hour had now passed. Marius would have no choice but to wait for the next full moon to claim my girl. That would buy me some time to start on working the secrets in her blood. This time I was determined to get it right. Buoyancy incited thunderous applause and jubilant cheers in the throng of vampires before their acclamations fused into one collective chant.

"Queen Avila! Queen Avila!"

She and Marius exchanged a smile. He gave her a nod and stepped back before she turned toward the audience, laughing. I knew she was still processing her part in all of this, but she was handling it rather well. I'd never seen her shine so bright. Her white dress illuminated heavenly against the iridescent candle flames to create an angelic impression as she took in the adoration offered by the people. I saw traces of grace and beauty borrowed by genes passed through her mother as her dark hair fell around her face when she gave a dramatic curtsey toward the audience, thanking them. Love and pride stole my heart as the crowd responded to Avila with deafening applause, but it was gone just as fast when a spine-chilling growl emanated from the side of the stage. The next thing I saw was the blood spreading over Avila's white dress and the wooden stake protruding from her heart before she collapsed.

"No—Avila!"

My voice was a strangled sound as I caught sight of Michal's grisly grin before I rushed to her side. Marius was there as I fell to my knees and yanked the stake from her chest. It clanked on the stage, but I heard nothing. *Nothing.* Sinister secrets clawed at my soul as I reached to cradle her.

"Livvie!" Marius cried out next to me, but I ignored him.

Blood leaked warm and sticky between my fingers and spread over the stage like a scarlet river. "A-Avila." Her skin hollowed against her cheekbones, fractured and ashen. I shook her gently. "Please—baby girl."

Please.

Marius stood up and growled as Sanguisa howls promised treachery and death in the night. In the next second, the five beasts were beside Michal and removing his limbs. My hair stood up as his wild screams echoed across the stage, but I felt nothing for him, vaguely recalling the innocent scientists he had murdered in cold blood before I had turned kindred. I was a fool to believe in him again. The sound of his tearing flesh and crunching bones snapped against the backdrop of splattering blood before his desperate cries stopped abruptly. My heart was a husk as I focused on Avila.

"I beg you," I told her. "Don't go from here, from me."

The assault was over. The Sanguisa had taken their retribution on my girl's attacker but her death was enough to reignite the supernatural bloodline butchery. No holds barred. The night filled with deranged screams and breaking flesh as Marius and Zaros led their men with a rage lit by the flames of hell.

I was aware of nothing but the silence of Avila's dead heart.

25

WAITING FOR THE DAY

*M*y vision blurred. The veins on Avila's temples spilt like shriveled vines beneath skin that only moments before flushed with lifeforce energy. I reached for her hair. The dark brittle strands crumbled between my fingers like dried straw. She was gone. *Gone*. The acute pain radiating in my chest resisted what I didn't want to know, and yet, I couldn't deny the sight of her fast degenerating corpse.

The timber podium vibrated to the strains of stomping boots and minced bodies as vampires stalked and menaced. It was a Sanguisa meat party. The beasts had rallied with Zaros and turned on Marius' men. A dozen more Mysticus guards had spilled onto the stage to fight in the name of who knew what? Nothing mattered anymore. Blood splashed in my face as I drew my girl into my arms and shook violently.

Avila.

Amalgamation was eerie sheiks, gruesome grunts and vile snarls pinging with the dull ache in my muscles. I closed my eyes and buried my face in her neck. Her arms floundered by her sides. She smelled sooty as I spoke against her thickening skin.

"I failed you again. I-I didn't see it coming."

My shirt soaked up the last of her life and I was as dead on the inside as she was. I started to rock her limp body. "I should have been someone better for you. I-I couldn't see past my own hatred—Avila. Y-you were right, I should've tried harder to accept the new world."

I gave an unrecognizable shriek as Sun appeared, yelling over raspy breaths, swinging stakes, and slashing claws.

"Jett! We've got to get out of here now!"

I looked up. Her eyes darted, jungli. The crowd, who had cheered Avila as their queen, had mostly dispersed save for the brave who chose a side and fought with vigor. A body thumped on the timber boards next to me, vacant eyes over a gashed throat and skin like aged cheese. I became aware of heat. Flames licked the backstage curtains. Candelabras were awry as smoke gathered above like a bleak fog. Burning flesh stunk like grilling pork. Sun yanked at my collar, jarring me.

"Jett!" She was breathless. "You've no time to think about it. Let's go!"

I couldn't think, but I wasn't leaving Avila here on the stage to become a trampled barbecued kebab. I gave a nod and stood, scooping my girl in my arms, and turning to follow Sun. I stopped short when I saw Marius facing the sharp, unremitting blows of a Sanguisa. The skin on his face broke in vermillion threads, and his attempts to ward off the monstrous vampire saw him take a fist through the stomach. His eyes bulged as the Sanguisa sniggered and played fisticuffs with his innards. Zaros charged into view, burning a path through brawling vampires to serve up a crescent kick to his jaw. Marius dropped like a bag of bones as Sun urged me forward.

"Come on!"

Damn. I hesitated. The world was nothing without my girl. Sun shook her head as I pushed Avila's body in her arms. "Take her home. I'll be right after you."

She went to protest but stopped when she saw the look in my eyes. I gave her a gentle shove, but I didn't wait to watch her leave. I whirled around with a bloodthirsty hiss before sprinting toward the Sanguisa who was now dragging Marius to his feet under Zaros' command. The overlord was about to become sausage stew.

Adrenaline felt like hot needles. I growled and launched myself on the Sanguisa's back, punching him in the neck with my right hand while piercing his throat with the other. He roared and released Marius, thrashing around hard enough to send me reeling. I hit a blood swamped floor, and Zaros was sneering in my face.

His black eyes were pitiless. "So, you've made your choice, even in the wake of her death."

He laughed. Lunacy chilled my spine. I glimpsed

Marius gasping and doubled over behind him. Blood dripped from the Sanguisa's chin as he rolled his head and growled. Zaros flicked a wrist at me. "Finish him."

I had no time to move. The Sanguisa screeched. Pink saliva sprayed in my mouth as he tackled me, walloping my forehead with a rock-hard headbutt. The back of my skull banged against the stage. In the next instant, his talons tore shreds at my ears and eyes. I pushed a fist into his gut, just breaking through his shirt enough to connect with flesh. The meat of his palm shattered my elbow as he forced my hand from his chest before he pinned me down and drew back his right arm to make the deadly play for my heart. His weight was like a moving truck.

A flashing red eye.

Inhale.

Twisting lips and blood-hungry intent.

Exhale.

The battle blasted all around, ringing in my ears as the Sanguisa splayed his razor-sharps over me. I squirmed and reached into my pocket to grasp Sun's crystal energy wand. I barely glimpsed Marius and Zaros as they growled and caged one another, going at it head to head.

Inhale.

The mutated creature crabbed his fingers and roared as he went to penetrate my ribcage, and at the same time, I roared and stabbed the wand into his throat with a force that surprised me.

Exhale.

The Sanguisa gurgled. His thick tongue hung from his

mouth as his eyes expelled yellow pussy gunk and he grappled for the wand that was buried in his neck. I shoved him off me and rolled out from beneath him. He started to gasp for air and writhe as I stood over him.

"Motherfucker," I said as I smashed my boot into his head. His skull cracked and caved in, and I became aware of Zaros as he shouted from some place behind me.

"Sanguisa!"

His next command was snuffed by the stake Marius speared through his chest. His face conveyed utter shock while a flood of Mysticus guards converged onto the stage. Zaros thudded heavily to the floor. His bloody talons wrapped around the stake and he spluttered. He opened his mouth to say something, producing blood instead. Then the surviving Sanguisa were at his side, their shoulders hunched as they stalked around him protectively. His other crew members left alive rallied together and fled from the scene.

Zaros' eyes rolled back. He groaned as Draven Sanguisa gathered him up, nursing him not unlike a mother nurses her child. The cold-blooded beast took his weight easily. His demonic eyes flashed, and his neck elongated with a drawn-out hiss as the guards barraged forward. A thousand footsteps pounded behind me.

His voice was something from the netherworld.

"Waiting for the day, doc."

I clenched my fists but said nothing as he lurched around, moving as if part of an incorporeal realm before he took off with Zaros, his fellow creatures following him from the stage.

Every vampire left standing remained silent. I didn't look around at the carnage left from the supernatural clash my daughter's death had incited. I didn't even look at Marius as he came up next to me, watching the Sanguisa disappear into the night. Their formless prints belonged to the shadows and went unheard, and the silence was broken by the occasional howl as the distance between us stretched.

Numbness took hold and I went to leave. Marius stopped me.

"Jett."

I wiped my brow and looked at him.

"Why?" he said.

"Because despite everything, the world would be that much worse without you." My voice cracked. "And you loved my daughter."

He gave a nod. "I'm sorry, Jett."

I nodded and he gestured at the Sanguisa left behind. The one I'd killed with Sun's wand. His body had deflated like a fossilized relic. A wilted version of a creature that shouldn't exist. Marius shook his head.

"How did you kill him?"

"I guess I uncovered their weakness."

"What?"

"Silver."

I started to walk away, and he called out after me.

"Where are you going?"

My heart seized in a violent implosion. I stopped walking but didn't turn around when I answered. "I'm going to wait for the day."

The day of Ascension.

The End

Author. Writer. Dreamer. Beautiful Delusions. Lover of coffee, summer storms, great books, the mystical, soul & people with heart – Come fly with me.

Kim Petersen is a *USA Today Bestselling* author of the new *Blood Legends* series, *The Ascended Angels Chronicles*, and co-author of the *Stone the Crows* series. Her debut novel, *Millie's Angel* received a gold award in the 2017 Dan Poynter's Global eBook Awards.

Join Kim's Reader Tribe and Grab a Free Read.
Subscribe to Kim's fiction newsletter and keep in touch!

Connections

Website: http://bit.ly/kimpetersen
Facebook: http://bit.ly/2MdNLjK
Twitter: https://twitter.com/kimpetersen_
Amazon: https://amzn.to/2APcSF0
Bookbub: http://bit.ly/2Tt8weC
Whispering Ink: https://whisperinginkpress.com/

BLOOD LEGENDS BOOK ONE EXCERPT

2070 - Three Streams Village:

Ten miles west of the Norbury City Ruins

Blood is treated like wine, or so I had heard from those fortunate enough to have lived to tell of cadaverous creatures. I lived in a hidden village nestled within the walls of an intricate web of caves miles from the ruined city. The elders called the village Three Streams because it intersected with three flowing, fresh rivers. They call us the Leavings. We are among the last surviving humans on earth, the ones the Vampiric Virus had left behind decades ago. About fifty Leavings called Three Streams home, needless to say it wasn't a shortage of water that threatened our existence. It was the kindred clans stalking us for the blood pushing through our veins that jeopardized the survival of humanity. We had become pawns between two vampire clans plaguing the land with a bloody war fought beneath the cloak of a night sky.

The vitality of the velvety, plasma-rich liquid that pumps through vessels, and fuels the hearts in all living creatures cannot be disputed. Without blood, humans could not exist. Now, blood has turned into a deadly, fast-moving commodity, during days when pale faces, cyclopean eyes, and sharp fangs reign supreme over the earth. Vampires now dominated the earth; humans had become the minority.

Some called me a Blood Legend. Those words weighed heavy on me. I resented every syllable. My parents had even named me Eva because of the rare blood flowing through my veins. Eva means 'life'. My parents were convinced that my blood, and the blood of my younger sister Kaia offered the life-force, the solution, perhaps, the legacy for the resurrection of humanity.

The birth of every Leaving child is followed with a simple blood test our predecessors had salvaged from the ruined city, that's how we come to know our blood types. It's how they'd discovered that Kaia and I happened to possess the world's most sought-after blood. The AB-positive blood type was rare even before the Vampiric era. Now, it had become priceless. The two clans that governed the ruined city lived their every moment in pursuit of our blood. Above all else, the Mysticus Clan and the Cruentus Clan scoured the desolate ruins for those with our blood type. It was their nucleus, the lore of their kind. The prize that would provide its host the power to defeat the other clan forever.

I guess you could say we were special.

Special was the last thing I felt right now, though. Beads of sweat stung my dark eyes and clung to my lashes as I wiped my brow with the back of my hand and clasped my wooden Samurai training sword with my other. Then I feigned a sigh, dropping my chin while gazing up at my sensei as if in defeat.

Astrid circled me warily. Her tightly bound ponytail hung glossy like liquorice under the morning sun as her supple feet glided along, her sword poised in slender hands. Her lips stretched briefly. I knew she thought she had me worn down for the session, but that's what I wanted her to think.

"Had enough, sunshine?"

She swivelled her sword between her fingers. The smooth timber saber followed her fluid movements gracefully.

I shrugged and grinned back, mirroring her motion with my own sword.

"Is that sweat glistening in your hair?" I asked. "Have *you* had enough, *sunshine*?"

Astrid was the type of person who made everything seem effortless. I had barely seen her break out in a smile, much less a sweat.

"I've had enough of your mouth," she said, scowling.

Her lips tightened as she moved like a firebolt and swung her sword toward my head.

I ducked and spun my boots in the earth while bringing my own sword around fast to connect with the back of her knees. I just caught the fleeting grimace on her face as her legs went slightly concave and she stumbled back.

I flashed her a wide grin and squinted at her brow line.

"It's sweat," I said, nodding before glancing around the training yard and spotting my best friend, Thayer.

He was sitting on a sandstone boulder at the side of the training range, sharpening a stake and watching the session. His thick eyebrows lifted with his grin as he paused to smile at me.

My small, sweet victory didn't last. I should've known; I had just broken the cardinal rule of combat. I had taken my eyes off my opponent, and this one had a nature like a Pit Bull Terrier out for blood. Astrid didn't take well to any kind of defeat.

In a matter of seconds, she was on her feet, her sword thrown aside in the dirt while her black almond eyes bore holes into the back of my head. I could've sworn I felt the heat of her stare at the same time as Thayer's face darkened in warning. But I was too late. She had already caught me in a headlock and I was crashing to the ground beneath her suffocating grip.

As much as I hated to admit it, Astrid was an excellent fighter, and highly disciplined in the principles of an array of Japanese martial arts. That's why Hendric, our village leader, had assigned Kaia and me under her care following our parents' disappearance. It was imperative that every village member learned to defend themselves to the best of their abilities, but considering our rare blood, Kaia and I had the most gruelling training regimen of all.

As I squirmed under Astrid's unrelenting, vice-like brace, I was certain the word 'care' might have been a little misleading in describing Hendric's selection of her as our guardian. The woman was nervy and as fearless as a summer storm. Seldom had I experienced her softer side, but I knew it was there somewhere – hidden beneath her hard-ass, Japanese exterior. Well, I thought it had to be.

"Enough now?" Her voice whisked into my ears like a warm gush of wind while her bony elbow pressed under my chin. It didn't feel so good.

I stamped my fists into the dirt before I choked to death, and glared at her as she released me and offered her hand.

"You looked away."

"Yeah," I muttered, taking her hand and rising to my feet next to her.

She shook her head, the ends of her long raven hair sweeping across her shoulders.

"Why?"

My eyes darted to Thayer and then back to her. I shrugged as I tried to push away the beginnings of a blush. I failed.

Her brows lifted, but she didn't say a word. Instead,

she took her stance before me and we bowed to one another, formally signalling the end of our session. I was grateful to graze my eyes over my feet for a few seconds.

By the time I'd straightened up, she was walking away from me.

"Now you can go to the fields and collect the supply of cabbages for the village before they turn," she called over her shoulder.

"What? Why?"

It wasn't my job to tend to the fields. When I wasn't on scouting expeditions, I took care of collecting fresh water and making sure our village barrels were always topped up.

Astrid whirled around and gave me a stern look. "Because collecting cabbages might remind you that distractions are a weakness in combat."

I rolled my eyes and loosened the elastic holding back my hair. I could feel a headache coming on.

"Seriously? I'm twenty years old. I think I know how not to be distracted in combat."

"Go tell that to the cabbage," she quipped before striding away.

My face screwed up with my scowl. Then I spotted Beck emerging from the clearing with his buddies, a smirk firmly impressed across his sharp features. My face began to ache at the sight of him.

"Got secrets for the cabbage, Eva?" he asked, picking up a training sword for his session. "I'll bet I know what your secrets are all about."

I was definitely feeling a headache coming on now. My fingers dug into my hips as I faced him, my jaw clenched. "I'll bet I know how to beat the living shit out of *your* secrets," I snarled, tossing my long, dark-amber braid.

He dropped the sword lower, holding it loosely by his side as he stalked closer to me. The ends of his short-cropped, sallow hair caught the sun and glowed over his scalp. His thick lips twisted.

"You wanna go there with me, cabbage-patch?"

I inflated my chest and squared my shoulders. No way was I going to back down from this dick.

"Anytime."

His brown eyes narrowed on me as he contemplated his options. We both knew I was the better trained fighter, yet he was a good foot taller than me and possessed a male's strength – which I obviously did not. Still, would he risk losing face in front of his friends?

We didn't have to find out because, suddenly, Thayer was practically stepping on my toes and pressing his nose against Beck's as he pushed himself between us.

"Alright, alright. Save your beef for our real enemies, you two!" he said, gesturing to the beyond with a nod. "You know those bloodsuckers are out there. Let's not lose sight of that fact."

His dark hair fell to the side while his inky eyes focused on me. I guess he did have a point, even if the three of us had never actually seen a vampire.

Beck shook his head as he began to wander away

with a shrug. "Maybe she needs to talk to the cabbage about them vampires before she ends up their main blood-cow. I hear cabbage helps with *distractions*," he added.

I scrunched up my face and gave him my filthiest look as his friends gawked and laughed behind him. *Asshole*.

"C'mon, I'll help you in the field, *cabbage-patch*," Thayer said, tugging on my arm.

I yanked my arm free.

"Eat shit, I'll do it myself!" I scowled, before storming away.

His laughter echoed behind me, his footsteps thudding in the earth as he gripped my wrist and pulled me to a stop. I whirled around with a belly full of anger and a whole lot of words ready to fling at him, but all of it melted somewhere at my feet when I caught sight of the smile in his eyes. I tried to ignore my flipping stomach as he squeezed my hand with his next words.

"I don't want to eat shit."

"You're an idiot."

He shrugged.

"Takes one to know one."

I laughed, shaking my head as I allowed him to lead me from the training grounds with his words still circling through my head. Vampires *were* the real enemies. Gone were the days of a world brimming with vibrant city lights and fast cars, when movies graced the screens of every household and fresh food was available at every street corner. That was a time when people could walk the city in safety, day and night. A time that preoccupied my daydreams and stirred an indescribable longing within me. But those days would forever elude me – they were stolen away long ago when the Vampiric Virus violated the world.

Nobody knows the real origins of the Vampiric Virus. Some say it was an experiment gone wrong. Others are convinced it began with a conspiracy. I think the real truth died along with the source. Either way, the rancid virus leached into the bloodstreams of millions like a merciless curse, leaving most of the population either infected or killed by the thirst of newborn vampires.

I had been trained to kill vampires from the moment I could walk, and I knew it was only a matter of time before they'd spill this far west. With that thought, I stifled the sudden giddiness in my belly.

Would I be ready to face the undead when the time came?

I wasn't so sure.

The air hung like a heavy blanket as we snaked deeper into the woods and trekked silently through a shroud of trees until the damp forest canopy gave way to a stretch of fields edging along a cliff-face.

I tramped through rows of cabbages and cauliflower until I reached the edge of the escarpment, where I dropped to my knees and squinted against the sun, breathing in the thin, warmer air blowing up from below. The ruined city of Norbury spanned out like a haze in the far distance. From here, the crumbling city appeared lazy and peaceful, much like a painting on a canvas. But I knew that was a farce. It was death and evil that lurked beneath those desolate buildings during the daylight hours.

As my eyes rested on the massive dome structure looming over one half of the city, I shuddered. The chrome sphere glistened bright under the reflection of the sun. My stomach began to churn. Thayer was right; it would be foolish to lose sight of our real adversaries. And I didn't know which clan was worse – the Cruentus Clan living and hunting in the ruins or the meticulously organized Mysticus Clan that farmed humans for blood under the protective UV dome structure beneath which they lived.